Some Sort of Crazy

Special Edition

Melanie Harlow

USA TODAY BESTSELLING AUTHOR

Copyright © 2022 by Melanie Harlow

All rights reserved.

No part of this book may be reproduced in any form or by any electronic or mechanical means, including information storage and retrieval systems, without written permission from the author, except for the use of brief quotations in a book review.

Tell me, what is it you plan to do
 with your one wild and precious life?

MARY OLIVER

CHAPTER 1
Natalie

I BLAME THE VODKA.

My sisters and I were out celebrating—oldest sister Jillian had finished her pediatric residency and gotten a job, middle sister Skylar was recently engaged and planning a fall wedding, and I'd just moved into my adorable dream house. It was only about eight o'clock but we'd consumed three dirty martinis apiece in the last hour and a half. Since we'd eaten nothing but the stuffed olives in our cocktails, we were functioning somewhere between Shhhh Don't Tell Anyone I'm Drunk and Oops I Missed the Barstool.

We managed to get out the door on our feet, sideways with arms linked, and I'm pretty sure everyone in the place was glad to see us go, since everything was hilarious to us and our laughter had grown increasingly loud and obnoxious.

"We need Uber," announced Jillian, breathless from giggling. Her hair was a mess—when she'd arrived at the bar it had been tucked into a pretty chignon but several rounds of arm wrestling had shaken it loose. She had spilled something on the front of her peach blouse too, right on her left nipple. It looked like she was leaking. "No way can any of us drive."

"We need food," I said. "Let's walk down to O'Malley's for a burger."

"Good idea." Skylar hiccuped. "Then I'll call Sebastian to pick ush up."

"Ush?" I elbowed her as we started walking down the sidewalk three abreast. But my tongue felt a little numb too.

"Hey, look!" Jillian stopped walking, but since we were still all connected we yanked her forward a few more steps and she stumbled. "Is that for real?" Detangling her arm from mine she pointed up to the second story of an old Victorian brick building.

I looked up and squinted at the hand-painted block-lettered sign in the window.

PSYCHIC MEDIUM
FREE READING!
OPEN LATE TONIGHT!

Skylar gasped. "Let's do it! Let's get a psychic reading!"

"No, I'm starving." And my bladder was suddenly at max capacity. How had I not noticed it three minutes ago? Vodka was insidious.

"Well, I want to." She looked around for a way into the building and took off for a narrow wooden door between two storefronts.

"Sky, you're already engaged! You don't need to know your future. It's Happily Ever After, The End." I hopped from one foot to the other and tried not to think about lakes and rivers and gushing waterfalls, which were of course all I could think about.

Skylar pulled the door open and looked over her shoulder at me. "So *you* get the free reading. Maybe she'll tell you whether Dan's going to shit or get off the pot."

"Dan and I already planned to get engaged this year. I don't need a psychic for that."

"You did?" Rolling her eyes, she went on, "God, you guys are so boring. OK, maybe she'll see a tall, dark, handsome stranger on the horizon for Jillian!"

"I'm in." Jillian made a beeline for the door and slipped through it.

Groaning, I gave up and followed her. If two of us wanted something, the third always ended up giving in. I hadn't meant to let that slip about getting engaged. It did make things a little anti-climactic if everyone knew it was coming... nothing like Sebastian's impromptu airplane proposal to Skylar. But then, Skylar was an impromptu kind of girl. I was more of a planner, and I sort of liked the knowing-but-not-knowing...the added anticipation of each date we went on this summer. Every time I got dressed, I'd think, *Will this be what I'm wearing when I say yes?*

Because of course I'd say yes—that's how a love story ends. We'd been together for ten years with only one bad rocky patch last summer when I'd discovered a dick pic on his phone. I wasn't snooping—it was an accident. I was looking for a shot he'd snapped at my birthday dinner, innocently scrolling through his photos, and there it was. It was definitely his junk, and I knew he hadn't sent it to me, so I felt justified in glancing at his texts after that. Why take a picture of your dick unless you're going to send it to someone, right? Dan is a bit self-indulgent and egotistical sometimes, but I didn't think he'd take that photo just for kicks.

Sure enough, he'd sent it to a girl at work, amidst a whole flurry of flirty activity. When confronted with it, he'd admitted to some "minor indiscretions," the details of which I hadn't wanted to know. He said they didn't sleep together, begged forgiveness, and promised to try harder, and after some thought, I forgave him and we moved on.

After all, ten years was a long time, and I hated to think we'd wasted it on each other if we weren't going to make things work for the long haul. All relationships take work.

Plus, I loved him and he loved me. We knew each other inside and out. We were comfortable together, had the same dreams for the future, had the same taste in music, sports, and takeout food. Those were important things, right? People had probably gotten married for worse reasons. Dan and I were compatible. Comfortable. Certainly not as passionate as we once were, and way less hot for each other than Skylar and Sebastian, but after ten years together, is it even possible to sustain that?

I asked myself that question a lot.

A lot.

"Come on, Nat. It'll be fun!" Skylar thumped me on the back as I passed her. "Live a little, why don't you! You're always so fucking sensible."

"I'm not being sensible, I'm being hungry. But fine, whatever. I hope the psychic has a bathroom otherwise I see wet pants in my future." Marching through the door, I followed Jillian up the narrow staircase beyond it. "It smells like cat pee in here," I whispered. At least I tried to whisper, but I was still inebriated so it came out a little louder than intended, and Jillian shushed me.

At the top of the stairs were two doors. The one on the right said 2B, but the one on the left had a sign on it:

MADAM PSUKA: *Psychic, Medium, Clairvoyant, Intuitive*

Palm Readings, Dream Analysis, Spiritual Channeling, & Numerology
FIRST READING FREE*

*does not include Spiritual Channeling

Jillian sighed. "Fucking spirits. So *expensive* all the time."

I laughed, crossing my legs at the ankle and squeezing my thighs together. "That's it. No one make any jokes until I find a bathroom."

"Do you think you pronounce that P in her name?" Skylar wondered. "Like, is it Madam *Puh*-suka?"

"No." Jillian looked back at Skylar with what we call her You're Dumb and I'm a Doctor face. "You don't say puh-sychic, do you?" Suddenly she looked down at the big wet spot on her boob. "Shit. When did that happen?"

Moaning in agony even as I laughed, I bent my knees and cupped my crotch as Jillian knocked. "I'm going to wet myself. I'm totally puh-serious."

Immediately the door opened and an acrid, smoky smell drifted into the hallway. The woman who'd opened the door looked nothing like what I'd imagined a psychic medium would look like—no purple turban or chunky gold jewelry or flouncy ruffled skirt. In fact, she looked more like an evening newscaster: blond helmet hair, too much makeup, horn-rimmed glasses. She was barefoot and wore jeans and a flowy black top.

"Velcome," she said in a thick accent. At least she *sounded* like a medium. She looked at each of our faces as we tried to stop snickering and appear presentable, which wasn't that easy since I was still holding my crotch, Jillian was trying to cover her left nipple, and Skylar hiccuped. "Hm. Three sisters."

Skylar poked me in the back, as if she were impressed, but I thought we looked enough alike that anyone could tell we were related, even though Jillian was dark-haired and built more like our dad, tall and thin, while Skylar and I were blonde and curvy like our mom.

"I am Madam Psuka," she said grandly, pronouncing the P. Out of the corner of my eye, I saw Skylar poke Jillian in the shoulder. "Vould you like reading tonight?" Madam Psuka's eyes narrowed. "I am getting verrrry strong energy from you."

"Yes." Skylar clapped her hands.

"Vonderful. Please to come in." The woman stepped aside and we entered a small, dimly lit front room. I was about to ask vhere the bathroom vas when color and texture and warmth bombarded me. The walls were covered in tapestries, rugs, and blankets in every imaginable hue and pattern. The windows overlooking the street were covered in dozens of sheer jewel-toned scarves, several of which billowed in the early summer breeze. In front of them was a round table covered with a Moroccan print cloth with a chair on each side. The floor was covered by faded Persian rugs in tones of ruby and gold and coral, and large square pillows in royal blue, hot pink, lime green, and leopard print lined the walls. On every available surface not covered with books, and sometimes even on top of the books, candles glowed—most inside lanterns, but some in glass holders or simply set on a plate. From the ceiling hung swooping strands of beads and charms and other trinkets, criss crossing the room clothesline style, and in the two front corners were huge green plants. My eyeballs hurt.

"Wow," said Skylar, turning in a slow circle. "This is amazing."

"Thank you," replied Madam Psuka, although the foreign way she pronounced the "th" sound made it sound more like *tank you*, which was highly appropriate tonight. She shut the door. "I am not here very long, but I try to make the space my own."

"It's beautiful," Skylar gushed, then hiccuped. "I love all the colors and patterns together. Very bohemian."

I made a face at Jillian and she wrinkled her nose. She and I had more understated taste than our fashionably trendy middle sister.

"What's that smell?" Jillian asked.

"Is burning sage. I just finish smudging." Madam Psuka sounded pleased with her puh-self.

"What's smudging?"

"Is ancient practice used for clearing away negative energy and purifying a space. You are very lucky to be my first reading after is done." She gestured toward the rug. "Please have seat."

"Can I please use your bathroom?" I asked, fidgeting uncomfortably.

"Of course. Is right over there." She pointed toward the small galley kitchen, and I found the bathroom right across from it. There was no door, just a curtain of beads, but at this point I didn't care. After relieving myself of what seemed like fifty pints of pee for every ounce of vodka I'd consumed, I washed my hands and joined my sisters and Madam Psuka on the rug, where they were all sitting cross-legged in a circle like Story Time at the library.

"She's going to do a short reading for each of us!" squealed Skylar.

"Normally I do only one reading per group for free," explained Madam Psuka. "But the energy is so good tonight that I feel the spirits vant me to be generous."

"Wait. Are there spirits here in this room?" Jillian asked, glancing over her shoulder.

"Of course." Madam Psuka gave my oldest sister a You're Dumb and I'm a Medium look. "Spirits are always among us."

A cool shivery feeling crept up my back, despite the warmth in the apartment from all the rugs and blankets and candles. Right away I shook it off. *Get a hold of yourself. There's no such thing as spirits or ghosts or even psychics. This is all just for fun.*

"So who is first?" Madam Psuka looked from one sister to the next.

"Me," said Jillian, scooting closer to the medium. "I'm the oldest, so I should go first."

Skylar and I exchanged a look. How many times had we heard *that* before?

Madam Psuka nodded and took Jillian's hand in both of hers. She closed her eyes, breathed deeply, and appeared to be concentrating very hard.

"Should I think about anything in particular?" Jillian asked, and my heart ached a little. I knew how badly she wanted to meet someone.

"Just relax. Let your mind wander naturally. Let energy of life flow through you."

Jillian closed her eyes and the room went silent for a moment, the only sound the sizzle of the candlewicks and the medium's breathing. Her nose made sort of a whistling noise, and I had to hide my face in my shoulder to keep from laughing.

Then she spoke. "Are you dirty?"

For a moment, I was on the verge of cracking up until I realized she meant *thirty*, but didn't pronounce her *th*'s very well. Still, I had to hide my face in my shoulder to stifle the laugh.

"Yes." Jillian sounded amazed. "I am thirty. And I *was* just thinking about my age."

"And you are caretaker—no, something stronger. You are healer."

Skylar gasped and my jaw fell open. Had we said anything about Jilly being a pediatrician? I didn't think we had. Could this woman have guessed?

"You are strong, sympathetic, generous." Madam Psuka spoke confidently, in amazingly good English considering it wasn't her first language. "You are always willing to carry more than your fair share of the load. You are loyal and trustworthy. You are often critical of others, but very hard on yourself. You have tendency to be controlling, and sometimes you meddle, especially if you think you know best." Madam Psuka paused and opened one eye. "Is this accurate?"

"Yes," Skylar and I said together.

Jillian glared at us as the medium went on. "You value visdom and compassion above all."

"Thank you," said Jillian, fidgeting a little. "Is there anything else? Anything about my career? Or my love life?"

"I cannot direct the energy," said Madam Psuka. "It reveals at its own vill." She was quiet for a moment. "But I do see children. Many children."

"Many?" Jillian said, her eyes going wide. "How many?"

"Hundreds."

Skylar laughed. "It's probably your patients, Jilly Bean."

"Oh." Jillian's shoulders slumped, and she took her hand back. "Right."

I felt sorry for her and reached over to pat her shoulder when she scooted back to sit next to me. We hadn't really talked about it, but maybe Skylar's wedding was kind of hard on Jillian. She was the oldest and the most traditional, and probably thought she'd be first to get married. She'd definitely talked about it the most as we were growing up. And now Dan and I would be next, and—

"Next?" asked Madam Psuka, jarring me a little. She was looking at me, too. It was as if she'd heard what I was thinking and was mocking me with the word.

"Me!" squealed Skylar, crawling over to sit directly in front of Madam Psuka and thrusting out her hand.

"Hmmm." The medium closed her eyes and did the breathing thing again. Meanwhile, my stomach started growling like crazy.

"You are creative and expressive. Your energy is bright, warm, effervescent, and sparkling."

Eyes closed, Skylar beamed, and Jillian and I exchanged an eye roll. How many times had we listened to people gush about our effervescent beauty queen sister? Good thing we weren't paying for this.

"You value harmony, beauty, and pleasure, and enjoy sharing your talents vith the vorld around you. You live life to fullest, often vithout care beyond the present. I am getting feeling that you are not good vith money."

I snorted, and Skylar sighed. "That's true," she admitted. "But I'm working on it."

"Romantic love is verrry strong influence in your life right now, and it will remain so. Its energy surrounds you in almost protective fashion."

"I'm getting married," Skylar said breathlessly. "This fall."

"Skylar! You're not supposed to tell her that." Jillian threw a hand up. "She's supposed to guess it."

Madam Psuka chuckled. "I might have guessed it. Is obviously very strong bond between them."

"Anything else?" Skylar said eagerly.

"Just the feeling of calm. I believe you are entering new phase of your life that will be long-lasting and peaceful and happy."

Skylar practically floated back to her spot on the rug. "Your turn, Nat."

I scooted in front of the medium and held out my hand.

"A skeptic." Madam Psuka sized me up correctly.

"Maybe I am a little skeptical," I admitted. "But what the heck? I'm here."

She took my hand and held it between both of hers, closing her eyes and inhaling deeply. Within seconds, I felt a sort of humming sensation in my arm, and it was more than a little disconcerting. While both of my sisters had closed their eyes during their readings, I kept mine open.

"You are organizer, planner, manager. You are dedicated and idealistic. Vhat you conceive in your mind you are able to achieve because you are practical, talented, and villing to vork. You know how to get a job done. But you may appear stubborn because once you make a decision, you follow it through to the end, right or wrong."

"Wow," Skylar breathed. "That's so right on."

I bristled a little. Following through wasn't being stubborn; that was tenacity.

"You must be careful not to get too caught up in the daily routine, because you might miss opportunities that—oh. Oh my." Madam Psuka frowned and she gripped my hand tighter.

"What?" My heart thumped a few erratic beats. "What do you see?"

"It is..." She muttered something in another language, maybe Polish. "It is total chaos. As if your entire life is turning upside down."

"What?" Jillian spoke up behind me. "Why?"

Madam Psuka turned her head to the side, forehead furrowed. "Because of man."

"Wait, man in general? Like mankind?" I asked.

"No. Vun man."

"Vun man?" Jillian repeated. "What is that?"

"*One* man," I clarified, relief easing between my shoulder blades. I mean, duh. It was the imminent proposal, of course. It was my boyfriend of ten years.

"Is his name Dan?" Skylar blurted.

"I don't know his name." She opened her eyes and looked at me. "And neither do you. He is a stranger."

Jillian clucked her tongue. "Oh, that is so unfair. *Natalie* gets the handsome stranger?"

"No. Don't be ridiculous." I pulled my hand back from Madam Psuka and stood. "Thank you very much for the readings, but we should go now."

"You are very velcome. I hope you come back again." She rose to her feet, as did my sisters.

We said goodbye and clomped back down the stairs, Jillian broody, Skylar dreamy, and me determined not to let some fake hocus-pocus ruin my night. A stranger was going to upend my life? What the hell? There was no way! I'd worked way too hard to get where I was, I had everything I'd ever wanted right in front of me, and no stranger, handsome or not, was going to change that.

Still.

I couldn't help but vonder.

CHAPTER 2
Natalie

"THAT WAS FUN," Skylar said when we were seated at O'Malley's twenty minutes later. She was across from Jillian and me, sitting cross-legged in the booth.

"That was absurd." I picked up my water and chugged, although I was kind of tempted to order another drink. "She doesn't really know what's going to happen with any of us."

"She might!" argued Jillian. "Look how she guessed all that stuff about us."

I turned to her. "Come on, you're a doctor. You believe in science, not magic."

"Can't I believe in magic too?" she asked wistfully. "I'd like to. She really nailed all our personalities."

"Maybe," I conceded, "but she knew you were the oldest, so she could have just spewed a lot of stuff about first-borns at you. And how hard is it to tell Glowy McSparkleface over here that she's beautiful and happy?"

Glowy McSparkleface wadded up a napkin and threw it at me. "Party pooper. Come on, we're supposed to be celebrating tonight."

I sighed. "Sorry, sorry. You're right."

The server arrived and set down three plates loaded with fat, juicy cheeseburgers and thick, hand-cut fries. My mouth watered.

"I'm thinking of trying a paleo diet this summer to lose weight for the wedding." Skylar announced this right before sinking her teeth into the doughy white bun of her burger.

"Ha! You'll last less than a day." Jillian poured ketchup onto her plate. "Trust me. I tried it last week. I didn't even last the morning."

"Why would you need to try it?" I looked at her incredulously. "You don't have a spare ounce on you." Skylar and I were always so jealous of Jillian's naturally skinny frame. I swam endless miles every week to keep extra pounds off my short, curvy body.

"To feel better." She shrugged. "I've heard people say they feel amazing on a paleo diet, but it was not realistic for me. I like bread too much. And pasta. And wine."

"Yeah, the wine thing could be an issue for me, working for a winery and all." Skylar set down the burger and dipped a fry in Jillian's puddle of ketchup. "Maybe I'll rethink it. So let's talk about Natalie's handsome stranger." Her eyes went wide with delight. "Who could it be?"

"She didn't say it was a handsome stranger, she just said it was a stranger." I reached for the mustard and squirted some on the top half of my bun. "And it was a load of horse shit anyway."

"You don't know that. What if it isn't?" Skylar waved a fry at me, a blob of ketchup dropping onto the table. "Everything else she said about you was spot on."

I replaced the bun and took a big bite, chewing slowly as I mulled that over. Was it true what she'd said about me? That once I make a decision I follow it through to the end, whether it's right or wrong? And wasn't that admirable, anyway? Why was it stubborn to see your goals through? I was where I was in life because of determination and hard work. At twenty-six, I was a successful entrepreneur who'd started my own small business and managed it daily; a loyal girlfriend to my very first love; and a homeowner thanks to my wise investments and frugal living.

So why were Madam Psuka's words so unsettling?

"Maybe 'upended' isn't a bad thing," I said hopefully. "Maybe it's just big changes coming."

"That's true." Jillian nodded enthusiastically. "She didn't say the chaos was bad or anything. And no one can sort out chaos like you, Nat."

"Thanks." I gave her a grateful smile.

"Good chaos could even be fun," Skylar put in. "Like getting engaged and planning a wedding. Or renovating your new house—that's gonna be a huge project."

I frowned at her. "It doesn't need that much renovating, not really."

Skylar's eyes bugged out. "Natalie. You have a sponge painted dining room. No."

"And that wallpaper in the guest bedroom is horrible," Jillian added. "Sorry if I'm meddling."

"And that ivy stencil in the kitchen." Skylar shuddered.

"That doesn't bother me so much. The master bedroom and bathroom are perfect. And I don't have money to redo everything at once anyway."

"What about Dan? Shouldn't he be helping you with these costs? Assuming he ever moves in," she muttered under her breath.

"He'll move in, eventually." I shrugged. "But he has to sell his condo first, and he'd remortgaged it to buy into the marina. Money is tight for him right now. Plus, I kind of like having the place to myself for a while. And I can afford it. I feel good about that."

Skylar splayed her hand over her chest. "OK, but please

let me help you in that kitchen. We'll strip that paper and paint it. I cannot handle the ivy."

Jillian laughed. "I'll help too, when I can. My hours will be so much better than before. Almost human, I think."

"Good. Then you can sign up for that online dating thing I told you about." Skylar gave Jillian a smug look before polishing off her burger.

Jillian sighed, picked up her water glass, and put it back down. "Anyone ready for another drink?"

"Yes," Skylar and I said together. We ordered glasses of wine from Abelard Vineyards, where Skylar worked and was planning to be married, and toasted our successes once more.

"To Skylar, may your wedding be the most beautiful event this town has ever seen," Jillian said, glass raised.

"To Jilly Bean, may your future patients appreciate how lucky they are to have the best doctor in the world," I said, clinking my glass to hers.

"To Natalie, may she always open the door of her new house to handsome strangers." Skylar's eyes glinted mischievously as she touched her glass to ours. "Sometimes a little chaos is a good thing."

A few days later, I was getting ready for work when my phone vibrated on the bathroom vanity. Surprised, I glanced down at it as I finished winding the elastic around my ponytail. It was four in the morning. Who did I know that would even be up at this hour?

Miles Haas calling, read the screen

I blinked.

Miles Haas was awake right now? *He's probably hammered,*

on his way home from a bar or a party or the bedroom of some girl who thinks he'll call her tomorrow. I bet he drunk-dialed me by mistake. He'd done that the last time we'd talked, about a year ago, but he hadn't admitted it until we'd been on the phone for almost an hour. Plus I was running late already, I was short-staffed today, and I had to make muffins for the coffee crowd and get the salads going for lunch. Tourist season was in full swing, and diners had cleaned me out yesterday. I did not have time for an early morning chat with Miles Haas.

Still, I took his call. I always did.

"Hello?"

"You married yet?" The gritty yet playful sound of his voice unlocked twenty years' worth of memories. Treehouse, mud puddle, sticky cotton candy memories of summers he'd spent at his family's summer house on Old Mission peninsula, where I grew up.

I smiled. "No."

"Good. That guy was a douche. He didn't deserve you."

"We're still together, Miles."

"*Still?* Jesus. That's even worse." Miles and Dan shared an intense mutual dislike for each other, which I'd never fully understood, since there had never been anything romantic between Miles and me.

Well, except for that one night.

The *almost* night.

"So what's up? Did you drunk dial me again?" In the mirror, I noticed my cheeks had gone pink.

"I'm perfectly sober, thank you."

"Then why are you calling me at four in the morning?"

"I'm bored with the girl blowing me."

"Oh my God." I squeezed my eyes shut. "Please tell me there is not actually a girl blowing you right now." It wasn't totally out of the question—Miles wrote an insanely popular blog called Sex and the Single Guy as well as articles for men's magazines, pieces with titles like "Should You Bang the Boss's Daughter? A Flowchart" and "Butt Stuff for Beginners: A Field Guide." Occasionally he wrote about topics other than sex, but his brand was built on his devil-may-care, hipster playboy approach to life. And that approach included a *lot* of banging, butt stuff, and blowjobs.

"No, I'm just teasing you."

"Good."

"She's tied up in the basement now."

"Oh, Jesus."

"You heading to work?"

I sighed. "Yes. I should be there already."

"I'm in town."

"You are?" I turned around and leaned against the vanity. I couldn't remember the last time I'd seen Miles in person—maybe two years ago? He'd gone to college and grad school out East somewhere and then moved around a bunch, but he hadn't come back up here very often. Last time we'd spoken, he was living in Detroit. "To your family's place?"

"Yeah. You busy later?"

I had to think for a second—today was Thursday, which meant Dan had his tennis league after work and I swam at the gym, but after that we always met up for dinner. We hadn't really seen much of each other this week. Could I break a standing date—for Miles—without causing tension? "I'm not sure," I hedged. "What time?"

"Whenever."

"Let me check on something. I'll text you this afternoon."

"Good. I'll have another round with Svetlana here, and I'll see you in a few hours."

"Svetlana?"

"Yeah, she's Ukrainian, some kind of acrobat. I don't know what the fuck she's saying half the time, but goddamn she's flexible. Maybe I'll send you a pic."

"NO." He'd done that before, and I'd had to quickly

delete the pic before Dan discovered it. "Don't you dare. I'm hanging up."

I ended the call and quickly finished getting ready for work. On the ten-minute drive to Coffee Darling, the small shop I'd opened downtown three years ago, I reminisced about those us-against-the-world summers when Miles and I had been close. His family's property bordered my family's cherry farm, and for as long as I can remember I'd looked forward to those eight weeks we'd have together while his family visited from their home outside Chicago. An only child, he was a year older than me, but about five years less mature, and growing up in a house with only sisters, I'd liked the idea of hanging out with a boy.

And unlike my bookworm sister Jillian or pageant queen Skylar, I'd loved nothing more as a kid than running around outside and getting dirty, climbing trees, swimming in his family's pool or the bay. As grade schoolers, we'd played pirates or spies or zombies. As pre-teens, we'd had swimming races and fishing contests and went to the county fair together, gorging on sticky carnival food and riding the Zipper or Round Up until we were sick and dizzy. And the weird thing was, as close as we were all those summers, we never talked during the school year. But when he arrived in late June for vacation, it was like we'd never been apart.

Things changed a little the summer after he turned sixteen, when he was suddenly tall and deep-voiced, and his body had acquired the muscular curves and lines of a grown man's. His face had changed too—it was more angular, stronger in the jaw and cheekbone, fuller at the mouth. *Miles is so handsome, isn't he?* my mother would remark. I'd rolled my eyes, because she wasn't the only female who'd noticed. Miles was suddenly every girl's crush, a role he relished, hooking up with every pretty girl with a pulse, including a bunch of my friends.

Secretly I agreed with my mother—Miles *was* handsome,

but his ego didn't need any boosting from me. When we hung out as teenagers, I endured his dirty, juvenile sense of humor and turned up my nose at his flirting, letting him know I was not impressed. Then I fell in love with Dan, which Miles did not understand at all—not only did he think Dan was an ass, but he thought relationships in general were stupid and told me repeatedly that I was missing out on all the fun.

As I pulled up behind the shop and parked my car, I recalled his last summer up here, after he'd graduated high school. He'd been moody and distant toward the end, not like himself at all. When I'd asked, he'd just said he had a lot on his mind, what with leaving for college in only a few weeks.

On his last night in town, he came over to say goodbye, and the memory of that hot, humid night returned to me with startling clarity. For several seconds, I held my breath, remembering how he'd come to my window in the middle of the night, how the wet heat blanketed my skin when I went outside to talk to him, how the air crackled with the electricity of an approaching summer storm. Nine years had passed, but I remembered every single word he'd uttered there in the dark, could still hear the low, raw sound of his voice, the thunder rolling softly in the distance. I'd never told anyone about that night, nor had Miles and I ever talked about it again. Not that anything had happened...

But we almost.

We almost.

I walked around the block to the front of the store, and stopped short at the sight of someone leaning against the door. My heart immediately pounded harder in fear—the street was still dark at this time of morning, and I wasn't used to seeing anyone but the occasional jogger. This was a guy in a hoodie and jeans.

"It's about time," he said.

I knew that voice.

"Miles? What the hell?" Hand over my heart, I resumed walking toward him. "You scared me half to death. I thought you were going to strangle me or something."

He came off the door and stood tall, feet apart, hands in his pockets. "Hey, I'm willing. If you're into that sort of thing."

I rolled my eyes. "Um, no." But for a crazy second, I pictured him with his hands around some girl's neck as he fucked her. *I bet he's done it. He's probably into that stuff.* It didn't repulse me or anything—in fact, it sort of turned me on—but Dan and I were pretty vanilla, and I was OK with that. He knew how to make me come, at least. Orgasms were orgasms, weren't they?

Not that I'd had one in a while. One that wasn't self-induced, anyway.

Stop thinking about orgasms.

When I reached Miles, I stood in front of him. He was tall and trim, with brown hair that was short on the back and sides, a little longer and messy on top. Still boyishly handsome, he wore black eyeglasses with thick frames and a satisfied smirk. "You're late."

"Yeah, somebody called me at four this morning and kept me on the phone for ten minutes."

"What an asshole."

"Totally." I smiled, reaching for him. "C'mere, asshole."

It was just a hug, and I'd meant it to be one of those friend hugs where just your shoulders touch, but as soon as his arms came around me, he pulled me close so my breasts pressed against his chest, and our torsos touched. Something fluttered again inside me, setting off a warning bell in my head.

Back off—it's dark and he's cute, and if someone sees you embracing out here like this, word could get around. Plus it feels kind of good, and how would you feel knowing Dan hugged women like this and got turned on by it?

I released him and took a step back, fumbling with my keys. For some reason I couldn't recognize the right one, even though I'd opened this shop practically every morning for the last three years. Finally I managed to get it in my fingers, and I unlocked the door. "Come on in. I'll get some coffee going."

After locking the door again behind us, I turned on all the lights. Normally I didn't do that until closer to opening time, but the prospect of being alone with Miles in the dark or even the dim made me feel a little edgy. We hadn't been alone in the dark since—

What the hell? Knock it off. He's your friend. Yes, he's a flirt, but he flirts with everybody.

No, he has sex with everybody! And writes about it!

Right. Miles Haas was *not* for me.

Dan was for me. Good old familiar Dan, the boat salesman. Maybe he wasn't perfect, but he was mine. Our lives were in sync. Our goals for the future aligned.

Wow, that sounds really unsexy.

Frowning, I put the coffee on, preheated the ovens and started mixing up a batch of strawberry muffins in the kitchen while Miles wandered around the shop. It wasn't very big—I could seat eight at the counter and sixteen at small tables lining the opposite wall. Long and narrow, the shop was the right side of a century old storefront that had been split in two. I'd kept the old wood floors and high tin ceiling, and lucky for me the place had been a cafe before I'd purchased the business, remodeled and revitalized it. The woodwork and wainscoting were painted a soft gray-green, the walls above it were a creamy white, and the counter top—my big splurge—was a gorgeous silver-veined marble.

"Congratulations, Natalie." Miles appeared in the open archway to the kitchen and leaned against it. "This is a beautiful place."

"Thanks. I'm proud of it." I poured batter into two muffin tins. *I forgot how blue his eyes are.*

"You should be."

"Make yourself useful and pour us some coffee, huh? Then you can come sit back here while I put together the lunch menu."

"You change it every day?"

"Not every day. It varies." I stuck the muffin tin in one oven and pulled two trays of unbaked cinnamon rolls out of the fridge. Normally I had a pastry chef/assistant manager here in the mornings, but he'd asked for a long weekend and would be gone today and tomorrow, so I'd stayed late last night to make up the dough and get the rolls ready to bake. "I use a lot of local produce and ingredients, so I change up the menu based on what's in season and available. Right now it's strawberry season. And rhubarb! I'm making a rhubarb pie later today. You like rhubarb?"

"I don't know." Miles set a cup of coffee near me and leaned back against the counter, lifting his to his lips. "But I love to eat pie. Can I taste yours?"

I stopped unwrapping the plastic sheet from the trays and glared at him. Over the rim of his cup, his eyes danced with glee. "You better be talking about rhubarb or I'm kicking you out."

"Sheesh. So sensitive." He sipped again. "I like the photos on the wall in there. The ones with the text overlaid? Is that Skylar?"

"Yeah. I took those."

He paused with his coffee halfway to his mouth. "Shut the fuck up. You did those?"

Pride made me smile. "I did. I was shopping with Skylar at this old antiques barn last fall and I found this old magazine from nineteen thirty-eight that had all these dating tips for girls, like 'Please and flatter your date by talking about his favorite subjects' or 'Never sit awkwardly or look bored on a date, even if you are.' We were cracking up." I stuck the two trays of rolls in the second oven and set a timer. "I'd always loved taking pictures, and I had the idea that it would be funny to create a series of modern photos with a quote from the advice on top."

"That's right. I'd forgotten how you liked to take pictures. You used to make those slide shows of us." He took another sip of coffee. "Those are great in there. Do you sell them?"

"Sell them?" I made a face. "Nah. It's just for fun. But I found this other article from eighteen ninety-four on advice for brides, and I want to do another series. It's unbelievable what people told women, like 'Clever wives are ever on the alert for new and better methods of denying their amorous husbands.'"

Miles chuckled. "Amorous. Great word."

"I wish I had a husband for that photo series but I doubt I could get Sebastian to do it."

"Who's Sebastian?"

"Skylar's fiancée. They're getting married this fall."

He nodded. "So why haven't you and the overly amorous Dan tied the knot yet?"

"Dan's not overly amorous," I said defensively. It was supposed to be a compliment to Dan, but it didn't come out right. And it reminded me again about the lack of sexual heat in our relationship—in fact, we hadn't had sex in two months. But this was *not* a fact I wanted to share with Miles.

"Ah. The fire's gone out, huh?" He nodded knowingly and sipped again.

"*No*, there is still *plenty* of fire, not that it's any of your business." My tone had gone snappish. "I just meant that things are fine. Comfortable."

"Comfortable?"

"Yes. That's what happens when two people are committed and together for a long time, which you wouldn't know."

"Got me there," he said easily.

But I was agitated. "Look, just because you make a living writing about your insane sexcapades doesn't mean everyone else's sex lives are boring." With jerky movements, I began pulling out ingredients to make chicken curry salad, slamming things onto the counter. "Dan and I have great fire, if you really want to know."

"Good."

"Hot, explosive fire." I plunked down a mixing bowl.

"Brilliant."

I turned to him and saw an amused expression on his face. "What's so funny?"

"Nothing. I'm happy for you and your fire."

Parking a hand on my hip, I cocked my head. "Did you come here at five in the morning just to make fun of me?"

"No. But not gonna lie, it's for sure an added bonus."

"What are you doing in town anyway?" I pulled a knife from the block and began carving up chicken breasts I'd poached yesterday. "Aren't there enough women to torment in the metro Detroit area? Or perhaps you've exhausted that supply and you're on to another city by now."

"I'm still in Detroit. And I don't torment women. I adore them."

"Several at a time, I bet."

He shrugged. "Occasionally. But hey, they all know the deal. It's just for fun."

Having only been with Dan, I couldn't imagine what it was like to have sex with random people outside a relationship, but Miles's sex life fascinated me in a sort of gawkerish way. "Yes, I know. I've read all about it." I dumped a handful of chicken in a large bowl.

"You read my stuff?" He sounded surprised.

My turn to shrug. "Occasionally. I particularly liked the one about going to a sex dungeon for your birthday."

"I didn't even have sex there."

"I know but you—did other stuff. Crazy stuff." I shook my head as I recalled reading what he'd asked the dominatrix to do to him. I'd been shockingly turned on when I read his account of it, and secretly I'd reread it a dozen times. Did that make me a pervert?

"It was slightly crazy. And a bit painful." He shuddered and adjusted the crotch of his pants. "Don't ever tie anyone's balls to a hook on the wall and then crawl around naked in front of him."

I snorted. "Please. I don't do that stuff."

"What do you mean 'that stuff?' What's wrong with playing around a little?"

"Nothing, if you're into that kind of thing." I tried to sound dismissive.

"Jeez. So judgmental."

"I'm not judging you, Miles, I'm just saying I'm not into the freaky stuff the way you are."

"I bet you'd like it. I bet there's a little freak in you just dying to get out."

My stomach flipped. "What? Don't be ridiculous. I'm a normal person."

"Normal people can be kinky, Nat. I'm telling you. You're missing out." His voice quieted. "And I bet there's a part of you, deep down inside, that's curious." He paused, moving closer to me, his tone low and serious. "I'd like to reach that deep part of you."

I went still, my skin prickling with heat. What the hell was going on here?

He burst out laughing. "You should see the look on your face right now."

Pressing my lips together, I focused on chopping chicken again, but my vision clouded for a moment and I nearly took off a finger. "Enough. You still haven't told me what you're doing here."

To my relief, he moved away and leaned against the counter again. "I'm working. I'm writing a piece about sex in haunted places, and I remembered that old asylum up near here. I drove up yesterday and snuck in there to get some pictures last night. Then I hung out a little to see if any ghosts popped up."

"Looking for a supernatural sexual encounter, are you?"

"Not necessarily, but that'd be awesome. I'd totally fuck a ghost if she was hot."

Shaking my head, I pulled a jar of homemade curried mayonnaise from the fridge and poured some over the chicken. "Sick. And ridiculous."

"What, you don't believe in ghosts?"

"No. But I did have a psychic reading a few days ago." Mixing the mayonnaise and chicken with a large wooden spoon, I shook my head as I remembered our vodka-fueled Sisters Night Out. "From Madam Psuka."

"Oh yeah?" Miles sounded interested. "What did she say?"

"A bunch of bullshit about my life being upended by a stranger. A man."

"Maybe it's me." Miles sounded happy about that.

I rolled my eyes, elbowing him aside so I could get to the plastic wrap in a drawer. "It's not you. She said it was a stranger. She said I didn't even know his name."

He paused. "Bet you don't know my name."

"What?" I stopped what I was doing and looked up at him, perplexed. "Yes, I do. It's Miles…" But I couldn't think of his middle name. What the heck was it?

He shook his head. "Miles is my middle name. Do you know what my first name is?"

I gaped at him. "Wait. Miles isn't really your name?"

"Nope. It's Edward." He looked smug.

"*Edward?*" I repeated, as if it were the most preposterous name in the universe. "I don't believe you."

Setting his coffee cup down, he pulled his wallet from his back pocket and took out his license. "Look."

And there it was. His full name, address, and vital stats right next to his grinning mug. I shook my head. Who the hell *smiles* in their driver's license picture?

Edward Miles Haas.

That's who.

CHAPTER 3
Miles

SHE LOOKED up at me as if she'd never seen me before. Fuck if I didn't wish that were true. Maybe if we were meeting for the first time, I'd say the right things or make the right moves and she'd forget all about Douchebag Dan and hang out with me tonight instead. Naked.

Not that I wanted to trade our past or anything—I loved our friendship. Natalie was like my favorite book, which is *Catch 22*. It's always there on my shelf, and even if I go a year or so without reading it, every time I pick it up, I'm reminded of why I connected with it so much in the first place. It's smart and different and always makes me laugh.

"Am I supposed to call you Edward now?" She gave me an amused smirk and went back to her chicken thing, adding spices and salt and pepper before giving it another stir.

"No. It's my dad's name, and I don't really want to share anything more than DNA with him."

She nodded, understanding. "What are your parents up to?"

"The usual, since the divorce. Dad jetting off around the globe with the new wife and Mom medicating herself so she doesn't have to think about her life too hard, which is pretty much the same thing she did even when they were married."

"I'm sorry."

I shrugged. "Eh, I'm used to it."

"So you're staying at the house?"

"Yeah. My mother usually spends summers up here, but she just decided to go on some quack spiritual journey in northern California, which I think is code for 'I'm having so much work done I'll need several months to recover before anyone can see me.'"

Natalie shook her head. "I don't get it. Your mom is so beautiful."

"She doesn't see that. She never has." It struck me as I watched Natalie work that I could be talking about *her*, too. I don't think she ever realized how beautiful she was. I don't even think *I* realized it until that last summer I spent up here. But by then it was too late—she'd had a boyfriend, and I'd been dating a couple different girls, and by "dating" I mean fucking them in the back of my car or in their basement or in a bedroom at somebody's party whose parents were out of town. If I couldn't have her, I might as well have fun, right?

But I *had* said some pretty serious stuff to her that last night before I left. Did she remember that?

Natalie shook her head. "Yeah, some women are like that, never satisfied with their appearance and panicking more and more as they get older, trying to erase every wrinkle and fill every line." She moved briskly, covering the big bowl of chicken salad with plastic wrap and pulling out several bags of green leaf lettuce. "I hope I don't get that way."

"I don't see that happening." I crossed my arms. "So tell me what's new with you."

She smiled at me, and my chest got tight. "I bought a house."

"You did? With Douchebag Dan?"

She rolled her eyes. "No, you big jerk. On my own. A woman *can* own property these days, you know."

"They can?"

She stomped lightly on my sneaker before moving to the sink, where she began rinsing the lettuce. "Yes."

"Well, congratulations. Where is it? I want to see it."

"It's on State Street. It needs some work, but it has a picket fence," she said gleefully, rising up on her toes. "And cozy alcove bedrooms and a huge clawfoot tub and a huge herb garden in the backyard."

"Sounds perfect for you." *Too bad the Douchebag will probably move in.* I couldn't believe she was still with that guy. She was way too good for him. Jealousy flared unexpectedly in my gut, a hot ball of fire. *The kitchen will probably smell like this every morning—fucking awesome, like sticky buns are in the oven. Haha, sticky buns. I could give her sticky buns. Oh, shit.* I adjusted myself a little in my jeans.

She glanced down at what I was doing, and her eyes flicked up to mine. "Nice."

"Sorry. Anyway, I'm only around for a few days, so as soon as you're ready, let me know. I can't wait to see it."

"A few days?" She turned off the water and dried her hands. "That's a short trip."

"Yeah, I just wanted to check out that asylum and catch up with you a little." *Because I've missed you. You've been on my mind a lot lately.*

But I wouldn't say that to her. Clearly her life was going exactly the way she wanted it to, and the last thing I wanted to do was fuck up our friendship, which sometimes felt like the one constant in my life. If only she wasn't so hot. It was distracting as fuck.

The timer went off, and she pulled the muffins from the oven. They were puffy and golden, sprinkled with cinnamon and sugar, smelling like heaven. My mouth watered. "Oh God, those look good."

"You can have one. Let them cool first, though."

A few minutes later, an employee arrived, a college student named Hailey, and the two of them went into full prep mode. I could tell I was in the way in the kitchen, so I went out to my car, got my laptop, and chose a table in the back to work at. Natalie brought my coffee cup out, refilled, and set down a plate with a muffin and a cinnamon bun on it, glaze dripping down the sides.

I looked up at her, unable to resist. "I really want to make a joke right now about glazing your buns, but I'm afraid you'll take this away from me."

Her eyes narrowed. "I will."

"How about buttering your muffin?"

She put her hand back on the plate and I grabbed her wrist.

"No! I promise I'll be good. A perfect gentleman."

"Ha. I'll believe that when I see it. Can I have my arm back please?"

I looked down at my fingers wrapped around her slender wrist, and felt my dick coming to life again. Letting her go, I sat back and smiled. "You can have anything you want." *Especially if it's in my pants.*

She sighed. "You know what I really want?"

"What? Sit on my lap. Tell me."

She glared at me. "Do you have to be such a flirt? What happened to the gentleman?"

He got hard. I sighed. "Fine, a chair."

"I can't sit anywhere. That's the thing—I'd really like a day off. A day of just doing nothing but relaxing. I haven't had one of those in a long time."

"So take one."

"I can't, silly. Not everyone works from wherever they want to. I have to be here every day; that's what being a business owner is."

"Are you open every day?"

"During the summer, I am."

"Can't you delegate? What about a manager?"

She shrugged. "Not that I'm good at delegating, but I do have an assistant manager. I can't afford to pay him for more hours or responsibilities right now, though. I have a pretty big house payment. And I'm still paying back loans I took out to open this place."

"What's a loan?"

She looked confused for a second and then she slapped my shoulder. "You trust fund babies. So out of touch with the real world."

"Kidding, kidding." I pulled the plate closer to me and looked up at her. "I do work for a living, you know. But is there something I can help you with? Do you need a loan from me to pay off the bank?"

"No." She shook her head vehemently. "Thanks, but it's kind of a source of pride for me that I'm doing this all on my own."

"Amorous Dan isn't helping?"

"Not at the moment."

Was it my imagination or had her jaw clenched a little before she answered? I decided to redirect. "How's your interest rate?"

She winced slightly. "It's OK."

"Well then, there's pride and there's being stubborn."

Something flitted across her face that I couldn't read—surprise? Anger? Whatever it was, it was gone a second later. "Thanks, but I'm OK."

"Suit yourself. I'm happy to help out a friend in need."

"I'll remember that." She patted my head like a puppy's. "Enjoy. I better get back to work."

"Do you mind if I stick around awhile? I don't want to monopolize this table if you need it, but I have some writing to do."

She gave me a smile soft and sweet as the cotton candy we

used to share. "Stay as long as you like."

A couple hours later, I could see why she wanted a day off. She was all over the place, doing everything from preparing food to serving it to pouring coffee to ringing people up, and she always had a smile on her face. As busy as she was, she made it a point to say hello to regulars and newcomers alike, and often stopped to chat with people she knew or someone with a question.

I finished my breakfast and tried to work on the novel I was writing, but I was distracted and tired. *Just go home and get some sleep. You've been up all fucking night.* But home up here was a huge empty house, and although I liked its creaky old floors and wraparound porch and the view of the Nixon cherry orchard next door from my bedroom window, something about being there alone saddened me. I liked it in here better. I liked the happy, caffeinated mood, the hum of conversation, the Billie Holiday playing in the background, the smell of muffins in the oven and coffee in the pot.

Besides, Natalie was here, and if I was honest with myself, I'd admit the real reason I came up North was to figure out why I couldn't get her out of my head. It made no sense—I wasn't looking for a relationship, I knew she was still with Dan, and I had no reason to believe she'd be interested in me even if neither of those things were true. And yet for months now, maybe even the last year, the thought of her just wouldn't quit me. Why the hell was that?

I'd told her I was up here researching sex in haunted places, and that was true enough. But the only ghost in my head was her.

I mentioned I'd fuck a ghost, right?

CHAPTER 4
Natalie

DAN CALLED me around three that afternoon. "Hey, babe."

"Hi." I exhaled and plunked myself onto a stool at the counter.

"Tough day?"

I rubbed one calf muscle. "Just long. Busy, which is good. But we're closed now, just locked the door."

"What are your plans?"

"After I finish up here, which will probably take me a while, since I'm short-staffed today, I was going to swim. You have tennis tonight, right?"

"I do, and then we were planning on going out for pizza and a few beers after that, since it's the last night this league meets. Is that OK?"

"That's fine." And it was fine, although I'd sort of hoped for some alone time with him tonight. Not because I missed him, but frankly I was a little wound up with sexual tension. A good hard bang sounded pretty damn good. Didn't he feel the same way? "But I'd like to see you tonight. Maybe we could meet up later."

"I'm not sure how late I'll be."

"Oh." Damn. If I was the kind of girl who had sex toys, I'd

pull them out tonight. At least I didn't have to feel bad about seeing Miles...but I did have to tell Dan about it. Crossing my fingers it wouldn't cause a fight, I said, "My old friend Miles Haas is in town. You remember him?"

"Who?"

"Miles Haas."

"The sex maniac?"

I rolled my eyes. "He's not a maniac, he's a writer. He blogs for—"

"I know who he is. I still can't believe that pipsqueak asshole gets all those girls. He's gotta be lying, or making shit up." Dan sounded mad about it.

"I have no clue. Maybe he does." I doubted it, but I didn't feel like arguing.

"So what's the deal? Are you meeting up with him?"

"Maybe."

"Where?"

"No plans yet." I took a breath. "Do you have a problem with my seeing him?"

A pause. "No."

"We're just friends. That's all we've ever been."

"I know." His voice had softened. "You'd never be interested in a guy like that."

"A guy like what?"

"A sleazebag."

"He's not a sleazebag. He's just a guy having a good time and writing about it."

"As long as he's not having a good time with you, I don't care what he does."

I smiled. "I'll make sure he has a terrible time. We'll probably just grab dinner or something. Catch up a little."

"All right. I'll see you tomorrow night. We have reservations at eight, right?"

"Yes. Skylar made them. Have fun tonight. Love you," I added, hating how rote it sounded. It felt kind of rote, too.

He hung up without another word.

Skylar was right. We are boring.

But what could I do about it? The truth was, we both had things we wanted to do tonight more than we wanted to see each other, and that happened a lot these days.

Oh well. I'd worry about that tomorrow. Tonight I'd just have some fun with an old friend.

I sat there a minute longer, realizing that I hadn't told Dan about Miles being at the coffee shop this morning when I'd arrived, or that he'd stayed half the day. I don't know why I didn't; it wasn't as if anything had happened. We hadn't kissed. We hadn't even almost.

It wasn't on purpose. You just forgot to mention it, said a sweet little voice in my head.

But deep down, I knew that wasn't true.

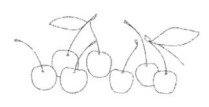

When I'd finished prepping food for the next day and closing up the shop, I sat at the counter again and called Miles. "Hi."

"Hey you." He sounded sleepy.

"Did I wake you?" I pictured him, hair tousled and chest bare, reaching for his glasses on the nightstand.

What? What are you doing? Stop that—put some clothes on him this instant!

"Yes," he said, clearing his throat, "but I'm glad you called. I was just having a dream about you."

I slammed my eyes shut, my mind immediately taking off his pants.

"We were at your shop, and I was eating a bagel."

"A bagel?" Relieved it wasn't a sex dream, I smiled. "Don't even have those here." Wait, was there something sexual about a bagel?

"Yes, a bagel, and you wanted to take my picture but you couldn't find your camera. And then you turned into a bear."

I burst out laughing. "A bear? Seriously? Not even a bunny or a cat or something sweet and cute?"

"Nope. A big old bear."

"And then what?"

"Then you called me."

"I saved you from the bear that was myself."

"Yes." He made a sound like he was stretching, and my mind drifted back into dangerous territory. "So what's up?"

"Well, I was going to go for a swim and then see if you wanted to meet."

"Oh yeah? Where do you swim?"

"At the gym."

"Come over here and swim."

I hesitated. "At your house?"

"Yeah. We have a pool here, remember? In which I repeatedly kicked your sorry state champ ass?"

"Ha! You never!"

"So you owe me another chance then. Come see if I've been practicing."

For a moment, I considered it. It would be fun, and the pool behind the Haas family's home was beautiful. But it just didn't feel right, going swimming alone with Miles at night. Other than the almost night, I had never been tempted to cheat on Dan, but there was some kind of spark between Miles and me that I worried could ignite if we were alone and close, especially the way I was feeling today. Better to avoid the situation entirely. "I don't think so, Miles. I'll just run over to the gym, get my laps done, and meet you later. OK?"

"Scared I'll be too tempting in my swim trunks?"

I laughed. "Yeah. That's it."

"I knew it. Plus there's no water in the pool here yet."

"Miles! What were you going to do if I said yes and showed up in my bathing suit?"

"Try to get you out of it."

I sighed, shaking my head. "I'll meet you at seven thirty. Jolly Pumpkin?"

"Sounds good."

Miles was sitting at the bar when I entered the restaurant, a little late because I'd gone back and forth so many times about what to wear. I wanted to look cute but casual, not too sexy but not too demure. Eventually I went with jeans and a sleeveless white top. Skylar probably would have added a necklace or something to look more trying-but-not-trying, but I didn't have time to hunt for the perfect thing, not that I would recognize it. The colorful flowers inked on my upper arm were usually enough ornamentation for me anyway. I did wear the shiny gold sandals Jillian had given me for my birthday last month, but only because they were flat and I knew I could walk quickly in them.

"Hi." I slid onto the seat next to him, a little out of breath from rushing. "Sorry I'm late."

"You're fine, I just got here." He reached up and mussed my shoulder-length hair, which was still damp from the shower. "How was the swim?"

"Good." I set my bag near my feet. "How was your afternoon?"

"Excellent. I napped a little more and then I took a run."

The bartender set a glass of beer down in front of Miles. "What can I get for you?" he asked me.

"I'll have the same." I gestured to Miles's drink.

"A Bam Bière? You got it."

"Could we get the pulled pork nachos?" Miles asked, looking at the menu. "And the truffle french fries?"

"Sure thing." The bartender glanced at me. "Are you sharing? Or would you like something else?"

"Um…" I glanced at Miles.

"I'll always share my pork with you, Natalie," he said tenderly. "I'll even let you pull it."

I sighed and looked at the bartender. "I'll share with him."

"Is this new?" Miles ran his fingertips over my tattoo, and the way I felt the effects of his touch between my legs made me shift in my chair. "It's beautiful."

"Not too new. I got it last year, when I turned twenty-five. A gift to myself." I shrugged, trying to ignore the way my female parts were tingling. "I'd always wanted it and finally worked up the nerve."

"What were you nervous about? The pain?"

I slugged his shoulder. "Come on, you know me better than that. I guess just the commitment. It is permanent, after all. Tattoos shouldn't be taken lightly."

Miles raised his eyebrows. "Well, for being nervous, you didn't hold back. How many sessions did that take?"

"Several. I figured if I was gonna do it, I was gonna be all in." I tilted my head. "I'm like that with a lot of things, actually."

"Does Dan like it?" He said it casually as he picked up his beer, but it sounded like a bit of a challenge. Should I admit Dan wasn't crazy about tattoos and was a huge reason why I'd waited so long to get mine?

"He does," I said carefully. "He's just not that into tattoos in general."

Miles nodded. "Think you'll get another one?"

"I don't know. Maybe. How about you?" Miles had gotten his first tattoo when he was eighteen, probably to spite his mother, but he'd added a fair amount of ink since. His left arm was pretty much covered. I wondered if he had anything on his chest or back and felt warmth bloom between my legs. So I crossed them. Tight.

"Maybe. If I feel like it. Like you said, it's a commitment." He set his glass down. "Probably the only kind of commitment I will ever make."

I elbowed him. "Probably."

Over a couple beers apiece, the nachos, french fries, and later a wild mushroom pizza, we caught each other up on family news, laughed over childhood memories and some of the articles he'd written, and talked about our jobs, our workout regimens, and our plans for the summer. He told me about the book he was writing, and I gushed about the new house. It was as easy to be with Miles as it ever was, and we went back and forth between serious topics and joking around.

What we didn't talk about was Dan. It's not like I was avoiding the subject, and I did mention his name once or twice, but Miles never asked me about him specifically, or about the relationship, nor did he offer any details about his own love life. But I was curious.

"So are you dating anyone?" I picked up a third slice of pizza, swearing inwardly that it would be my last.

He swallowed the bite he was chewing. "Define *dating*."

"Just the two of you. You pick her up or she picks you up or you meet somewhere, like a movie or a bar or a restaurant."

"Sounds OK so far," he said hesitantly, furrowing his brow.

I smiled. "And then you do this repeatedly, like several times a week."

"With the same person?"

"Yes."

"Hmm." He adjusted his glasses. "You lost me there."

I slapped his arm. I liked the shirt he was wearing—dark blue, short-sleeved, with a collar and white piping. It had a light blue chest pocket with a little penguin logo on it. I liked the way he smelled too. It was cologne, but it wasn't overly powerful. Or maybe it was his hair product or something. He looked like the kind of guy who'd use it in the effort to look like he didn't. "You're terrible. Aren't you worried you're going to end up old and bald and alone someday?"

"I think I'd look good bald, actually. I have a really nice shaped skull." He took another bite of pizza.

I shook my head. "What about a family? Don't you ever want a wife and kids?" In light of how attractive I was finding him tonight, I thought it might be helpful to remind myself how different we were, how we didn't want the same things in life. Not that I was putting any stock in the whole Madam Psuka thing, but just to reassure myself...because I was having a little too much fun, and he was looking a little too good to me. Sitting a little too close.

"A wife and kids? My dad said those things are expensive," he said with his mouth full. "And that whole loving someone completely and forever thing? I don't think that's for me. I'm too selfish. Doesn't sound fun."

There. See? He's selfish. All he wants to do is have fun. So just keep your pants on. I sighed dramatically, reaching for my beer. "Fine. I give up. Be alone forever."

He swallowed his bite. "Hey, you didn't say *you* would be the wife. I might change my answer if that's the case. Because your buns are amazing. And your muffin? Out*stand*ing."

Setting my empty glass down, I looked at him with one brow cocked. "You'd marry a girl for her buns, huh?"

He held up a hand. "Not all buns are worth matrimony, Natalie. Yours are."

I giggled, the two beers I'd had making me feel warm and tingly. "My buns aren't available to you."

"I know this. Your buns have never been available to me. It's really unfair."

"What is?"

"Pretty soon your buns are going to be permanently off the market and I never got the opportunity to glaze them."

I held up a hand. "Please. You were very busy glazing other buns every summer we hung out. You did not look lonely. You still don't, for that matter."

He placed his palm over his heart. "My loneliness is on the inside, Natalie. You can't see it, but every morning I die a little, knowing your buns are on some other man's plate."

"Oh my God." Rolling my eyes, I gave him a punch on the shoulder. "Enough. Tell you what. You get a girlfriend, I'll give her the recipe."

"I don't want a girlfriend."

"Of course you don't. So what *do* you want?"

He looked at me, and a shivery feeling brushed up my spine unexpectedly.

You.

I swear to God, I thought he was going to say it, and my entire body seized up with panic. And want. And confusion. And need. But instead of answering the question, he picked up his beer and finished it. "I want another beer. You?"

"Um, water for me please. Or I won't be able to drive home." Suddenly I was feeling a little dizzy. "I'll be right back. I have to go to the bathroom."

My legs wobbled as I made my way to the ladies room. What the hell was wrong with me? Why was I acting like this? I didn't want Miles. I wanted Dan. D-A-N Dan, right? I kept reminding myself of that as I used the bathroom, washed my hands, and stared hard at myself in the mirror over the sink. *You are not a cheater.*

And I wasn't. It's not that I never found other people attractive, but as Skylar always joked, I got the monogamy gene. I enjoyed being in a relationship, and I'd never felt stifled by it.

It's just that Miles was doing something to me.

I have to get out of here.

As I walked back to the bar, a pretty female bartender was leaning over the bar chatting with Miles, and he was clearly turning on the charm, judging by the grin on her face. Jealousy kicked me in the gut. Not only of the way he was looking at her, but at her freedom to write her number on a coaster and slide it over to him. He'd call her, wouldn't he? Anyone would. She had super long blonde hair and big breasts and a great smile. A Barbie doll. Maybe he'd even meet up with her tonight. Maybe they'd fuck at his parents' house, in his old room. I'd slept in one of those beds once when we were seven or eight. Our one and only sleepover. Would he fuck her in my bed? And brag about how great it was tomorrow?

I was irrationally angry by the time I got to my chair. Angry at him, angry at her, and angry at myself. I was even angry with Dan for going out with the guys tonight. Why didn't he want me like he used to? Why was our relationship so boring? And why was I here flirting with Miles, envying the bartender he'd probably bang heartlessly later on? I didn't want that. I wanted to be banged with heart! And I wanted it *tonight.*

"There she is." Miles turned to me. "I was just telling Jamie here about Coffee Darling. She's new in town."

Jamie gave me a friendly smile, which made me feel even worse about hating her. "Can I get you anything besides water, hon?"

"No, thanks."

"Oh, come on." Miles slung an arm around my neck, pulled me close and rubbed his knuckles on my head. "We don't see each other enough, so you should get drunk with me. You don't have to drive; I'll drop you off. Or better yet, spend the night at my house. Give me one night to convince you to leave that asshole and run away with me."

"Knock it off." I pushed him away and ran my hands over my hair. "You're crazy."

"She doesn't want me," Miles said sadly, his expression crestfallen. "She never has."

Jamie laughed. "Then maybe she's the crazy one."

He sat up straighter. "I think so too. So what are *you* doing later?"

"Oh, lordy." I pulled my wallet from my bag. "You know what? It feels late, and I get up early. What do I owe you?"

Jamie disappeared to pour Miles's beer, and he put a hand on my arm. "Hey, I was only kidding about her, Nat. Don't go."

"It's not that. I really do have to go to bed." I avoided looking at him, because I knew he could probably convince me to stay, and it was too dangerous. He was too tempting. I needed to go have sex with Dan, remind myself that what we had was real, and loving, and good.

It was, wasn't it?

"OK." He took his hand off me. "Put your money away. You treated me all day long. This one's on me."

"Thanks." I put my wallet back in my bag and threw it over my shoulder as I stood. Glancing at Jamie, I added, "She's hot. Looks like you'll have fun tonight."

He shrugged. "Eh, she's no Natalie Nixon."

My face warmed, and I shook my head. "You are *such* a flirt."

"I know. And I love the way it bugs you. Hold on, I'll walk you out." He signaled to Jamie he'd be right back and put his credit card on the bar before following me to the exit. Stepping around me, he opened the door and allowed me to pass through first. "Where are you parked?"

"Just down the street."

He walked next to me, hands in his pockets. "You don't believe me, do you?"

"About what?"

"That I think you're more beautiful than that bartender."

I snorted. "No."

He said nothing more until we reached my car. "Do you

remember what I said to you the night before I left for school?"

It was still warm, but a shiver ran through me as I unlocked the door. *Don't do this to me, Miles. Not here in the dark with no one around. You're confusing me.* "No," I lied. "What was it?"

"You really don't remember?"

I laughed nervously. "Should I?"

He paused as I opened the door and stood behind it. "No. Never mind. Drive carefully."

Sliding behind the wheel without hugging him goodnight, I dropped my bag on the passenger seat and gave him a too-bright smile. "I will. Have fun tonight."

I started the engine and he shut the door, lifting one hand in a wave. Then he stood there as I drove away, looking sadder than he had a right to.

Well, maybe he had a right. What he'd said to me that night, the almost night, was unforgettable.

The Almost Night

MILES

It was hot, the hottest August we'd had in years. And the heat was mean, the kind that made you feel exhausted all day long but refused to let you sleep at night. I don't know how long I stood beneath her window, toying with the rocks in my hand, sweating my balls off and arguing with myself. Should I tell her or not?

Yes. She deserves to know.

No. It's none of your business.

All summer I'd listened to Natalie ramble on about Dan, a thick-chested, empty-headed jerk-off I'd seen making out with another girl in his car at the fucking gas station two weeks ago. And I knew it was him because of his stupid license plate that read DAN 32 for his football number. Why the fuck I didn't pound on the window and punch that bastard in the face, I have no clue. And I said nothing to Natalie, either, although it made me crazy to keep it from her. But it wasn't like I was in love with her or anything. What the hell did I know about love? I was eighteen, for fuck's sake. I loved sex and blowjobs and nachos.

But she *mattered* to me. And she could do *so* much better. It killed me to think of the way he'd betrayed her trust. I thought relationships were the worst idea ever, but if you were going to be in one, you should fucking be in it and not dick around. Especially on a girl like Natalie.

Fuck, it's sweltering. I need to do this or go home.

Impulsively, I tossed the first rock, and then the second. She appeared at the window a moment later and opened it.

"What are you doing?" she whispered.

"Come down." This was not the kind of conversation you had through a screen.

"OK." She closed the window and disappeared from view. I loved how she didn't even question why I wanted to talk to her in the middle of the night. She just said *OK* and trusted that there was a good reason. This was a good reason, wasn't it? The truth?

But then she came out of the house and tiptoed across the deck toward me, and my chest got tight. She wore shorts and a little white top that showed off her swimmer's arms and the tops of her breasts. I'd stared at them a lot this summer when I hoped she wasn't looking and got myself off daily to the thought of them. Her ass, too. She had the most unbelievable ass you can imagine, and in my wildest jerking-off fantasies she let me come all over it. Sometimes I felt guilty thinking about my friend like that, but not enough to stop.

"Hey," she said quietly. Even in the dark, I could see the concern on her face.

"Hey."

"God, this heat." She reached behind her neck and piled her hair on her head. My dick jumped to life. She had no idea how sexy she was. "So what's up?" she asked. "You OK?"

For a long moment, I just stared at her. A strange hollow formed in my chest, creating an ache I'd never experienced before and couldn't name. Or maybe wouldn't name. But one thing was certain—I couldn't hurt her. The truth wasn't a good enough reason.

"Yeah. I just wanted to say goodbye."

"Goodbye!" She dropped her arms. "But you aren't leaving until next week."

"I changed my mind. I'm going in the morning." Until that moment, I hadn't planned to leave early at all. But standing here with her, seeing how perfect she was and knowing that she was giving herself away to that asshole was too much to handle. She'd told me sex with him was "beautiful" and "fast" and I couldn't decide whether to laugh or hurl.

"Why are you leaving so soon?" she asked.

"I don't know. Just ready to get out of here, I guess." I glanced toward the driveway. "Saw Dan's car here earlier. You guys get back together?"

"Yes."

My hands curled into fists inside my pockets. "Why?"

"What do you mean, 'why?' Because we want to be together. We shouldn't have broken up in the first place. They were only rumors. I was just being jealous and stupid."

Jesus. She thought it was her fault? How could she be so smart and so stupid at once? "Yeah, I was gonna tell you that."

Exasperated, she put her hands on my chest and shoved me backward, and I smiled at her feistiness.

"Kidding, kidding. You know I'd never think that about you."

"No, I don't." She stuck her hands on her hips. "You say that stuff to me all the time."

"That's only because your reactions are fun. I love making you mad." That was true, but right now it also felt safe. Her body was looking way too good to me right now, and my shorts were way too tight in the crotch.

"This is what you had to tell me before leaving? How you really feel about me?"

Oh, Jesus. I put my hands back in my pockets and tried to adjust myself. "How I really feel about you. You don't want to know that." I'd sort of meant it as a joke, since I was dealing with an uncooperative erection at the moment, but Natalie's face was serious.

"Yes, I do. Tell me."

Oh, fuck. What was the right thing to say here? The thing that wouldn't ruin our friendship forever?

I decided to go with *a* truth, if not *the* truth. "I think Dan is the fucking luckiest bastard on this planet, and he better fucking realize what he has and treat you right."

"That's what you think about *Dan*." Her eyes dared me to answer differently. "What do you think about *me*?"

Thunder growled above us, and the rain would start any minute. The air was hot and heavy with it.

Fuck it. I'm just going to be honest.

"I think you're the most beautiful girl I've ever met. I think no one will ever be good enough for you, least of all me, but all I want to do right now is kiss you. Well, that's not *all* I want to do. But it's a start."

She gasped and went perfectly still. And then the most amazing thing happened. She swayed forward, lifting her lips toward me as if she actually wanted me to do it. My hands clenched and my stomach muscles contracted. God, if it were any other girl, I'd have grabbed her and pulled her down on top of me in the grass already, impending thunderstorm or not. But it wasn't any other girl—it was Natalie, and I knew she'd regret this. I had to do the right thing.

"But I can't." I tore my eyes away from that waiting mouth.

"Huh? I mean, no. You can't." Flustered, she backed away from me, her hands knotted in front of her.

Thunder rumbled again; the storm was getting close. "You should get inside," I told her. The longer we stood out here like this, the less I cared about doing the right thing.

"OK." But she didn't go. She threw herself at me, her arms wrapping around my waist, her cheek pressed against my chest. *Oh fuck, she feels good.* I put my arms around her and held her tight, trying desperately not to think about her breasts crushed against me. This was the closest we'd been physically in years, maybe ever. Did it mean she wanted me that way? Was she really going to cheat on her boyfriend?

A little sob and then another escaped her, giving me the answer.

No, she wasn't. And it was better this way.

It made goodbye easier, it made our friendship easier, it made my life easier.

"Hey." I gave her shoulders a little shake. "Enough. You'll get snot on me."

She laughed and stepped back, wiping at her nose. "You deserve it for saying that stuff to me."

"You're probably right. But you asked how I felt."

"Yeah, I guess I did." She sniffed and shook her head, like she couldn't believe what was happening.

Lightning illuminated her pretty face, making my chest ache again. Had I just fucked up my one and only chance with her?

"Email me, OK?" Her voice was quiet. "Let me know how school is."

"OK." I watched her scurry back across the lawn and over the deck as rain began to fall. When she was safely inside the house, I walked back home and sat on the porch a while. Probably I should have gone in and started packing since it was too hot to sleep anyway, but I didn't. I just sat in an old wooden chair and stared out at the rain, wondering if I was a nice guy or the biggest fucking idiot on the planet.

Damn this heat.

It was making me crazy.

CHAPTER 5
Miles

I WAS ONLY KIDDING about taking that bartender home. Well, if I hadn't been there with Natalie, I probably would have done it, but for some reason it felt wrong to go back in the bar where I'd just been sitting with her and try to pick up another woman. Anyway, I didn't want to be with another woman tonight—I wanted to be with her. Not necessarily in a sexy way; I just wanted to hang out. I'd almost forgotten how fun she was.

Actually, that's a lie. I wanted sexy too.

Fuck, why did she still have to be with that shithead Dan? I bet he was still cheating on her. Guys like that who fool around and lie about it don't change. That's not to say I'm an angel or anything, but I don't lie to women, unless it's a white lie to boost her ego like *fuck yeah, you're the best ever, don't stop* when my dick is in her mouth, or to spare her feelings, like *of course those pants still fit you* when she's trying to wear her 8th grade jeans. I always make sure, when it comes to sex, that it's perfectly understood I like to have a good time and hope they do too. If a woman is seeking commitment, I make it clear I am not the Friday night fuck she's looking for, and she should mosey on down to the other end of the bar. Lucky for me, though, there are always plenty of hot girls who just want to have fun.

And it's not because I'm super ripped (I'm not) or have a twelve inch penis (alas) or make a million dollars a year (not even close). It's because I'm good to them. I treat the women I'm with like goddesses. I make sure they have at least one orgasm, I always give a warning during a blowjob, I never complain about wearing a condom, and I encourage them to tell me exactly what they want in bed. Then I do it.

Also, my face. I'm kind of adorable.

But you don't need an adorable face to make a girl scream your name. Guys are always writing me asking how to make a woman come, and every time, I say it boils down to this: Slow down. Pay attention. Give a fuck. And even though I've told them all my best clit-sucking, finger-fucking, and pelvic-grinding techniques (NO JACKHAMMERING), I also tell them you have to *ask her* what she likes, and you have to listen both to what she says, and what she doesn't say. Because even if she's too shy to tell you with words, a woman will let you know with her body what she wants.

As I walked back to the bar, I wondered what Natalie would be like in bed. The thought was enough to make me stumble a little on the sidewalk. I'd thought about it a thousand times before, maybe even closer to a million, but I was usually alone in the shower with my dick in my hand. Every now and then I fantasized a woman I was fucking was Natalie, which is kind of shitty, I guess, but it doesn't hurt the woman any, and for all I know she's imagining it's Ryan Gosling banging her. Doesn't bother me.

Back at the bar, I finished my beer and flirted half-heartedly with Jamie a little more, but turned down her offer to meet up later. I just wasn't feeling it. When I got home, I sat out on the front porch with a glass of scotch, thinking about the last time I'd been out here late at night.

Did Natalie really not remember what I'd said to her

before I left for school? I guess it was possible, although sort of depressing. I'd never said words like that to any woman since. Was *that* why I couldn't stop thinking about her? Was I subconsciously worried that I'd never meet anyone who measured up?

Not that I'd tried. I'd had a few extended fuck flings in my life, but nothing I'd call a Relationship. I had a lot of girl friends, Natalie being the oldest and most important to me, but I'd never had a serious girlfriend. Did I want one now? Was I lonely or something?

Frowning, I took stock of myself and decided not. I wasn't the lonely type, not really. Sometimes around the holidays I got a weird hankering to snuggle with someone in a completely nonsexual way, and this felt kind of like that, but it was only June. Cuddle weather was at least four months away.

Leaning back in the rocker, I brought the glass to my lips and stared across the orchard in the direction of the Nixon place. I remembered much preferring their busy, cluttered farm house with its comfy couches to my parents' drafty old Victorian with its formal furniture and silent rooms. And the Nixon house always smelled delicious because Mrs. Nixon usually had cherry pies in the oven to sell at their farm stand. *Natalie's new house will probably smell good all the time too. And she'll marry Dan, and fill the house with kids, and it will be just as hectic and noisy and fun as her own house was growing up. Perfect for her.*

But what about me? Did I want that? Letting the scotch roll over my tongue, I wondered if some part of me was tired of the parade of girls in and out of my bed and ready for something more. But that was crazy, wasn't it? What twenty-seven-year-old guy would give up the freedom and fun I had just to settle down and be an adult? I mean, technically I was an adult, but I wasn't a very adulty adult. I wouldn't call myself serious or mature. Responsible? Usually. Good with a deadline. Hard working. But I liked sleeping in. Not wearing pants. Eating cereal for dinner. I made stupid dirty jokes, I used plastic forks and paper plates at home to avoid having to do dishes, and I'd been living in my apartment for two years already and I still had no curtains on the windows, no pictures on the walls, and no plants. Was that pathetic? Was I supposed to stop playing at being a grown up and start living like one? Commit to silverware? A woman? A rubber tree plant?

I thought about my buddies with curtains and girlfriends, and the one with a wife. Were they happier than me? I didn't think so. Maybe the married guy, but they were still newlyweds. That glow wouldn't last. It certainly hadn't for my parents. Sure, maybe wedded bliss made for some cozy Sunday mornings in bed, but were the Saturday nights still as hot?

And maybe feeling that someone would love you unconditionally for the rest of your life would be nice, but wasn't that a lot of responsibility? You had to make the same promise, right? How would you know if you could love someone *forever*? Did I even have it in me to love someone that deeply? She'd probably want me to do things like wear pants every day and have brunch with her Republican parents and answer my phone. I just didn't see that happening. Frowning, I took another swallow.

One person. Forever.

Fuck that.

But what if that person was Natalie? said a voice in my head. *You think you couldn't love her like that?*

"Well, it's not her," I muttered, tipping back the last of my scotch. "It can't be her. So fuck it."

CHAPTER 6
Natalie

INSTEAD OF GOING HOME, I drove to Dan's condo after leaving Miles in the parking lot. I had it in mind to surprise him in bed wearing something sexy—except that I had nothing sexy, not at Dan's and not even at my house. I slept in tank tops and shorts. One Valentine's Day, Dan had gotten me a red lace nightgown but it wasn't the right size. I took it back and picked out a fuzzy pink robe instead. Red lace wasn't really my thing.

Now I was beginning to panic that *sexy* wasn't really my thing. Maybe *I* was the problem in our sex life—was I boring? Passive? Uninspiring? What could I do to spice myself up a little?

I thought of Miles letting some woman tie his balls to a wall and felt like a cloistered nun. It wouldn't even *occur* to me a man might like that! I could sort of understand something like a blindfold or whipped cream, but really? Being tied up felt good? Maybe I'd been missing out. Not that I was going straight to bondage tonight, but after bragging about our fire to Miles this morning, I could at least try to light one.

Dan wasn't home yet, so I hurried into the master bathroom and rummaged around in the vanity drawers. Maybe I had some scented lotion or something, and we could give each other massages. That was sexy, right? Or at least sensual? Unfortunately, I couldn't find anything other than unscented Eucerin, which did not say *unbridled passion* to me.

Frustrated, I threw it back in the drawer and decided to hunt around for a candle. I managed to find one fat, short pillar in the linen closet, and I found the lighter in the kitchen junk drawer.

In the bedroom, I lit the candle, took off all my clothes and slid beneath the covers. Immediately, I thought of Miles. Was he still at the bar? Or was he getting it on with that bartender by now, his face buried in her breasts, his hands on her ass, his hard cock driving deep inside her? Jealousy stole my breath for a moment.

Don't think about it. It's none of your business.

I checked the time on my phone and discovered it was nearly eleven. I hoped Dan wouldn't be too much longer since I had to get up in about five hours, but I didn't want to call him to check. That would ruin the surprise. Maybe I could take a nap—that was a good idea, right? I could nap, and I'd wake up all refreshed when I heard him come in. Then I'd attack. I'd be aggressive and confident. I'd whisper dirty words, tell him exactly what I wanted him to do to me, and that would turn him on so much he'd be unable to hold back. That worked in the movies, anyway.

Closing my eyes, I lay back and thought about what to say.

I want you to fuck me.

Gasping, I pulled the sheet to my chin. Could I really say that? Dan would probably have a heart attack. Not that I was totally silent during sex; I made the appropriate noises and all, said the usual *that feels good* and *mmmmm* and *yes yes yes, oh oh oh* kind of thing, but I'd never been more explicit than that. Neither had Dan, really. He cursed a lot, and he grunted and moaned and breathed hard, but he wasn't a talker. Maybe it stemmed from having to be quiet when we were teenagers and we used to do it in our parents' houses. Back then we had to be silent and quick or risk discovery. Dan was still the master of quick, and he'd learned how to get me off pretty fast as well, so maybe the habit of being quiet had stayed with us too.

Not anymore, I decided. We were going to change it up. We needed something different, something to revitalize us. We were too young to be boring! I liked that we were first for each other and would be last for each other, but we didn't have to be the *same* for each other all our lives, did we?

I want you to fuck me.

Just thinking the words made me feel sexier. *I want you to fuck me.* Without thinking about it, I slipped one hand between my legs and touched myself, imagining a warm body between my thighs, a hard chest brushing against my nipples, a low voice in my ear.

You want to get fucked?

Oh, shit. My eyes flew open. I knew that voice, and it wasn't Dan's. Heart racing, I quickly placed my hands flat on the mattress next to my hips and squeezed my legs together as if I'd been caught doing something wrong. I did not want Miles to fuck me. I couldn't want that.

I must have fallen asleep, waking when I heard the front door to Dan's condo shut. The candle was still burning, but it was much lower, and I picked up my phone to check the time. One twenty-seven? Where the hell had he been all this time?

His brawny shape filled the doorway. "Natalie? What are you doing here?"

"I was waiting for you." I propped myself up on my elbows, squinting at him. "How come you're so late?"

"I told you. We went out after playing." He made a beeline for the bathroom, so I thought he was going to use it and come right back out, but a minute later I heard the shower running.

Confused, I sat all the way up. Why was he showering now? Hadn't he cleaned up at the club like normal after playing tennis?

I blew out the candle, switched on the bedside lamp, and got out of bed. After pulling on my underwear, I knocked on the bathroom door. "Can I come in?"

"I'll just be a minute."

I crossed my arms over my bare chest, cold all of a sudden. "Didn't you shower at the club?"

He didn't answer right away. "No."

I backed away from the door and went into his walk-in closet, pulling a clean t-shirt from a drawer. After slipping it over my head, I got back between the sheets and waited for Dan to finish up in the bathroom, trying to think about what he'd been wearing before jumping in the shower. Was it tennis clothes? I didn't think so, which meant he must have put on clean clothes without showering, and then gone out sweaty. Granted, it was just pizza and beers with the guys, but it was weird to me that he wouldn't have cleaned up first.

A few minutes later, he came out of the bathroom wearing a towel and went into his closet, coming out in his underwear. He set his alarm before climbing into bed and dropping his head on his pillow, eyes closed. "Can you turn off the light? I'm fucking exhausted."

"Sure." But I stared at him for a moment. His face was so familiar—the same dark brown hair, square jaw, and high forehead I'd been looking at for the last ten years. I knew his features as well as I knew my own. Why did he look different to me right now?

"The light please, Nat?" He sounded annoyed.

"In a minute."

He opened his eyes. "What?"

"I came over here to surprise you."

His eyes closed again, but he managed a small smile. "Thank you. It's nice."

I took a breath. "I was hoping to seduce you."

"Seduce me?" He chuckled.

"Yeah." I slid down under the covers, put an arm around him, and pressed my lower body against his, trying to work up more enthusiasm than I actually felt. "We haven't done it in a while. I was hoping to remedy that." I felt nothing stir between us. Or within me.

He patted my back. "Not tonight, babe. So tired."

Don't be boring. Be fiery. Even though I wasn't really feeling it, I reached between his legs to encourage him a little and he jumped, pulling away from me. "Hey. Not tonight, OK? I said I'm too tired."

"Oh. Sorry." Feeling rebuffed, I turned away from him, reached out and switched off the lamp, then got back under the covers. Dan started snoring right away, but I lay on my back for a while, staring at the ceiling.

This was not the rekindling of desire I'd hoped for. On the contrary, it was awkward and embarrassing, and it forced me to take a good hard look at the truth.

Something was off.

Something had been off for a long time.

After work the next day, I went home and took a two-hour nap. I'd felt like the walking dead since my alarm went off, going through the motions of my work day without speaking any more than necessary, and nearly dozing off ten different times. The moment I got home, I collapsed onto my bed fully clothed. Facedown, I slept hard, and I woke up to the sound of my cell phone ringing. It was Dan.

We hadn't spoken at all yet. I'd gotten up and left for the shop without waking him, and he hadn't called me from work. The shower thing had been bothering me all day, because the only explanation that made any sense at all—that he'd been with another woman—was so unpalatable.

It's not that I was mad—I couldn't really blame him for spoiling my seduction scene, since he hadn't known about it in the first place, and by one-thirty in the morning, I was tired too. Still, I'd been willing to have a go at it, and it rankled a bit that he hadn't even been interested in trying. He was twenty-seven, for heaven's sake! Weren't guys his age supposed to be ready to go all the time? *I bet Miles never turns a woman down because he's tired.* In fact, all day long, I'd been shoving the image of him and that bartender out of my head. I had no idea why it bothered me so much—I'd been reading about his sex life for years without being envious or judgmental. But now it felt different.

Frowning, I rolled onto my back and accepted the call. "Hello?"

"Hey, babe."

"Hi."

"You about ready?"

For a second I was confused, and then I remembered we were having dinner with Skylar and Sebastian tonight. "Oh, crap. I forgot. I've been asleep for two hours."

"Want to bail on dinner? I'm tired too."

"No." I sat up and ran a hand through my hair. "We can't do that. Just pick me up in twenty. I can get ready fast."

"OK."

I pinned up my hair and quickly jumped in the shower, the warm water reviving me a bit. As I soaped, I thought about Miles's fingertips on my tattoo last night, and felt an unwelcome pull in my stomach. *Jeez, Miles, get out of my head already!* But as I dried myself off, I wondered what he'd done today and what he was up to tonight. Did he have other friends in town? Would he see Jamie again? Would he spend the night in alone? I entertained a brief fantasy of us just hanging out on the couch watching TV together before getting mad at myself.

Stop thinking about him, and don't even bring his name up tonight. You've got enough to deal with in your relationship without adding any jealous tension. Forcing Miles from my thoughts, I chose a black sundress and sandals from my closet, and had just enough time after putting them on to shake out my hair and put on a little makeup. Dan knocked just as I was tucking a few things into a small purse, and I grabbed my keys on the way out the door.

"Hey," he said, kissing my cheek. "You look great."

"Thanks. So do you." Dan always looked good in a suit. I liked the way his big shoulders filled out a jacket, although he always complained it made finding the right size difficult. *Built totally different than Miles*, I thought, foiling my plan to stop thinking about him. *Both have nice, athletic bodies, but Miles has a leaner frame. A soccer player's body, not a linebacker's.*

On our way to the restaurant, I noticed Dan kept biting one of his thumbnails, which he did when he was nervous about something. He wasn't talking much, either. *Maybe he's embarrassed about last night.* "Everything OK?" I asked.

He dropped his hand to the wheel. "Sure. Why?"

"I don't know. You seem worried or something. You're so quiet."

"Oh. Sorry." Glancing at me, he made an attempt at a smile, but it was pretty weak. "I'm just tired."

I groaned. "Me too. I stayed up too late." I was hoping he'd take the chance to say something about last night, even make a joke, but he didn't. Eyes on the road, he drove the rest of the way in silence, his thumbnail finding its way back to his lips.

He seemed like his usual self during dinner, conversing with Sebastian about sports and politics and a few mutual acquaintances while Skylar babbled nonstop to me about the wedding. She'd completed her bridal registry that afternoon, and was all excited about the china pattern she'd chosen.

"I don't know where she thinks we're going to keep all those dishes." Sebastian shook his head. "I'm going to have to build a second cabin on the property just to house our wedding gifts."

"Oh, stop. It's not that much stuff. We're only having a hundred or so guests anyway. It's not like it's a giant affair."

That had surprised me, actually. Jillian too. We'd both imagined Skylar would want nothing short of an epic bash when she got married since she'd always adored a big production, especially if she was the star. But she was really trying hard to keep things more intimate. Mia Fournier, the woman Skylar worked for at the winery, had previously been a wedding planner, and the two of them were in their glory planning this event. Apparently it was going to be photographed for a spread in a wine magazine, so every detail had to be perfect. I had no doubt it would be—when it came time for my wedding, I hoped Skylar would help me plan it too.

If I ever have a wedding. I looked over at Dan, who was cutting a piece of New York Strip and asking Sebastian about his truck. "I'm thinking of getting one like that," he said.

I blinked at him. "You're selling the Mustang?"

"No. I'd keep that and use the truck for more work-related stuff."

"I didn't know you were thinking of doing that." A new truck would be expensive. Where would he find the money?

He shrugged. "I haven't decided anything yet."

I dropped my eyes to my plate of salmon and asparagus and said nothing, but from my left I felt Skylar staring at me.

After dinner plates had been cleared and we'd ordered coffee and dessert, she stood. "Nat, come to the bathroom with me."

"OK." I picked up my purse and followed her back to the ladies lounge. We each used a stall, and then stood washing our hands next to one another. In the mirror, I could tell she was looking at me strangely. "What?"

"I was about to ask you that," she said, taking a towel from a basket on the vanity and drying her hands. "You've been acting weird all night, and it's obvious there's tension between you and Dan. Is it the house?"

"What about the house?"

"I keep thinking you want him to move in and he's putting it off for some reason. The money excuse sounds kinda flimsy to me, especially since he's talking about buying an expensive new truck."

I sighed. "It's not the house. You know what, I don't even care that he's not making plans to move in. Which is part of the problem—I should care. I should want him to live with me, and I feel completely ambivalent about it."

"Then is it Miles?"

I coughed. "Miles Haas?" I said, like it was the most absurd thing she'd ever said.

"Yeah." She put the towel in the hamper and took her lipstick from her purse. "I ran into him today at the grocery store. He said he'd seen you last night."

"We had a beer and some food at the Jolly Pumpkin, that's all." I hated how defensive I sounded. "Why should that cause tension?"

My sister rolled her eyes. "Because he's always had a thing for you and Dan knows it."

"What?" I screeched, throwing my towel in the hamper. "That's ridiculous. Miles and I have never had a thing."

I think you're the most beautiful girl I've ever met.

"I didn't say you *guys* had a thing, I said *he's* always had a thing for you." She capped the lipstick and rubbed her lips together. "At least, *I* always thought he did. I was surprised you two never hooked up."

"I've always been with Dan," I said, unhappy with the way my heart was skipping beats at the thought of hooking up with Miles. It was too late for this.

I think no one will ever be good enough for you, and all I want to do right now is kiss you.

"I'd never cheat on Dan," I went on, as much for my benefit as for hers. "And besides, you're crazy. Miles doesn't have a thing for me. He's just a flirt."

Well, that's not all I want to do. But it's a start.

Skylar raised her eyebrows. "If you say so. But I saw the look on his face when he was talking about you today."

"What look? What did he say about me?" For someone who just denied any kind of *thing* with Miles, I knew I sounded way too eager, but I couldn't help it.

"He was going on about how awesome the shop is, how proud you should be, how good you are at everything you do, from baking to managing to taking pictures." Looking at herself in the mirror, she played with her hair and fussed with an earring. "And he said you two met up last night and had a really nice time."

"We did." I took my lip gloss from my purse and applied it with shaky fingers, staring at my mouth in the mirror instead of my pink cheeks and guilty eyes. *A very nice time. Too nice. I wish I was hanging out with him again tonight, and I feel horrible about it.* "But we're just old friends who don't get to see each other often enough. That's all."

"So what's with Dan, then? I *know* there's something."

I put the lip gloss back in my purse and faced her. "Honestly, something *is* wrong there, but I can't figure out what it is. And I'm scared." My eyes filled unexpectedly, and I fanned at them.

She pulled me over to a small chaise in the powder room adjacent to the bathroom. "Come here. Sit. Talk."

"We have to go back to the table," I said, fighting off the tears. "And it's probably nothing. I'm just so tired."

"*Talk.* We're not going back until you do." She folded her arms. "I'm the big sister, and I say so."

Sniffing, I laughed a little. "It's dumb, really. After hanging out with Miles yesterday—you know how he is—I started to feel like Dan and I needed a little boost in the sex department."

"The sex department?" She wrinkled her nose. "What's that about?"

I played with the hem on my dress. "It's been a couple months, that's all."

"A couple *months*?" Skylar was dumbfounded. "Why?"

"We've just been busy and tired a lot, I guess. I don't know. And we've been together so long, we don't feel the urge as much as you guys do."

"No one does," she said seriously. "We are animals."

I sighed again, louder. Why couldn't I be animals with someone? "So I went over there with the idea of surprising him." I told her what happened and watched her expression change. "What's that face you're making?" I asked, scared to hear the answer.

"Why would he need to shower again? Did he have to wash someone's sex stink off?" Skylar still hadn't forgiven Dan for last summer's transgressions.

I winced. "I don't know. I've been trying not to think about that."

She harrumphed. "And what about after he came to bed? Did you do it?"

"No. He said he was too tired."

"You tried? And he turned you down?"

I nodded, feeling pathetic and helpless. "I didn't try very hard. But yeah. He went right to sleep. And you know what, I wasn't even that disappointed—I was more confused than anything else."

Skylar's eyes narrowed. "Something is off."

"I thought the exact same thing."

"It could be nothing, Nat. Maybe it was just late and he was tired. But *something* is up. With you, too, and you guys need to talk about it."

"Me?" I put a hand on my chest. "Why do you say that?"

"Because I know you, and you are not acting like yourself. Maybe it's this thing with Dan, maybe it's Miles Haas, mayb—"

"It's not Miles Haas." Irritated, I stood up. "It's just a little rocky patch, nothing Dan and I can't work through. We've done it before. I'm not giving up."

Skylar stood up too, her expression dubious. "If you say so. But Nat, I hope you're not sticking with him or with a dead relationship just because you've put so much time in. It's not giving up if you're unhappy."

"I know that. I'll figure it out." We went back to the table, and Dan held out my chair. When he took his seat again, he smiled at me, and I reached for his hand, making a promise to myself. *I'll make a bigger effort to rekindle things with us. I will put Miles Haas out of my head and focus on the solid commitment Dan and I have and the plans we've made.*

If only I felt more excited about it.

CHAPTER 7
Natalie

WE SAID goodbye to Skylar and Sebastian, and drove back to the house. "Come on in," I said as he pulled into the drive. "I have a bottle of wine we can open."

"Actually, I'm really tired, Nat." He yawned with perfect timing. "I think I'm just gonna head home."

I stared at him, open-mouthed, and finally cracked. "What's going on, Dan? Why are you so tired all the time, and why do I feel like you're avoiding me?"

"I'm not," he said feebly.

"Well, that's what it feels like. We haven't had sex in months! Why don't you want to? Is it me? Is there someone else? Just be honest, please." I was surprised the tears that threatened to spill over in the bathroom earlier didn't make an appearance. I actually felt more angry than anything else. "I'd rather know the truth."

"It's not you, it's just—" Dan ran a hand over his chin. "It's me. *And* it's you. It's us."

"What the fuck are you talking about?"

Dan sighed. "I hate it when you swear."

"Too fucking bad. Now what it is?"

He turned to face me. "OK, I feel like we've been together

for so long, and now we're talking marriage, and..." He struggled with what to say next.

"And what? You don't want to get married? You fucked someone else last night? You don't love me anymore? Just say it, Dan!"

"No, of course I love you." He took my left hand and looked down at it. "I love you, Nat, I do. You're the perfect woman. And I want us to get engaged—eventually."

"Eventually?" I raised my eyebrows.

"Yeah, but not right away. I've been thinking about this a lot lately. We're only twenty-six and twenty-seven, you know? And we've only ever been with each other." He flicked a nervous glance at me. "So before we commit to marriage, maybe we should...take a break from each other."

"A *break*?" I gaped at him and yanked my hand away. "What the hell does that mean?"

"Just step back a little. Spend some time apart, be free to see other people."

"So you did fuck someone else last night." I shook my head, tears of humiliation burning my eyes. "Oh, God. And then I tried to—"

"Natalie—"

"Please just admit it." I looked him in the eye. "Be a fucking man, and admit it."

He swallowed. "Fine."

I felt an inexplicable rush of relief, followed by anger when he spoke again.

"That's why I think the break will be good for us. I think we need this time to really be sure we're right for one another."

"I think you're fucking insane. This is not how it works. Either we're together or we're not. And right now, I think not." Opening the door, I elbowed my way out of the car and slammed it shut. Dan jumped out as I was stomping my way to the front door.

"Natalie, wait!" He ran up and grabbed my arm, forcing me to face him. "I don't want this to be the end of us. I just want some time to breathe. We've been together for so long. Don't you ever feel like you want some space for yourself? See who you are when you're not just half of Dan and Natalie?"

"No," I said through clenched teeth, although hearing him say that made something start ticking in my brain. "Because I *like* being part of a couple! It's never occurred to me that I would need time and space away from that. From the person I've spent ten years of my life being devoted to. The person I *thought* loved me the same way." But even as I said it, I felt kind of horrible because a truly devoted girlfriend would probably not spend as much time today as I did thinking about Miles Haas naked. Was Dan right? Did we need to step back instead of forward, make sure what we were planning was right? But it had to be right! We'd put ten years of time and effort into this!

"I do love you. It's not about that." Frustrated, Dan let go of me and fidgeted with his keys. "But I need to do this, Natalie. Or I'll always feel trapped."

I stuck my hands on my hips. "Fine. You go do what you need to do." I lifted my chin as my eyes finally filled, because I saw this for what it was, even if Dan didn't. "But I won't be waiting around for you once you're done with your alone time or your other people or whatever."

He pressed his lips together. "Don't say that. This isn't the end, Nat."

"Goodnight, Dan." Without another word, I marched to the door and let myself in. Slamming it behind me, I locked it and went straight for the booze.

Unbelievable! I thought, as I pulled the top off the vodka. A few tears fell as I poured myself a generous shot, slammed it, and then another. Sniffing, I swiped at my eyes with the back of one hand, my mind a swirling mass of confusion, anger, hurt, dread.

How dare he think he can treat me this way! How dare he fuck someone else and let me sleep in his bed? And how long has he known he was going to do this! He should have been honest from the start. I feel like a complete fool!

I slammed a third shot, and somewhere from underneath all the turmoil in my head sprang a little well of relief. Finally, the truth was out there. Things weren't perfect between Dan and me, and I didn't have to go on pretending they were. I didn't have to wonder why the sex wasn't passionate. I didn't have to worry that something was wrong with me. Because there wasn't! I was hot, dammit! Maybe I wasn't as gorgeous as Skylar or as thin as Jillian, but I had some nice assets of my own. Miles said my buns were amazing.

Miles.

My blood warmed at the thought of him. Or maybe it was the vodka.

But Miles wanted me, right? Miles would never turn me down.

I took another swig of vodka, right from the bottle. Little seeds of want planted themselves inside me.

I want to kiss Miles.

I want his hands on me.

I want to touch him everywhere.

I watered the seeds with more vodka, and they multiplied.

I want to hear him say he wants me.

I want to see him lose control over me.

I want to feel him inside me.

I tipped back the bottle again and admitted to myself what I'd been denying for two days.

I want to fuck Miles.

And now I can.

After one final shot for courage, I grabbed my phone, ordered myself an Uber, and punched in Miles's address. In the five minutes I had before the car arrived, I used the bathroom, changed from my usual plain underwear into something with lace, and brushed my teeth. What I didn't do was think too hard about the actual act of seduction.

Whatever. I'd wing it.

My stomach was jumping with nerves, so I took one more swallow of vodka, grimacing as it burned its way down my esophagus. When I saw headlights in the driveway, I bolted out the door, pulling it shut behind me. The booze hit me as I hurried toward the car, but I managed to stay on two feet and get myself into the back seat.

On the ride to Miles's, I texted him.

Hey are you home?

The reply came immediately. **Yes. Writing tonight. What's up?**

Yay! I'm coming over!!!

Should I put on the gimp suit?

I snorted. **That's funny you're funny I like you.**

WTF are you drunk?

Cackling with glee, I tossed my phone back in my purse. Miles was hilarious. And cute and smart and sweet and he did have a thing for me, didn't he? He wanted me, right? And when he saw me in my underwear, he wouldn't be able to resist me. Not like Dan. "Asshole," I muttered, right before another hiccup.

"I'm sorry?" said my driver.

"Nothing." Dang it, weren't we there yet? I was coming out of my skin with excitement, bouncing around in the backseat like a puppy. This was the best plan ever!

Finally, the big old house came into view, and my heart beat quicker when I saw the light on in Miles's bedroom window and the living room. "Thanks," I yelled, jumping out of the car before it even came to a complete stop. I ran up the front steps and banged on the big wooden door. Miles pulled it open, and before he could say anything, I lunged for him, smashing my mouth against his and throwing my arms around his neck.

I knocked him backward about five feet, his heels hit the bottom step of the staircase, and he went down on his ass. I ended up straddling him, one knee on either side of his legs, which I thought was perfect. Congratulating myself on the excellent choreography, I wiggled my hips a little.

"Natalie...what the hell?" Miles tried to pry my face off his. His glasses had been knocked askew, but he looked absolutely delicious. His hair was messier than usual, and he hadn't shaved in a few days, so his scruff was more like a beard. Dan was always clean-shaven, so kissing Miles felt totally different and thrilling. *I'm kissing Miles! Finally!* Nine years of suppressed desire bubbled to the surface.

"I want you to fuck me, Miles," I breathed, right before a hiccup. "And you want to."

"What?" His voice cracked, and he adjusted his glasses. "Whoa, whoa, whoa, crazypants, what is this?"

"This is fire." I planted sloppy, drunken kisses across his face. "Hey, your beard is softer than I spected. Ex-spested. *Expected.*" I rubbed my face on his jaw.

Miles laughed uneasily, pressing me back by the shoulders. "What have you been drinking tonight, Jezebel?"

"Wine. And vodka." Biting my lip, I reached beneath his t-shirt and ran my hands up his sides. "Take this off. I wanna see you naked."

"Oh, Jesus." He grabbed my wrists and held them away from his body. "What is *with* you? Where's Dan?"

I pouted. "I don't want to talk about that asshole."

"Why?"

"Because. He doesn't want to have sex with me."

Miles looked incredulous. "He doesn't?"

"No. But you do. You're always talking about it." I tried to lean over and kiss him again, but he held me off, so I bounced on him a little, riding him like a kid on a merry-go-round pony.

"For fuck's sake, Natalie, will you stop it? Just wait a second." Somehow, he got to his feet and set me on mine, then went behind me to shut the front door, which was still wide open. When he paused with his hand on the handle, probably trying to gather his wits, I launched myself at his back, wrapping my arms and legs around him. Burying my face in the crook of his neck, I inhaled deeply.

"Mmm. You smell so good." I licked him below the ear. "You taste good too."

He groaned, grabbing me beneath the knees so I didn't slide off, and walked into the dark living room. In front of a long, floral-upholstered couch, he turned around and sat down, trying to deposit me on it. "Get off."

"No." I clung even tighter. "Are we going to do it on your mother's expensive couch? I don't think she'd like that."

"No, we are not."

"So take me to your bed. Blindfold me. Tie me up. Fuck me!"

"Jesus, Nat, the only place I'd take you tonight is the loony bin. Now let go so I can turn on the light and get you some water. Or a tranquilizer dart."

"Come on, you want me," I cooed. "I know you do." I reached beneath his arms and ran my hands up and down his torso. He sighed exasperatedly, but he let me. Beneath his soft black t-shirt I felt the ridges of his abs and giggled. "I like your nice muscles. They're hot. You're hot stuff." One of my hands strayed south to his belt. Putting my lips right by his ear, I whispered, "Why don't you take off your pants, hot stuff?" This might have had a more seductive effect had I not punctuated it with a giant hiccup.

He shook his head. "You know, I've had a lot of fantasies about you. A lot. But they never went like this."

"I was less daring?"

"You were less drunk." He put his hand over my wrist. "Just how much alcohol have you had?"

"Dunno." I shrugged. "Doncare."

He sighed again. "Yes, you do. You will."

"No, I won't! Now why aren't you being fun? Your whole life is all about sex and fun and now that I'm ready for some, you don't want me?"

"It's not that." He tried to get up but I hung on tight.

"Then what?" I succeeded in sliding my palm over his crotch, and I could not resist a squeal of delight when I felt the solid bulge there. "Ha! You do want me!" I hiccuped loudly in triumph. "You're hard!"

"Of course I'm hard!" he snapped. "A hot girl has her legs wrapped around me and her hand on my junk. And you're not wrong—I do want you. I've always wanted you." Two seconds later, he had me on my back, my wrists pinned over my head. His face hovered right over mine, his breath warm on my lips. "But not like this."

"Like what?"

"Impaired." His eyes searched mine. "Angry. Hurt. I don't know what the fuck is going on with you and your asshole boyfriend, but I'd be the biggest dick in the world if I took advantage of you right now."

"You wouldn't be! I want this." His knee was wedged between my legs, and I squeezed it with my thighs. *God, that feels good.* "I need this."

Miles closed his eyes and exhaled. "Yes, you do. You need this and want this because you're looking to get back at Dan. But I'm not interested in those terms."

"Since when do you care what the terms are?" Angry that he'd fuck a stranger at the bar and *had* many times, I got in his face. "Casual sex is your thing, right single guy? Just treat me like another body or whatever."

He laughed, brittle and quick. "That's out of the question."

"Why? Why is it OK for you to have sex with total strangers, even two at a time, and not me?"

"It just is."

"Fuck you, Miles! You're a tease!" Panicking that he was going to reject me too and I'd die of frustration, I changed tactics, wiggling anxiously beneath him. "Look, I need this and want this because I haven't had sex in months, and I'm all hot and bothered right now, and you're gorgeous and you're here and I like you, so just shut up and do it already, OK?"

"Oh, fuck. This is a nightmare." He glanced toward the ceiling. "I hope you know the sacrifice I'm making here. You could at least give me a bestseller after this."

"Miles, please. Please." Lifting my head, I brushed my lips against his scruffy jaw, softening my approach. "Say yes."

He groaned and looked down at me again. "I can't. Because tomorrow, when you and Dan make up from whatever fight you've had, the way you always do, I'll be the asshole that fucked you when your defenses were down, and you'll never speak to me again."

Oh, God. He really was saying no. Just like Dan had. I turned my head to the side so he wouldn't see the tears of humiliation in my eyes.

He squeezed my wrists tights. "Look at me, Natalie. *Look* at me."

His tone was so forceful, his grip on me so tight, I had to do as he asked.

"Believe me when I say I want nothing more right now than to tell my conscience to fuck off, take you upstairs, blindfold you, tie you up, and spank you for being such a bad girl. Then I'd spend the rest of the night making you come over and over and over again. I'd fuck you so hard you'd forget your own name, let alone your stupid boyfriend's." He lowered his lips to my ear. "But if and when I fuck you, it's going to be about you and me, and no one else. Understand?"

A shiver moved through me, making my entire body tingle. In fact, for a second I thought I might come just from hearing Miles say those words to me. "Yes," I whispered.

"Good." Releasing my wrists, he stood up. "I'll get you some water and put some coffee on."

He left the room and I shut my eyes, putting both hands over my stomach. *Oh God, oh God, oh God.* I didn't know which was more powerful, my humiliation at being turned down or my raging lust. Had Miles really just said all that to me? It sounded so *good.* Not once in twenty-six years had I been talked to that way, or treated the way he'd described.

I wanted it.

I wanted it *so badly.*

I understood why he'd refused me, and maybe I did need to examine my motives for coming over here so soon after Dan admitted he'd cheated and asked for time apart. Did I really want to sleep with Miles? Had I just raced over here out of spite? Or was it because I was hot in the pants and thought he'd be a sure thing?

Jesus. This was so embarrassing. I'd been rejected by not one but *two* men in as many days: my own boyfriend, and a guy who once had sex in an airplane bathroom with a flight attendant whose name he had forgotten by the time he told me about it.

(How was that even possible? There is no room in those bathrooms!)

What the hell was wrong with me? Bringing my hands to my face, I curled up in a ball and wept into them.

A week ago, my life had seemed right on track.

What had gone wrong?

CHAPTER 8
Miles

IT TOOK every ounce of strength I had, and some I didn't, to walk out of that room. There she was, desperate and needy and begging me to fuck her, this beautiful, perfect woman I'd idealized and adored, and I'd had to turn her down.

Fucking hell.

I braced myself with both arms on the granite island in the kitchen, grimacing as I willed my dick to give up the dream and retreat. *You can stop being hard now. It's not happening tonight. I know that's a shock, but just relax already. I'll pay attention to you later.*

After a few deep breaths and some concentrated thoughts on unsexy things like my great aunt Mildred, the smell of pigeon shit, and doing my taxes, my heart rate slowed and my cock seemed to get the message.

I made a fresh pot of coffee, dumping what was left over from this afternoon. The words hadn't been flowing too well today, and I'd hoped a caffeine infusion would help. But mostly I'd spent the day brooding over Natalie, annoyed that I couldn't stop thinking about her. But there was nothing I could do about it. She was a relationship person; I was not.

The End.

But fucking Dan! What had he done to her tonight to make her show up here like this? It was torture! I'd fucked girls with boyfriends in the past, I'd fucked friends in the past, and I certainly had no hang-ups about no-strings-attached sex, but something inside me would not go there with her. She was different.

She was also drunk.

She had to be, throwing herself at me that way, saying those things. That wasn't like her at all. Blindfold her? Tie her up? Jesus, I loved the thought that there might be a kinky side of Natalie to explore, but the circumstances here were too fraught with the wrong kind of tension. Until I was confident that she wasn't coming after me just to spite her boyfriend, I wasn't going to risk ruining our friendship over one night of hot sex. It was bad enough I said those things to her… although I'd meant them.

Fuck yes, I'd meant them. I wanted nothing more than to tease her, play with her, make her vulnerable for all the right reasons. I wanted to see her naked and needy beneath me, her skin slick with sweat, her legs open for me. I'd make her come with my tongue first, use my fingers inside her, and when she was drenched and panting and whispering my name, I'd slide into her, slowly at first, make her feel every inch of my hard—

Oh, for fuck's sake. Again?

Adjusting myself so my erection wasn't pinned painfully inside my jeans, I briefly considered going upstairs to jerk off before the coffee was done. It would only take a minute. But then I heard a few muffled sobs coming from the living room, and my chest caved a little. She needed me more than my dick did. *Sorry, buddy. Usually I put you first, but not tonight.*

I found some Motrin in a kitchen cabinet, poured a glass of water and then some coffee, and I put everything on a tray I saw lying on the counter. Feeling pleased with myself, I carried the tray into the living room, set it on the coffee table, and switched on a lamp.

She was curled in a ball on the couch, her shoes on the floor, one bare foot covering the other one. Her dress had ridden up, and I willed myself not to peek at her crotch.

OK, I peeked. She was wearing black lace panties. *Fuck.*

But her face was buried in her hands, and her whole body shook with sad, pitiful sobs.

"Hey. Come on. It's not that bad." I sat down next to her and put a hand on her back.

"Yes, it is," she wept.

"Talk to me. What happened tonight?" I patted her as she kept crying, feeling a little awkward. Usually when a woman cries, I find any possible escape hatch, but I wanted to comfort Natalie, who had never been a crier, even as a kid. The only other time I'd ever seen her cry, in fact, was the night we said goodbye up here. Another near miss for us. Were we always destined to have this bad timing?

I reached for her arm and pulled her up to a sitting position, then gathered her close so her cheek rested on my chest. Immediately she brought her knees up toward her chin, tucking her little feet between my legs. Her arms were folded into her chest, and I wrapped my arms around her whole body, legs and all. The tears stopped, and her breathing slowed. I lowered my face to her hair and inhaled.

God, she smells delicious.

I tried not to think about tomorrow, when she'd go back to that fucker, and he'd be the one who got to hold her.

Eventually she pulled away from me, putting her feet on the floor. "I have to blow my nose. I'll be right back," she said, hiding her face from me as she hurried from the room.

I heard the bathroom door open and close, and she was gone for several minutes. For a moment, I worried she was sick from the alcohol, but she reappeared in the living room looking puffy-faced and pink-eyed, but otherwise OK.

I picked up the Motrin from the tray and held them out to her. "Here. Take these."

"Thanks." She dropped onto the couch and took the pills from me, then popped them in her mouth. After drinking the entire glass of water, she picked up the coffee cup and sipped.

"Better?"

"Yeah. The world is just a little topsy turvy right now. I'm a bit dizzy."

"Been there. Want to get some air?"

She inhaled and exhaled slowly. "Yes."

We went out on the wraparound porch, and I pulled the front door shut behind us, making sure it was unlocked. To our right was a swing, which was probably not what she needed right now, and to our left were a few wooden chairs.

"Want to sit?" I gestured to the chairs, and she nodded. I sat next to her but didn't say anything right away. I wondered what she wanted to hear—should I ask what happened? Should I just wait for her to spill? Should I apologize for turning her down? She understood why I had to, didn't she?

Finally she spoke. "I'm sorry. This was such a bad idea."

"It's OK."

"No, it's not. I put you in a really bad position."

I paused. "Actually you had me in some really nice positions."

She slapped my wrist lightly, but she smiled a familiar smile, and I felt infinitely better. "You know what I mean."

I nodded. "I do. And I will probably regret my decision for the rest of my life, especially if you get back together with the Douchebag tomorrow. I'm running out of chances with you."

She tilted her head. "What do you mean?"

"Well, tonight. And then…" I looked out across the orchard toward her parents' house. "That night before I left for school. I wanted to—whatever, but I didn't."

"Why not?"

"Because you were with Dan, and even if we *had*—" I struggled to find words.

"Whatevered," she supplied.

"Right. Even if we *had* whatevered, I felt like you'd have regretted it and our friendship would have suffered. And our friendship was important to me. So I forced myself to leave you alone." I laughed a little at the way things had come full circle. "It's funny, I remember coming back home and sitting right here on this porch, wondering if I was an idiot or a gentleman."

She took a sip of coffee, holding the cup in both hands. "And tonight?"

I smiled wryly. "Exactly the same."

"Well, I think you're a gentleman."

"Aha. See?" I pointed at her. "You agree that it would have been a mistake. You'd have been sorry tomorrow. I was right."

"I'm not saying that," she said defensively. "I'm just telling you that you're a gentleman, not an idiot. *I'm* the idiot, coming here and throwing myself at you." Her cheeks flushed scarlet, and she rolled her eyes. "God."

"Natalie." I put my hand on her arm. "Many women have trouble controlling their sexual urges around me. You need not be ashamed."

She groaned. "Promise you're not going to make fun of me for this the rest of our lives."

"No way. I'm not that big a gentleman."

Her face went pale. "But you can't tell anyone about this."

"Sure I can. But I won't. In return, you tell me what the fuck happened tonight that made you lose your marbles."

She sighed and looked across the fields toward her childhood home. "Dan wants time apart. Either that or we broke up. I'm not sure."

"What? Why?"

"He said he wants a break. He said it would be good for

us to see who we are when we're not a couple." She sipped her coffee. "He said we should be free to see other people and do what we want for a while before we get married."

I blinked. That was so fucked up. He had her, and he wanted other girls?

"I lied to you yesterday when I said things were great sexually between us. They're not." She stared into her coffee. "He doesn't seem to want me like that anymore, yet he says he still loves me. He...he cheated on me last night. And I think he's done it before."

Furious, I clenched my fists in my lap. "God, I'd like to punch that asshole right now. If he wanted other girls all this time, he should have said something and you guys should've broken up a long time ago. That's the thing about having a girlfriend—you don't get to fuck other girls. He doesn't get to have it both ways." Maybe my anger was hypocritical, since I'd been with girls who had boyfriends before, but goddammit, this was twice now I'd refrained from touching Natalie the way I wanted to, the way every bone in my body was aching to. OK, so I wasn't exactly doing it for *him*, but he was a tangential reason why I wasn't fucking her right this minute, and I was livid about it.

"He's not asking for both ways." Natalie bristled a little. "That's why he asked for the break."

"You're defending him now?" It came out louder than I'd intended, but I couldn't help it. I could write a fucking encyclopedia about all the ways he didn't deserve her.

"No! I mean, not really." She sighed, her eyes closing. "I'm just trying to decide if there's anything left there to salvage, I guess. But I don't even know what I want anymore. I'm so confused. And so tired. And I have to get up so early tomorrow."

My anger dissipated. *Be a friend, not an asshole. This isn't about you or your dick.* "Come on. I can take you home." I stood up and she grabbed my hand.

"No." She looked up at me, her cheeks going a little pink. "I don't want to be alone tonight. Can I stay with you?"

I blinked. Wow. God really wanted to test me tonight. "Uh. Sure."

"I'll just open a little later tomorrow."

"I can take you early. I don't mind." *See, God? I'm such a good person right now. I'm not even going to get myself off while she's in the house, even though I really, really need to.*

She cocked a brow. "Like four AM early? I have to go home first for work clothes."

I shrugged. "Sure. Or you can take my car. Whatever you want." I gave her hand a quick squeeze and dropped it. "There are no sheets on the beds in any guest rooms. Let me make one up for you real quick."

"Can't I stay in your room?"

Really, God? "You want to stay in my room?"

"Yeah. Don't you have two beds?"

I shook my head. "My mother replaced them with a queen."

"Oh." Her eyes fell for a second, but then she lifted her shoulders. "Well, I don't care if you don't."

You don't care that you'll be sleeping in the same bed as my erection all night long? Great. It's a plan. "Um, OK."

Upstairs, I gave her a clean t-shirt and she went into the bathroom to change. In my room, I undressed down to my boxers, which was how I usually slept, but decided to throw on some pajama pants. The more barriers between her body and mine, the better. But then she came into the room, looking adorably sexy and clean-faced in my shirt, and I didn't even try not to stare at her nipples, which poked through the thin white cotton. My cock jumped, and I rushed across the hall into the bathroom, where I vigorously brushed my teeth and thought about Aunt Mildred until blood stopped rushing between my legs.

The light was off in my room when I returned, and I could

barely make out her shape under the blanket. Leaving my glasses on the bedside table, I slid between the sheets, careful to stay on my side. When was the last time a woman slept in my bed without orgasms being involved? I couldn't think of one time, actually. I didn't even know what to do with myself.

I lay there for a while on my back, hands beneath my head, breathing slowly and deeply, trying to stay calm. But I could smell her perfume, and it was making me hard again. Fuck! Was she asleep already? Could I rub one out without her knowing? I braved a look at her, and my eyes had adjusted to the dark enough to see that she was facing away from me, curled up on her side. Long, agonizing, minutes ticked by, during which I imagined rubbing my cock along the crack of her ass, which was sticking out in my direction. Taunting me.

"I lied to you last night." Her voice was so soft, I thought I might have imagined it. Or dreamed it.

"Huh?" *Stop thinking about her ass.*

She rolled to her other side and faced me, tucking her hands beneath her cheek. "I lied last night. I told you I didn't remember what you said to me the night we said goodbye. The night before you left for school."

I blinked in surprise. "Oh."

"Did you really mean the things you said?"

"Of course I meant them. I stand by every word I've ever said to you." *And my cock is standing straight up right now. So if you could please stop being beautiful and sexy and vulnerable, I'd appreciate it. Thanks.*

She took a shuddery breath. "And yet...tonight, you wouldn't—"

"Tonight was not about us, Natalie."

"But...what if it was?" She paused. "What if it could be?"

Fuck, was she serious? Because I wanted that. I wanted a night that was just about us, wanted to show her what it was like to be with someone who appreciated her. Just *one night*, even if it was all we ever had. But I couldn't be the one to initiate it, not without knowing it was really OK.

"Natalie," I started, but she interrupted me.

"I'm lying here thinking, a week ago my life seemed so complete, everything in order. My relationship. My business. My house. I had everything I wanted."

"And now?"

"Now I feel like I've been missing something. Like maybe I was wrong about what I wanted. I feel…lost." She looked at me with her huge, round blue eyes, making my whole body heat up.

"You're not lost." Rolling onto my side, I met her forehead with mine. "You're right here with me."

And I kissed her. Just like that, I kissed her.

I'd kind of intended it to be a quick, friendly, reassuring sort of kiss, but then I couldn't stop.

I kissed her again. And again. I couldn't help it.

She put a hand on the back of my neck, threading her fingers through my hair. "I can't stop thinking about you, Miles." Her words came breathlessly, as if they were taking her by surprise. "That's why I came here tonight. I know you think it was about Dan and not you, but ever since you called me yesterday morning, I can't get you out of my head. And the things you're doing there…" She breathed deeply, inhaling and exhaling as her eyes traveled down my chest to where the blanket covered me to the hips and back up again. "The things you said to me on the couch…I want that. I want you."

Oh, yeah. This is happening. Tonight.

I gave her a wicked grin. "Good. Because guess what?"

"What?"

I scooped her up and rolled over, pinning her beneath me. "The gentleman is on a break."

CHAPTER 9
Natalie

HE KISSED me deep and hard, his mouth slanting over mine, his tongue sliding between my lips. I welcomed it, sliding my fingers into his hair, tasting him for the first time. *It's Miles! I'm kissing Miles! In his bed!* I had first-time butterflies in my belly and felt the tingle all the way to my toes. It had been so long since I'd even kissed another guy—everything felt new and different, and I couldn't catch my breath. I reveled in the weight of his body over mine, his hips between my thighs, his hard length trapped between us. I ran my hands down his bare back, tilted my hips to meet his, my entire body hot and alive, radiating with desire.

This, I thought as we frantically tore off each other's clothes. *This is fire.*

Miles knelt between my thighs, and my heart clamored in my chest. His body was *beautiful*. Ever since I'd walked in on him shirtless in his pajama pants, my nipples had been hard and my panties damp. I'd had to look away, scared my arousal was too obvious and he'd go sleep on the couch or something. Now I stared unabashedly at his muscular chest and stomach, the ink covering his arm, the V lines low on his torso that pointed directly to his thick, hard cock. Having only seen one dick in my entire life—and frankly, it was nowhere near as impressive as this one—I felt like I'd just unwrapped a shiny new toy, and I couldn't wait to get my hands on it. I sat up and reached for him, but immediately he pushed my hands away and tipped me backward again, bracing himself above me.

"Want something?" The sly grin was back.

"Yes," I panted.

"What do you want?"

He wanted to hear it again? Perfect, because I'd say it all night long. "I want you to fuck me. Hard."

"Hmmmm." Sitting back on his heels, he put his palms on my quivering stomach and slid them up to my breasts, squeezing gently. Then he began circling his thumbs around my nipples, making them tingle and ache without even touching them, a sublime little torture. "I love hearing you say that, and you're so fucking beautiful," he said, finally brushing the backs of his fingertips over the taut peaks. Then he pinched them, hard, and I cried out—in pain and relief. "But you were a bad girl today, weren't you? Coming over here in your black lace panties telling me to fuck you." He pinched me again. "Pretending *all this time* to be the innocent girl next door, teasing me with what I could never have, when you really just wanted to get fucked."

I started to protest, to tell him I hadn't been pretending, that I really was sort of innocent where sex was concerned, but he immediately clamped a hand over my mouth, hard.

"No excuses, Naughtalie Nixon. You misbehaved, and now I have to punish you." Suddenly he flipped me over onto my belly and hitched up my hips so I was on my knees. When I tried to get up, he grabbed a handful of my hair and held my head down, pushing my cheek into the mattress. "Don't. Move. Or you won't get what you want."

I'd always liked the low, gravelly sound of his voice, but

now it made me so hot I wanted to scream. It was Miles, but it was a side of him I'd never known, still playful but also commanding, and it almost made him seem like a stranger. I could feel his cock pressing against my ass, and I shivered in anticipation, biting my lip. What would he do to me?

He sat back, letting go of my hair. "Say you were a bad girl."

I giggled—mostly from nerves—and he cracked one palm hard across my ass, making me yelp.

Fuck! That kinda hurt!

But it made me want to please him.

He put his hand over the stinging skin. "Say it."

"I was a bad girl," I said softly, coquettishly.

He smacked the other cheek even harder, and I cried out again. "Louder, Natalie."

"I was a bad girl!"

"Good." He smacked me a third time. A fourth. "Tell me to spank you harder."

"Spank me harder." Wincing, I braced myself for the sting, but it didn't come.

"Say it like you mean it, please."

"Spank me harder!" I yelled. *Crack!* His palm slapped my ass with enough force to bring tears to my eyes, but I was so turned on I was smiling deliriously.

"Good girl." He rubbed both hands over the burning skin. "Fucking hell, your ass is phenomenal. I could punish you all night."

"No," I said breathlessly. "You promised to fuck me."

"That's right." Reaching beneath me, he turned me onto my back and slipped a hand between my legs. "I promised to fuck you hard, didn't I. Are you wet for me?" He stroked me shallowly, finding my pussy slick with desire.

"Yes." I whimpered as he slid one finger easily inside me, and then two, his thumb rubbing my clit.

"Good."

I rocked my hips against his hand, panting in frustration. "Miles," I begged. "Now."

"So impatient," he chided. "It took me years to get you into bed, honeypot. You have to let me play a little." Moving down the bed, he lowered his head between my thighs and replaced his thumb with his tongue, licking my clit with long, firm strokes. "Mmmm, don't come until I say so, OK? You are absolutely fucking delicious, and I need to savor every bit of this meal in case I never get to eat out at this restaurant again."

"Oh, God." My entire body was so coiled up with sexual tension, I was nearly in tears, yet he could still makes jokes and tease me.

He bit my inner thigh as he twisted his fingers inside me, putting pressure where I'd never felt it before, a spot that had my eyes rolling back in my head.

"If you don't want me to come too soon, you better stop touching me like that."

"You like that?" His fingers plunged deeper inside me as he teased my clit with the tip of his tongue, his lips, his teeth.

My legs twitched. "Fuck yes. Oh God."

"Don't come yet, you naughty thing. Wait for permission." But then he buried his face in my pussy and sucked my clit into his mouth, flicking it hard with his tongue.

I felt myself spiraling upward, and had no idea how to control it. Unable to help myself, I rocked my hips instinctively, grinding against his mouth. "Oh God, I'm sorry, it's been too long, and you're too good, and I'm going to come so hard, and oh fuck—Miles. Yes. Yes! *Yes!*" I moaned in agony and delight, my hands clawing at the sheets as the orgasm reached its highest peak. At the moment of release, I grabbed his head, fisting my hands in his hair as my body released all the tortuous tension inside it in blissful pulsing waves.

"Fuck." Miles crawled up my body, licking his lips. "That was so hot. But you are a very bad girl to come before I said you could. I knew you were just pretending to be such a goody two shoes all these years."

I laughed, trying to catch my breath. "You know what? Maybe I was."

"And inside you was a wanton little harlot just waiting for me to let her out."

I reached between us, finally wrapping my hand around his cock. "I want *you* inside me."

"Yeah? You want my cock inside you?" He closed his eyes, his game face slipping slightly as I worked my hand up and down his hot, hard length.

"Yes. But first." I shimmied down between his legs until my head was right between his thighs.

"What's this?" Miles looked down at me in surprise.

"What if I never get to eat at this restaurant again?" I asked coyly, angling his cock toward my mouth and rubbing its smooth tip on my lips. I had never, *never*, acted this boldly before, but Miles was inspiring me to let my instincts take over, play a little, take my time and enjoy this for what it was —good, dirty fun. How had I gotten to be so serious about sex?

"Ah. I see. In that case..." He tipped forward, bracing himself against the headboard. "Bon appétit."

Keeping one hand wrapped around the base, I swirled my tongue around the tip, closing my eyes and focusing on the velvety feel of his skin, the salty-sweet taste, the sound of his labored breaths above me. Lifting my head off the bed, I took the head in my mouth, sucking gently at first, and then harder. With my other hand, I reached between his legs and played with his balls, cupping them gently and sliding my finger along the sensitive spot behind them. When he moaned, I picked my head up further, taking his cock into my mouth as far as it would go, letting the tip hit the back of my throat.

"Jesus," he rasped above me, his hips beginning to move.

"That feels so fucking good. You are invited to this restaurant eight days a fucking week."

Grabbing his ass, I pulled him toward me, jerking him into my mouth with one hand and sucking greedily. He began to thrust faster, his hips pumping in deep, forceful jabs that pushed my head back onto the bed. A tingling rush of heat swept up my center as I imagined him driving into my pussy that way. Moaning appreciatively, I slid one hand up the front of his body. Really it was just a cheap feel of his abs and chest, but when my fingertips brushed over his nipple, he inhaled sharply and groaned in pleasure.

What's this? Miles Haas has sensitive nipples?

It's hard to smile with a dick in your mouth, but I was pleased as punch when pinching one resulted in another quick intake of breath and a throb of his cock.

"Christ," he growled, pushing off the headboard and taking my head in his hands. "Is this real?"

I looked up, our eyes met, and something happened between us, shifting the mood from playful to serious. His expression was hot and dark as he curled his fingers in my hair, pulling it as he slid his cock deeper into my mouth, so deep I nearly choked.

"I love how deep you take me," he whispered, holding still. "I love watching my cock slide between your beautiful lips. I love the sounds you make. I could come so hard right now."

I was totally willing to let him, so I was surprised when he pulled out of my mouth and stretched out over me.

"But I've been waiting to get inside you for so long, and if I only get one chance with you, this is what I want."

"Yes," I breathed. "It's what I want too."

The hot, wet tip of his cock teased my pussy. "Do you... Let me get a condom."

For a second I thought he wanted to do it without protection, and the way I felt right now, I'd have let him. Still, I was glad when he got out of bed and rummaged through a bag on the floor near his closet. In less than a minute he was back, rolling on the condom before positioning himself between my legs.

I touched his cheek, overcome with affection for him. "See? You *are* a gentleman, Miles."

He kissed me. I thought he would tease me some more, make me wait, order me to say something dirty, but he didn't. He just kissed my lips and slid inside me silently, reverently, my breath still as he reached the deepest spot.

"Are you OK?" he asked.

"Yes." Closing my eyes, I smiled at the perfect fit.

"Can I keep going?"

My eyes flew open. "There's more?"

He smiled, making my heart flutter furiously in my chest. "Yeah."

I took a deep breath, wrapping my legs around him. "Give me everything."

He pushed in even deeper, going slow, allowing me time to get used to his size.

"It feels like the first time," I whispered, gasping at the way he filled me, at the way the twinge of pain only added to my arousal.

"It is." When he was completely sheathed inside me, he closed his eyes. "It fucking is the first time."

"Miles," I whispered, my body igniting again. "Your voice does things to me."

"My voice, huh?" He began to move over me, rippling, rolling undulations of his body that had me sighing. No wonder he wrote about sex—he was so *good*.

"Yes." I ran my hands down his sides, up his back, digging my nails into his skin.

He groaned. "Everything about you does things to me.

Fucking everything. Your eyes, your laugh, your perfect mouth. And don't even get me started on your ass." He moved his hips a little faster, but stayed tight to my body so the base of his cock rubbed my clit.

"Oh God, that feels good." The lovely storm inside me built again, and I knew without a doubt Miles would indeed give me a first—two orgasms in one night. "You're gonna make me come twice. I've never done that."

"Oh, fuck." He moved his hands beneath me to grab my ass, tilting my hips as he drove into me, and at first it hurt because he was hitting me so hard and deep, but then something started to happen inside me—it felt like an orgasm was building, but it wasn't centered in the usual place. I mean, one was building there too, but this was something else. Muscles deep within I didn't even know I had were tightening around him like a vise and suddenly I couldn't see or speak or even hear. My world went white as the contraction reached its apex and it seemed like I would balance on the precipice forever, suspended there between purgatory and nirvana. My mouth hung open, and I dropped my head to the side, desperate for climax, as he slowed down, the tip of his cock teasing that perfect spot. Oh God... I was going to die.

"You want it?" Miles growled in my ear, the little pulses of his hips driving me mad. "You want everything?"

"Yes!" I cried, near tears. "Yes!"

He rocked into me hard and fast. Then it began—the longest, most intense orgasm of my life. An orgasm that jarred my bones, stopped my heart, stole my breath. It was more powerful, more potent, more euphoric than any orgasm I'd ever experienced. It was a *moregasm*, and I never wanted it to end.

In the final throes, Miles changed his position a little and lasted only about two seconds before I felt the skin on his back ripple with gooseflesh and his body went stiff above me. I lifted my hips, giving him more friction, and he moaned as his cock throbbed deep inside me.

He dropped his head into the crook of my neck. "Oh my God. Natalie."

I ran my hands through his hair, overcome with affection for him. "What?"

"I... I can't find words."

"No?"

"No. Wait, yes. Hold on. I need to breathe. I'm not thinking straight." He laid his cheek on my chest.

Every part of my body was still tingling as I cradled his head. "It's OK, honey."

"Wow." He inhaled and exhaled. "This is crazy. I have spent a lot of time fantasizing about fucking you. Like, a lot. But the real thing just blew the fantasy out of the water."

"Oh, stop."

"No, I mean it." He picked up his head and looked down at me. "In general, I'm a fan of sex, but that—that was something else entirely."

"I agree. What the hell did you do to me in there? I've never felt that before."

"Good." He kissed my collarbone. My breast. My cheek.

"We must have really needed that, huh?"

"Well, I did. That's for sure. Nine years, I've been waiting. And yes, you were worth it." His whole body shivered.

I giggled. "Oh yeah?"

"Definitely."

"Good. Maybe I won't make you wait another nine before we do it again."

He looked elated. "Seriously?"

I shrugged. "That was the most fun I've ever had in bed, spankings and all."

"Sweetheart, you keep being bad like you were tonight, and I'll spank you as often as you like."

"We'll see," I said slyly. "Now you better let me get some sleep because I have to get up and go to work in like an hour or something."

Miles rolled off of me, put his glasses on and picked up his phone. "You have to get up at four?"

"Yes. What time is it?"

"You don't want to know."

"Tell me."

"Two fifteen."

"Oh God. Tomorrow is not going to feel good."

"But tonight did."

I smiled. "Yes. It did."

Miles went across the hall to the bathroom, and when he came back, I went. After cleaning up a little, I looked at my reflection in the mirror and actually felt like smiling. My hair was a wreck, my eyes were still puffy, and my face was a little scratched from Miles's scruffy chin, but I looked happy. Relaxed. Satisfied.

With a spring in my step, I went back into Miles's room and jumped into bed next to him. Immediately, he pulled me into his arms, spooning me.

"This is what I wanted to do earlier," he said, his arm tight around my waist. "Before the sex happened."

I laughed, snuggling back into him. "This probably would have led to the sex anyway."

I felt a little nudge against my ass.

"Um, it still might."

I sighed, but secretly I was thrilled. "OK, but a quickie this time. No eating at the restaurant first."

"No promises." He kissed the back of my neck, my shoulder blade, my upper arm. "It so happens that I have a taste for buns right now, and you, my sweet, have the best buns around." He kissed his way down my arm and threw the blankets off, putting his lips on my hip. When he sank his teeth into my ass, making me shriek, I realized I didn't care if I ever slept before the sun came up.

Who knew what tomorrow would be like—maybe we'd

go back to being just friends, maybe not. I was just as confused about my feelings as I had been before.

But if I only had one night with Miles, I wanted to make it count.

CHAPTER 10
Miles

JESUS. Fucking. Christ.

How was it possible that Natalie was even better in my bed than she'd been in my head? No woman should have been able to live up to the idealized version of her that I'd dreamed about, but not only did she look gorgeous naked, have a deliciously sweet pussy, and insist on sucking my dick, but she was playful enough to let me spank her, submissive when I wanted her to be, and yet unafraid to take what she wanted from me. To ask for it. And the way she looked up at me when I was inside her—like she'd never been with anyone else. Like she'd waited for me all this time. Like she was mine.

It was almost enough to make me believe it.

But then, everything with us was always *almost*.

I almost lost control when she pinched my nipple.

I almost asked to fuck her without a condom.

I almost told her I loved her when it was over.

Almost.

She'd changed the subject and gotten out of bed before I could embarrass myself, thank God, and I'd had a few minutes to regain my fucking sanity. Then we cuddled up close and I'd had every intention of letting her close those big blue eyes and get some sleep.

But her ass...it was right there next to my dick, and I cannot be responsible for ideas my dick gives me when it's close to her ass. I just can't. Even when the idea is to bite it so hard she screams.

And then it was like magic, because instead of telling me to fuck off and leave her be, she turned to me and opened her arms. And her legs. And her lips. It didn't even feel real. Was it just make-believe, like all the games we used to play?

I want you, she said.

I trust you, she said.

Give me everything, she said.

That was my favorite—give me everything.

I would. I would give her everything.

Even if it was only make-believe.

CHAPTER 11
Natalie

THE NEXT DAY at work should have been miserable. I think Miles and I might have slept for half an hour, but even after we did it a second time, we found it hard to sleep. Our bodies were tired, but we kept making jokes, or kicking one another, or bringing up a childhood memory that made us laugh. The entire night was just ours, like we existed outside of time, in our own little world. Granted, the beginning of the evening was a bit shaky, and there were plenty of cracks on his part about my drunken attempt at seduction, but by five AM when we stumbled out to his Jeep, shushing each other because my parents' house was right next door, exhausted and sore and smiling, I was convinced it had been the best night of my life. Not just because of the sex, but because it was the lightest I'd felt in I couldn't remember how long. I had no clue what the hell was going on with my life, but for once, I didn't care.

Miles drove me to my house and dozed on the couch while I took a two-minute shower and changed, then he insisted on coming into the shop with me and helping me open up. I told him it wasn't necessary, but he said he'd work for buns, so I let him stay.

We were like two goofy kids all morning, snickering whenever we made eye contact, making jokes about glazing buns, and sometimes just dropping everything to kiss—he'd back me up against the giant stainless refrigerator, I'd jump up and straddle him out of nowhere, he'd corner me in the walk-in pantry.

It was silly and sexy and exactly what I needed, so I didn't dwell on the fact that in the three years since I'd owned this shop, not once had Dan ever come in to help me open up. I don't even think he'd ever offered—if I'd stayed the night at his place, he drove me to my condo and went right back home, or he'd let me take his car.

But Miles...Miles stayed with me.

So all morning I ignored my phone when I saw that it was Dan calling, and I never opened any of his texts. If he showed up, I'd kick his sorry ass right out.

When Hailey arrived, I could see her looking back and forth between Miles and me, wondering what was going on with us. I'd introduced him as an old friend the other day, but even though she was barely out of her teens, I think she knew better. The air between us crackled with sexual energy.

At around noon, the caffeine buzz started to wear off. "Oh my God," I said, slumping onto the kitchen counter. "I'm dying. I'm not gonna make it."

"Yes, you will." Miles was on dish duty, loading cups and plates and silverware into the washer since I'd asked Hailey to be more visible up front today. My puffy eyes with dark circles underneath were not fit to be seen out there.

"I'm not. I'm gonna die. Need sleep."

"We're gonna nap so hard when we're done here, Nat. I'm serious. Fucking gold medal nap."

"Nap. Naaaaaaaaap," I moaned.

"A couple more hours. You can do it." He came over and took me by the shoulders, straightening me up. "Hey. You're taking the day off tomorrow. You work too hard."

I laughed weakly, but I felt like crying. "I can't do that."

"Yes, you can. And you will. If I have to pay your staff myself, you are doing it."

I sighed. "Michael will be back. He can probably handle things for a day."

"He can. I am sure of it."

"You don't even know him."

"Doesn't matter. You hired him, so he's talented and competent. He can run a goddamn diner for a day."

I made a face. "It's not easy, you know."

"I know. Believe me." He gathered me close, and I rested my head on his shoulder, thinking that if he just stayed still, I could sleep like this, standing up. "There's a reason I chose writing as a profession. I don't want to be in charge of people. I'm barely good at being in charge of myself. But you're amazing at it. You're so amazing that Michael has picked up on exactly what to do to keep this place going in your absence for a day. Or a week."

I pulled away from him. "What week?"

"A vacation. You need a week off, I think." He rubbed his hand over his jaw, then snapped his fingers. "A road trip. That's it."

"You're insane. I can't leave here for a week!"

"A road trip to…" Miles went on as if I hadn't spoken. "Detroit!" His face lit up. "We'll drive down to Detroit, spend a few days there hanging out, and I'll show you all my favorite places. How about it?"

"A week? No way." I folded my arms. "Can't do it."

"Then three days." Miles took me by the wrists and shook my arms. "That's all I ask. Three days of relaxation and fun with me, and then you can come back here, be a grown up and make that frowny face all you like."

I snatched my arms away. "I don't make a frowny face!"

He burst out laughing. "You do. It looks like this." He set his jaw stubbornly, his bottom lip a little pouty, and squinted.

I winced. "Please tell me I do not make that face."

"You do," he assured me. "But I would too if I dealt with managing people day in and day out. Or if I just got out of a dead end relationship and needed to have some fun."

I looked away, a little sadness seeping into my bloodstream for the first time today. I'd successfully avoided thinking too much about Dan, for the most part, unless it was to make unfavorable comparisons to Miles. But that wasn't really fair. Miles wasn't here to stay, either.

A week. That was his best offer.

Should I take it?

"I don't know," I said. "Let me think about it."

Miles grabbed my face and planted a big kiss on my lips. "You're adorable when you're serious. It makes me want to spank you."

"Shhhhhhhh!" I shoved his hands down. "Someone might hear you."

"Good." He grabbed me again, pulling my head to his chest and yanking on my hair. "Everyone should know the real you, you dirty slut."

"Oh my God." I pushed him away, but I had to laugh. "You are a horrible person, and I am too tired to deal with horrible people right now. That's the whole reason I'm back here today."

"Fine. I will go out and charm your customers for you." He adjusted the crotch of his pants. "You're welcome."

Two hours later, Miles drove me back to my house, and I had a hard time staying awake on the ten-minute ride.

"Want to come in and nap with me?" I asked. "Then when

we wake up, I can give you a tour." I did want to show him the house, but honestly I just didn't want to part with him yet. The moment he left my side I'd have to deal with the fallout of my relationship, including the fact that Dan had cheated on me, and I didn't think I was ready to face that yet. Miles was the perfect distraction, and I was giving myself permission to be distracted for the time being. Something I'd *never* done before.

"Hell, yes." He turned off the car, and pulled the key from the ignition. "You were right. Working that place is exhausting."

I smiled. "Only on no sleep. Otherwise it can be fun. Come on in."

Bleary-eyed, we stumbled into my house, managed to get up the stairs, and tumbled across my bed sideways, me on my stomach and Miles on his back, our legs hanging off the side. We didn't even take off our shoes, didn't say another word, didn't move for hours, waking only when my phone rang. I heard it, but it sounded far away, like it was in a dream. Eventually I realized what it was and reached into my purse, which rested near my head. The screen said Skylar.

"Hello?" I croaked.

"Hey, where are you?"

"I'm home." I wiped drool from my mouth and frowned at the wet spot on my comforter. "Why?"

"Dinner at Mom and Dad's, remember?"

"Oh crap. No, I didn't."

"Well, come over. We're waiting for you."

I thought about making an excuse and turning her down. What could I say? My mind was a dead zone, and all I could do was whine. "But I'm tiiiired."

"Come on, Mom's grilling Italian sausage." She laughed. "And you need some sausage."

"Hahaha."

Miles opened his eyes, rubbed his face with one hand, and looked over at me. "Did someone say sausage?"

Ten minutes later, we were on our way to my parents' house.

"Do not say anything to them about anything," I warned. "Not Dan, not us, not anything."

"Why? Are you ashamed of me?" Miles feigned offense, putting a hand on his chest. "I'm hurt by this, Natalie. You want to hide our love."

I rolled my eyes. "Look, I'm sure this is all fun for you, but breaking up with Dan is a big deal for me. I'm not ready to announce it yet."

He went quiet for a moment. "Is it because you're not ready to face it yet?"

"I don't know. Maybe." I glanced over at him. "Is that OK?"

"It's fine." He put his hand on my thigh, which was bare since I'd changed from my work shorts into a short white skirt I'd paired with a soft gray t-shirt. "I think the guy was an ass, but you loved him for a lot of years. I'm sure that doesn't just turn off overnight because you're mad. No one would ever stay married if that were the case, not that many people stay married, anyway."

"Right." Sighing, I rolled down my window and closed my eyes, letting the wind hit my face. I *was* mad, not as mad as I'd been last night, but still. Dan should have been honest with me from the start about feeling trapped. But then again, wasn't he right about me needing time apart too? Hadn't I felt relief when I realized I could run straight to Miles and not feel guilty about it? What did that say about me?

"Stop thinking so hard." Miles rubbed his hand on my leg.

"I can't help it. I was totally shocked and hurt when he said he'd cheated and wanted time apart, but look how quickly I jumped into bed with you." I twisted my hands together in my lap. "Am I a bad person?"

"No. Jesus Christ, Natalie." He shook his head. "You're a great person. And you were totally faithful to him for ten fucking years. You jumped into bed with me because A, let's face it, who wouldn't? And B, we've always wondered what it would be like. At least I have."

"I have too," I admitted. *And it exceeded all my expectations. I didn't even know sex that good was possible.*

"That doesn't make us bad people, it makes us two consenting adults who had fun together. You didn't cheat on anybody, you didn't hurt anybody, and the world did not explode because you had someone else's dick in you."

"Felt like it did."

One side of his mouth hooked up. "Good."

We stopped at the wine store because Miles didn't want to show up empty-handed to dinner, and he lectured me while I perused the selection.

"You're way too serious for being so young. You always have been. The rest of us have been fucking up our lives and having a damn good time doing it for years. Now it's your turn."

"To do what? Fuck up my life? I'll pass, thanks."

"No, just…treat yourself. Go a little crazy. All that mature, responsible behavior cannot be good for your mental health."

I looked at him over my shoulder. "And I suppose going a little crazy involves a trip to Detroit and lots of sex with you?"

He put his hands out toward me, palms up. "I am totally willing to sacrifice my time *and* virtue to help you reclaim your lost youth."

I gave him the frowny face. "I'll think about it."

After I chose two bottles, a red from the winery Skylar worked at and a white from another local vineyard, we headed up the peninsula highway. It was sunny and warm, the perfect summer evening.

"What a pretty day," I sighed.

"It is pretty up here. Think you'll always live in this area?" Miles asked as he pulled up in his driveway.

"Well, considering I own a business here, my family is here, and I just bought a house, I suppose I'll say yes." We got out of the Jeep and started to walk over to my parents' place. "What about you? You like Detroit?"

He shrugged. "Yeah. I like anywhere for a while. But I'll probably move again eventually. I don't like to stay in one place too long."

It was a good reminder that whatever there was between us was temporary, all in fun, but something in my chest ached a little when he said it. *Don't get carried away with this*, I warned myself. *And definitely don't get attached. As fun as it is to mess around with Miles, he'll be gone in a few days and you'll still be here like always.*

But at least being with Miles had reminded me of what good chemistry feels like. That hum in the air, that flutter in the chest, that pull deep in the belly.

I wanted those things. I deserved them, didn't I?

"You OK?" Miles whispered as we approached the back deck where my family was gathered, "I see those wheels spinning."

I took a deep breath. "Yeah. Just thinking."

"Stop that. No thinking allowed."

"Hey, everybody," I called as we climbed the few steps to the deck. "Brought a friend. Hope that's OK."

"Miles!" My mother flew over to give him a hug and kiss. "I saw the car in the driveway yesterday and wondered who was in town. How are you, dear? Is your mother up too?"

"I'm great, Mrs. Nixon. No, she's in California this month. I'm here by myself, so thanks for letting me crash Sunday dinner."

"You're always welcome, honey." She patted his cheek. "So handsome."

I rolled my eyes and took the brown paper bag from Miles's arm. "We brought a couple bottles of wine."

"Great. There's one open on the table, too. Help yourself. Is Dan coming?" My mother looked at me quizzically.

"Uh, no. He had some things to do."

"Oh." She looked satisfied with that. "Well, Miles can sit at his place then. I already set the table."

"Perfect."

My dad came over and shook Miles's hand, my sisters both gave him a hug, Skylar sending me an impish grin over his shoulder, and then I introduced him to Sebastian.

We poured some wine and sat chatting on the deck a few minutes, and when my mother called us in to eat, Miles pulled out my chair and sat me before taking his place on my right.

Skylar kicked me from the left.

She kicked me again when Miles raved about my coffee shop, telling everyone how he'd helped out there today and had a new appreciation for running a place like that.

"My shin is going to be black and blue! Will you knock it off?" I whispered in her ear.

But she kicked me a third time when he praised my photography skills, again when he complimented my baking, and yet again when he boasted that he'd gotten me to agree to a few days off.

"Wow," laughed my dad. "I didn't think Natalie was familiar with the concept of 'days off' during the summer. How'd you convince her?"

"I have my ways." Miles smiled cockily, and I kicked him under the table.

"What are you going to do, Nat?" Jillian asked, scooping more pasta salad into her plate. "House stuff?"

"I haven't exactly decided yet." Flashing Miles a murderous look, I reached for my wine.

"I'm trying to convince her to go on a road trip with me." Miles smiled at me with *gotcha* eyes.

I continued glaring at him. *Stop*, I mouthed.

"A road trip, how fun!" Skylar squealed while everyone else at the table looked from Miles to me and back to Miles again, trying to figure us out. "Where will you go?"

"I want her to come stay with me in Detroit for a couple days. If she says no, I'm going to kidnap her." He put an arm around my neck, his hand over my face.

Jesus. Could he be any more obvious? I shook him off, guzzled the rest of my wine, and looked around the table at the perplexed faces. My mother's fork was stopped halfway to her mouth. Sebastian looked like he was trying not to laugh. And Jillian was blinking rapidly.

"Dan and I broke up!" I blurted.

"What?" said at least two women at the table, maybe three.

"When?" Jillian asked, her eyes wide.

"Last night." I scanned the shocked, concerned faces of my family. "Look, it's not something I want to talk about right now, and I'm not really sure if it's permanent or just some time apart, but when I'm ready to talk, I promise to fill you in."

"Are you OK?" my mother asked, her blue eyes concerned.

"I'm fine. And Dan's fine. Everyone's fine." I gestured to my right. "And I have Miles here to take my mind off things."

"Well, I think you guys are smart," Skylar said. "You've never been apart for any length of time, not in ten years. You were just kids when you got together. It's hard to know who you are as a person when you've always been part of a couple, don't you think?"

"Yes. That's exactly it." I picked up my fork again, anxious to end the conversation. Jillian caught my eye, and I sent her a silent plea. She nodded.

"Sky, fill me in on wedding details. What's new?"

Perfect. I shot her a grateful look, and she smiled.

It was good to know that no matter what changes in my life were ahead, I had my family, and they'd always be there for me.

Family was what mattered most. I could hold on to that.

CHAPTER 12
Miles

"WANT TO COME IN FOR A WHILE?" I asked Natalie as we walked back toward my house.

She scowled at me. "No. You and I are in a huge fight."

I laughed. "Why?"

"Because you shouldn't have said that stuff to my family. I didn't want them to know about Dan yet."

"Hey, *I* didn't tell them about the breakup, *you* did."

"I had to! You were running your mouth about me going on a road trip with you this week. Girls with boyfriends don't take road trips with other guys."

I shook my head. "That is why no one should be in serious relationships. Everyone should be free to take road trips with random people any time they want."

"Well, I still haven't decided if I'm taking one with you, so you better behave."

"I'll try. So what about tonight? Want to hang out?" I sort of hated how desperate I sounded to be with her, but I had all her attention for the first time ever.

She sighed. "I do, but I should go home. I have to get ahold of Michael and make sure it's OK to take tomorrow off."

"Ask him if he can cover 'til Thursday on his own." She groaned, but I took it as a sign she was coming around. I slung my arm around her shoulders. "Come on. It's gonna be fun! I can show you where I live."

She looked up at me suspiciously. "Your apartment doesn't have a sex dungeon, does it?"

"No, smartypants. I wasn't even thinking about sex." And I wasn't—that was crazy, wasn't it? That I'd have her to myself for three days, and I wasn't planning on holing up in my loft and banging her endlessly? I mean, I'd be lying if I said I wasn't hoping for banging too, but it wasn't the only reason I wanted to get her to myself. I actually wanted to be with her.

Wait a second.

Just wait.

I slowed my steps as the harsh realization sunk in.

Was I...*growing*? Like...*maturing*? *Emotionally*?

No. That wasn't possible. Guys like me took decades to grow up and have Emotions, didn't they? One night of mind-blowing sex with the girl next door hadn't turned me into an actual adult with Feelings, had it?

Maybe I should slow down.

"Just kidding," I added quickly, taking my arm from her shoulders. "I'm always thinking about sex."

"I know this about you. And yet I'm still considering your offer. What does that say about me?"

"That after years of suffering and deprivation, you are finally ready and willing to enjoy yourself."

She sighed. "OK fine. You win. I'll ask about taking three days off. But I need to go home. Do you want to drive me? Or should I take your car?"

"I'll drive you. Pack up while you're there, too. Then we can leave whenever we want."

"Slow down, cowboy. I haven't talked to Michael yet."

"Sorry. I'm just excited to get you all to myself." *Oh, shit.* "You know, for all the sex."

Rolling her eyes, she thumped me on the chest. "You're an animal," she said. But she actually looked happy about it.

On the way to her house, she called Michael, her pastry chef, who was back from his long weekend and more than happy to manage the shop for her the next three days. She double-checked with both waitresses scheduled to work this week, and each said she would be glad to pitch in with extra hours if needed.

"See? Everything is under control," I said.

"Seems like it." She chewed the tip of her index finger. "And they can always call me if they need to."

"Exactly. But they won't. And you know what? This tells me you're an awesome boss. You've trained them well."

"Thank you." She shook her head. "I can't believe I'm actually taking a little vacation. I haven't—oh shit."

"What?" I glanced at her and followed her gaze down the street. Daylight was just starting to fade into dusk, and I easily made out the red Mustang in her driveway and the burly douchebag in a suit getting out of it. "Oh, shit. What do you want to do? I can keep driving and we can pretend we never saw him, I can wait for you in the car, or I can walk you in. Your call."

She eyed me. "If I say come in with me, can you manage not to get in a fight with him?"

"Possibly." I pulled alongside the curb, noting unfriendly stance of said douchebag, who looked like he was ready to throw a punch. "But unlikely."

"Oh, God. Please don't, OK?"

But Dan was already stomping across the lawn toward us, chest first. In general, I'm a lover not a fighter, but I have a big enough mouth that I've gotten myself into trouble a few times. I took off my glasses just in case, popping them into the glove box under Natalie's worried gaze.

Dan yanked open the passenger door. "Can we talk?"

"Not right now," she said breezily. "Dan, you remember Miles. Miles, Dan."

I leaned over her and smiled. "What's up?"

He ignored me. "I really want to talk to you."

"Well, give me a call at the end of the week." She got out of the Jeep. "I'm going out of town tomorrow."

Score! I thought, hopping out and following her up the front walk. *Now please, please ask where she's going and with whom.*

Dan walked on the grass to get ahead of her. "Out of town where?"

"None of your business," she said, pulling her keys from her purse.

We reached the front porch, and Dan stepped in front of the door. "Where were you last night? I came back to talk to you, and you weren't here."

She shrugged. "That's none of your business either."

Goddamn, I was proud of her. If he tried to touch her, I was going to move in, but as long as she could hold her own, I thought it was best to let him see her stand tall without any help.

Dan flicked his beady douchebag eyes at me. "What's he doing here, anyway?"

"He's my friend. Now get out of the way so I can go into my house."

"Not until you agree to talk to me."

"There's nothing to say right now, Dan." Natalie threw a hand up. "Go be free! Enjoy your space! You were right. We need a little time apart, a little distance to reevaluate what we want out of life."

Dan looked nervous. "You're reevaluating your life?"

"Yeah. I am." She sounded just as surprised as he did. "Just because you had a plan doesn't mean you should follow through with it, right or wrong. There's dedication, and then there's blind stubbornness."

"But…" He ran a hand over his hair. "But what if the break was the wrong plan?" He lowered his voice. "I couldn't sleep last night at all."

"Sorry to hear that. But you know what? I didn't get much sleep either."

I snorted. I couldn't help it. But then I thought Natalie might kill me, so I tried to turn it into a cough. She gave me a nasty stink-eyed stare over her shoulder before shoving Dan out of the way. To my surprise, he gave up, standing there slump-shouldered and dejected while Natalie opened the door and gestured for me to go in. "Go on, Miles. I'll be in in a minute."

Reluctantly, I slipped past her into the front hall and eavesdropped on their conversation through the partly open door.

"You're punishing me. I deserve it," said sad sack Dan. "I know I do." I rolled my eyes and gave him the finger through the door.

"You cheated on me, Dan. That hurts." Her voice was like steel.

"I'm sorry."

"Was it more than once?"

I didn't hear anything so he must have nodded or something, because she laughed coldly. "I should have known. God, was I just stupid?"

"No! Look, it happened but we can put it behind us now, Natalie. I don't want anyone else."

"Until the next time."

"There won't be a next time. I promise."

"I'm not interested in your promises anymore, Dan. What are you even fighting for? It's time we admit things between us haven't been good for a while now—they've been forced, and that's partly my fault, because I didn't want to face it. Now we have to."

"I don't think it was forced," he said, his tone defensive. "I think it just got comfortable, and I took you for granted."

"Whatever it was, Dan, there has to be something better. I've decided I'm too young to settle for comfortable."

God, I wanted to tackle hug her for that so hard.

"But I love you, Natalie. I still want what we had planned. I just didn't want it so fast."

"I get it. And I'm glad you were finally honest with me. It's giving me a chance to take a closer look at what *I* want now. To figure out what's really going to make me happy."

"I hope it's still me."

It's not you! I felt like shouting. *You don't even know about her G spot, you fuckwad!* Unexpected rage curled my hands into fists and flared my nostrils when I thought about him having sex with her. About his mouth on her, his hands on her, his stupid lazy dick. And if she went back to him, he'd get that spectacular body to himself. He'd get to eat that sweet little muffin. He'd get to glaze her buns.

That was fucking unacceptable.

I wanted to glaze her buns.

Molten fury rose in my chest, and I clenched my fists at my sides.

"I don't think it's you anymore, Dan. I'm sorry. We'll talk next week, OK? Goodnight." She came in the house and shut the door, leaning back against it, breathing hard.

"Oh my God. I can't believe I just did that." She put her hands over her stomach. "I broke up with Dan. For good."

It was dim in her front hall, and I didn't have my glasses on, so I couldn't read her expression too well. "Are you OK?"

She nodded, her eyes wide. "Yes. But I'm in shock. I think I just drastically changed my life."

I smiled. "Fuck yeah, you did. How does it feel?"

"Good. Liberating. I'm filled with all this..." She waved her hands around frantically. "Insane energy right now."

I leaned toward her, boxing her in against the door with both arms. "Want some help burning that off?"

"Yeah," she breathed, running her hands up my chest. "I think I do."

CHAPTER 13
Natalie

DON'T THINK, I told myself as his lips slanted over mine, his tongue stroking inside them. *Don't panic, don't worry, don't analyze. Forget about everything but the way this feels.*

I gave myself over to Miles, to the smell of his skin, the feel of body against mine, the way his breathing changed when he got close to me. I slipped my hands beneath his t-shirt and ran them over his warm abs and chest, brushing my thumbs over his nipples, making them hard. He moaned lightly and reached under my skirt, rubbing me over my cotton panties. His mouth moved down my neck, his tongue warm and wet against my skin.

"Want to know what I've been thinking about all day?" he said in my ear, working his fingers in circles over my clit. "Getting my mouth right here. Tasting your sweet little pussy. Making you come again with my tongue."

"Really?" I put one hand on his crotch and rubbed the bulge in his jeans. How did he get hard so fast? Had he been like this already?

"Really. And I don't think I can wait any longer." He dropped down in front of me and pushed my skirt up, putting his mouth on me without even taking my panties off.

"Oh God, that feels good." Breathing hard, I threaded my fingers through his hair, watching him soak my underwear with his mouth—or maybe it was me soaking them. He flung one of my legs over his shoulder, kissing and licking and biting my inner thigh before moving my panties aside to get his mouth on my bare skin. God, I loved the way he didn't rush, loved the languid strokes of his tongue up the slick, hot seam at my center, the decadent swirls over my aching clit, the sweet, slow way he devoured me...I felt like he loved making me come as much I loved doing it, like he'd be happy to do this all night, like he didn't care how long it would take me.

Not that it would take long.

"Fuck," I whispered, the tension coiling tight at my center. "How do you do it? You make me come so fast."

"Good." He switched to hard, quick flicks with the tip of his tongue, then sucked the hot little bud into his mouth. When he slid two fingers inside me, my leg trembled and I dropped my head back against the door.

"Yes, yes, yes, like that," I whimpered, my fingers clutching his hair. I clenched the leg he'd thrown over his shoulder, pulling him into me. "Right there, oh my God..."

He plunged his fingers deeper and sucked harder, and when I looked down at his head between my thighs, I cried out as I watched him take me over the edge, my clit throbbing inside his mouth, my core muscles contracting around his fingers.

"Fuck yes," he said, his breath warm against my wet skin. He bit my inner thigh once more. "I love the way I can feel you come. I love it so much, I want it again." He pulled my drenched panties down and I stepped out of them. When he stood up, I grabbed the hem of his shirt.

"Take this off. I love your arms and your chest," I said. "I want to see them." He reached behind his neck and pulled it over his head, tossing it aside before caging me against the door with his arms. "Yes," I whispered, biting my lip as I ran my hands over his upper body. I kissed his collar bone, the ink on his bicep and forearm. Reaching between his legs, I rubbed my hand over the erection straining hard against the denim, and circled his nipple with my tongue. It was hard already, and I stroked it, kissed it, flicked it. When I bit it gently, Miles exhaled sharply and grabbed my ass.

"Fuck, that feels good," he said, his fingers sliding low to penetrate me from behind. "Mmm, you're so wet. I want to get my cock right there. You want it?"

"Yes." I looked up, meeting his eyes, and he grabbed my jaw roughly with one hand.

"Say please."

My core muscles clenched. "Please."

He kissed me hard, and I tasted myself on his lips and tongue, felt the dampness on his chin. Quickly I unbuckled his belt and unzipped his jeans, desperate to get my hands on him. The moment I freed his cock, he leaned forward, one hand braced against the door again. While I stroked him with both hands, I teased his other nipple with my tongue, sucking it into my mouth and biting down a little harder than before.

He groaned. "That feels so fucking good. I could make a mess all over you in ten seconds."

"Do it," I breathed, pumping him harder. "I want you to."

"But there's something I want more right now." His hands gripped my waist. "Now wrap those legs around me, because I'm going to fuck you senseless against your front door." He picked me up, pinning my back against the door, my skirt bunching up at my hips. I twined my legs around him and braced myself on his shoulders while he angled his cock underneath me.

He hesitated. "Oh. Is this gonna be OK?"

It took me a second to realize he meant not wearing a condom. I hadn't even thought about it, because Dan and I hadn't used them since I'd been on the pill. I had none here. But fuck—*fuck!* Miles was no angel. Was this safe?

As if he'd read my mind, he said, "I'm clean. I get tested often and I can show you the results. I always wear a condom, too. Always—and I haven't even been with anyone in months. But if you don't—"

"It's OK." Possibly it wasn't, but my decision-making capacity was impaired by the smell of his skin and the blue of his eyes and the tip of his cock brushing my wet pussy. "Maybe I'm senseless already, but I really, really want to get fucked against my front door. And since you're here…"

"Allow me."

I sucked in my breath as he penetrated me one hot, wet, bare inch at a time.

"Yes. Go slow like that," I whispered. Our eyes met, and I held my breath.

"I love how tight you are." His voice was low and raw. "I love how deep you take it." When he was buried inside me, he dug his fingers into my ass and moved me against him in slow, grinding circles, my upper back against the door.

"Oh God, I love this door," I sighed. "I really fucking love it."

"I bet you looked at this door every day and thought, 'I wish Miles Haas would come over and fuck me right here.'" On the word *fuck*, he thrust violently hard, making me shriek.

I smiled, clutching him tight around the neck. "Had I known how good it would be," I panted, "I would have."

"Do you know how much I thought about this?" He switched to holding me steady and thrusting up with deep, slow strokes. "Do you know how many times I got myself off just thinking about it? My cock gets so fucking hard for you. Can you feel it?"

"Yes." I met his eyes, which looked dark and hungry. "It's so deep it hurts, but I love the way it feels."

"You love my cock deep inside you?" He pumped into me

a little more violently, hitting that spot that made me whole body clench into a hot ball of fiery tension.

"Yes!" I cried, hanging on tight.

"Say it," he ordered through gritted teeth.

"I love your cock deep inside me! Oh God, don't stop!"

"Not until you come all over it," he growled, driving into me, steady and fast. "I want to feel that sweet little pussy come all over my cock."

Fisting my hands in his hair, I bit his shoulder as my entire body pulsed with white hot ecstasy.

"Fuck!" His hips went still and he grabbed my ass, jerking me roughly up and down his cock as he came long and hard inside me.

"Jesus," I whispered when he finally slowed down. "Maybe we should just stay here for three days. I've got a lot of other doors."

Miles laughed. "I have doors at my place too. And tables and closets and a couch and chairs and a bed." He turned his head, spoke low in my ear. "And ropes and beads and wax and silk scarves and a ball gag."

I gasped. "Really? You have all that stuff?"

He straightened up. "Well, maybe not the gag. But we can stop and pick one up if you'd like."

"That's OK. Really."

"Chicken." He bumped his forehead to mine before he set me down and pulled out. "Uh, can I get you anything?"

"It's OK. I need to clean up anyway. Let's go upstairs."

I was going to take a shower, but Miles had another idea once he saw my big bathtub. "Let's get in it."

"A bath?" I wrinkled my nose. "It will take forever to fill. And it's a pain to wash my hair in a bath."

Miles put a hand on his chest. "I will wash your hair. In fact, I will take care of everything. You go away, and I'll call you when it's ready."

I sighed. "OK, fine." Shaking my head, I went into the second bathroom and cleaned up a little. With the adrenaline rush over, my mind started to wander back to the conversation I'd had with Dan. Was it really over? Why didn't I feel more devastated? Was it because it had been over already and I'd just been clinging to an idea? Was it because he'd cheated on me? Maybe I was still in shock and it would hit me later, but mostly what I felt was relief.

I wandered back to my bedroom, where I heard the water running through the closed door to the bathroom. I also heard drawers being open and shut as well as the vanity cupboards. What the hell was he doing in there?

Inside my closet, I undressed and pulled on a short robe. From a high shelf I took down a small suitcase, opened it on the floor and dropped a few things inside it. I wondered if I needed anything dressier than shorts and jeans, and if I should pack a swimsuit.

A few minutes later, Miles poked his head in. "Ready."

My pulse picked up at the sight of his bare chest, even though I had just been thoroughly pounded not thirty minutes before. Was I turning into an animal too? Smiling, I followed him into the bathroom, where he'd dimmed the lights and lit the candles on the windowsill. He'd also filled the tub with bubbles, and the air was warm and humid and scented with vanilla and cinnamon. "Wow. I'm impressed."

"Good." He slipped the robe off my shoulders and hung it on the back of the door. "Go on, get in."

I slipped beneath the warm, fragrant water, the bubbles up to my shoulders. "Coming in with me?"

He set the plastic container I keep under the sink to water my plants on the sill too and unzipped his jeans. "Definitely."

"What's the container for?"

"To wash your hair, like I promised."

I smiled. "You don't really have to do that."

"Well, I want to. So shut your face."

Laughing, I watched him get undressed and noticed he

wasn't fully hard for once, although the size was still impressive. It felt oddly intimate, seeing him like that, somehow more intimate than seeing his giant erection in front of my face. Why was that? I looked away as he stepped into the tub behind me.

"Scoot up a little bit." He stretched his legs on either side of me, and I leaned back against him as he gathered me in close. "There. Isn't this nice?"

"Yes." It was nice. I was more of a shower person since I got up so early and was always in a rush, but it felt good to slow down and relax a little. "I don't think I've used this tub more than once since I've lived here."

"How long is that?"

"Three months. And I've definitely never been in it with another person."

"Can't say I'm sorry about that." We were silent a minute, the only noise the crackle of the bubbles and sizzle of candle wicks. "So was Dan boring in bed or what?"

I sighed. "I don't know."

"You don't know?"

I tried to think of a way to explain it. "Well, you know how you have a favorite pair of sweat pants or something, and they're really comfortable and feel good every time you put them on?"

"Uh, I guess so."

"Well, sex with Dan was sort of like that."

"Like sweat pants?"

"Yeah, you know—something comfortable and familiar that feels good. Does that make sense?"

"I guess so, but if any woman ever said sex with me was like sweat pants, I'd fucking shoot myself."

"Well, I didn't know any better, OK? We both had orgasms, so I figured we were doing fine, but clearly we weren't, because he went elsewhere to get what he really wanted, and I..." I stopped, unsure of how to finish the sentence.

"You what?" In front of my chest, Miles linked his fingers with mine.

I'm having way more fun—and way better orgasms—with you than I ever had with him. But I couldn't say that. Miles would probably freak out and think I wanted him to be my next boyfriend or something. And I didn't want that. I knew we were just friends doing this for the hell of it, enjoying the kick. For all I knew, sex with Miles would become routine after a while too.

Although that didn't seem possible.

"You what?" he prompted again.

"I'm learning things about myself." I grinned at him over my shoulder. "You're a good teacher."

"And what have you learned so far?"

"Hmmmm." I settled back against his chest. "I like it when you say dirty things to me."

"Good."

"I like when you get bossy with me."

"Even better."

"I think I might like to get bossy with you sometime."

"Sweetheart, you can boss me hard and often."

I giggled. "Wash my hair. *Now.*"

"Not exactly what I meant, but OK," he said, reaching for the plastic container. "Sit up."

I sat up and crossed my legs, tipping my head back. "Like that?"

"Yes. Perfect." He poured water over my head and shampooed my hair, massaging my scalp as I sighed contentedly. When the conditioner was on, I turned around.

"Your turn."

He let me wash his hair, and I giggled as I sudsed him up. "You should get a mohawk," I said, forming one on the top of his head.

"No, thanks."

"Or grow a grizzly beard." I scooped up some bubbles and spread them around on his face, covering it completely. "There. Big improvement."

He lunged for me, trying to smear bubbles on my face, and pushing a huge tidal wave over the edge of the tub in the process. I squealed and fought back, suds and water flying everywhere. He ended up cradling me across his lap, but instead of dunking me, he kissed me, sealing our wet mouths together. I looped one arm around his back and one around his neck, my belly flip-flopping as his hand moved up my ribcage. He teased my nipple with his thumb, making it harden and tingle.

"Ever had an orgasm in this bathtub?" he whispered, his hand moving lower.

"No." I gasped, my stomach quivering as his fingers rubbed soft little circles below my belly button and spiraled down to just above my clit.

"I love giving you firsts," he said, keeping his hand in that spot, making me yearn for him to go lower.

I closed my eyes and opened my legs, my body relaxed and humming. "I only wish there were some firsts left for me to give *you*. You've done everything already."

He stopped moving and shook me gently. "Hey."

I opened my eyes and saw that his expression was serious.

"Everything is different with you. Everything feels like a first."

"Is that good?"

He smiled, making my heart skip. "Yes. It is." Sliding a finger inside me, he lowered his lips to my ear. "Now be a dirty little slut and tell me to make you come."

"Want to stay over?" I asked Miles as we dried off. "I can finish packing my bag and we can leave first thing in the morning."

"Sure." He shook his head like a wet puppy, flinging droplets at me. In fact, the entire bathroom was a mess. Water was *everywhere*.

"I'd better mop up this floor." I hung up my towel and reached for a dry one on the shelf.

"I'll do it. You pack."

"Seriously?" I smiled happily. *Holy crap, Dan would never have offered to clean up that mess.* "Hey, do I need to pack a dress and heels for any reason?"

"Definitely." He knelt down and started sopping up the water.

"Oooh, what's the reason?" I asked, clasping my hands together.

"Sometimes I like wearing a woman's shoes while I fuck her." He looked back at me and rolled his eyes at my stunned expression. "Because I want to take you somewhere nice, Natalie. Jeez."

"Oh. Sorry," I said, laughing. "But with you I never know."

I finished packing my bag, adding a white strapless sundress and some nude heels, a bathing suit, and my camera. When I was done, I went into the bathroom and pulled an extra toothbrush from my vanity and offered it to Miles. "Want this?"

"Yes, thank you."

We brushed our teeth side by side at my sink, Miles in his boxer briefs and me in boy shorts and a tank. As our eyes met in the mirror, I felt a funny little flutter in my chest. For all his egotistical jokes and promiscuous ways and his complete refusal to seriously commit to anything except ink, he really was being very sweet to me. He'd make a good boyfriend or husband if he ever decided to get serious. *Too bad he's content to be a man-child his whole life. He's got a lot to offer someone besides just sex.*

He finished up and caught my eye in the mirror. "You look funny when you brush your teeth."

So much for sweet. I spit and rinsed. "Shut up, I do not."

"You do, and you get toothpaste all over your face. Look at you, you're a mess." He grabbed a hand towel and smashed it over my mouth, tucking me under his arm. "I could make a mess on your face."

"OK. That's it." I took the towel, threw it down, and took him by the shoulders. "You've threatened me enough times with a mess. You should fucking do it already." I marched him backward into my room and pushed him down onto the bed.

"Is this you bossing me around?" he asked, leaning back on his elbows as I yanked his underwear off.

"Yes."

He grinned. "I like it already."

CHAPTER 14
Natalie

I WOKE up feeling rested and happy, Miles's arm still curved over my belly, the sheet pulled up to our hips. Smiling, I stayed wrapped up in him a few more minutes before carefully sliding out of bed to use the bathroom. When I came back into my room, he was on his back, one arm over his head. I snickered at his hairy armpit, his messy hair, the scratches on his shoulders. I'd be surprised if there weren't teeth marks too. I'd been a little out of control last night.

But holy hell, it had been fun. The most fun I'd ever had in bed—and I had three more days of it to look forward to. Three days of guilt-free, uncommitted, mind-blowing, earth-shattering sex. Beyond that, I didn't even care.

I poked Miles in the shoulder. "Wake up, sleepyhead. You talked me into a road trip and I'm ready to go!"

"Oh God, what time is it? How can you get up so early?"

"It's not early, it's nine already!"

He groaned, but he sat up and blinked. "I need my glasses. Where the hell did I leave them?"

"In the glove box of your car," I said, already heading into my closet. "Let me throw some clothes on and grab them while you wake up."

"Thanks. Keys are on the table in your front hall."

I put on denim shorts and a soft white t-shirt and tugged my Converse sneakers on my feet. Snagging the keys off the table near the door—my belly cartwheeling at the memory of my back against it—I went outside and practically skipped to the Jeep in the sunshine. What a perfect day to start my vacation.

Ten minutes later, Miles had loaded my bag in the car and we were on our way to his house so he could pack. I suggested stopping by Coffee Darling for a couple cups to go, but Miles saw through my plan to check up on things, and we hit Starbucks instead.

At Miles's house, he packed up a duffel bag while I stripped his bed—we'd left it a mess yesterday morning. When he was done and I'd put fresh sheets on the mattress, he announced he had to write a quick blog post.

"Right now?" I paused in the middle of slipping a pillow into its case.

"Yes, before I forget any of the details of that fuckhot blowjob you gave me last night, although that is not likely to happen in this lifetime. If ever anything was unforgettable, that was it."

My cheeks got hot. "You can't write about me giving you a fuckhot blowjob!" I shrieked, although secretly it delighted me to think I might be the subject of one of his lurid posts. Me, of all people. *Me!*

He laughed. "I love when you say fuck. Listen, men and women depend on me. I make the world a sexier place, therefore a *better* place, when I share these things. And you're helping me do that. You should feel proud of yourself."

I chewed on my bottom lip. "Fine. But don't use my name."

"I never use real names."

"Why not?"

He shrugged. "It protects the innocent, and it keeps things light. Fun."

While Miles wrote, I sat on the porch with my coffee and a book from the house's dusty library, a volume of poems by Mary Oliver. I'd never heard of her before, and I didn't know much about poetry, but hers was so beautifully easy to understand, and so personal, I felt like she was speaking right to me. One poem in particular, called "When Death Comes," made chills sweep across my back and down my arms. I sat up straight and read it again, then I looked out across the orchard, half expecting to find the poet herself standing there, pointing a finger at me. I looked at the words again, trying to memorize the final line.

I don't want to end up simply having visited this world.

It was such a simple statement, and yet so powerful an idea. I knew exactly what she meant. That feeling had inspired me from the time I was young to go after what I wanted and do my best to achieve those goals. Swimming, good grades, Dan, a college scholarship, my own business, my house…but I could see now how fear of change, or maybe fear of failure, had shaped that ambition into a careful, tidy, safe sort of life. And when my life was over, did I really want no mistakes on my record? No messy lessons learned? Nothing that made me say, *I can't believe I did that!*?

I wasn't planning to, as Miles said, fuck up my life. But I was planning on taking a few more chances. Living out loud a little more. If I made mistakes, so be it—I'd own them.

Miles came out onto the porch with his duffel, his computer bag, and his coffee. "Ready?"

"Yes. Just let me put this book back."

He tipped his head too read the cover. "Ah. That's a good one. I got it for my mom for Christmas one year after hearing Mary Oliver on NPR. I doubt she ever opened it. Want it?"

"I can't take your mom's book," I said, rising from my

chair. "But I might buy my own copy. I really like it." After I replaced the book on the shelf, Miles locked up the house.

"Want to take the top off?" he asked after throwing his bags in the back and his coffee in a cup holder.

"Sure." I put my coffee in the car too, helped him remove the roof panels and stow them in the back, then jumped in the front seat.

Miles slid in behind the wheel a moment later and surprised me by grabbing my face and planting a huge kiss on my lips.

Butterflies took flight inside me. "What was that for?"

"For being brave," he said, starting the car. "I'm so fucking proud of you." He threw an arm across the back of my seat and looked over his shoulder as he reversed out of the driveway.

"Thanks. I'm kind of proud of myself, even though my life feels a little upside down right now."

He grinned as we started down the highway. "Told you it was me."

It took me a few seconds to realize he meant Madam Psuka's prediction. "Oh, stop. That wasn't real. You didn't upend my life, you just helped me see that I needed to make some changes. Have more fun. Explore a new side of myself." I cocked my head. "Hey, what did you call me in your article, by the way?"

"Cinnamon Buns."

"Cinnamon Buns!" I yelled, my eyes bugging. "That's the anonymous nickname you gave me?"

"Yeah, why? You don't like it?"

"No! For one thing, it will be totally obvious to anyone who knows what I do for a living, and for another, I thought it would be something sultry and glamorous, like Svetlana."

"Mmmm, Svetlana."

I hit him on the leg. Hard.

"I'm kidding," he said, laughing. "You're much hotter

than Svetlana. Beautiful girl next door with hidden dirty streak beats Ukrainian acrobat any day. And anyone who reads this article will agree with me. Trust me, it's *highly* complimentary."

"When can I read it?"

"Right now if you want. It's live."

"It's *live*? I thought you were going to let me see it first, at least!" Diving into my purse, I scrambled for my phone. "Oh, God. I'm scared."

"Don't be. I'm telling you, it's all good."

My heart thumped hard as I searched for his blog, my body prickling with heat. What had he said about me? I saw the right link in the search results, clicked on it, and began to read.

Want a Better Blowjob Tonight?

I thought so.
And I'm here to help.

Last night, I had quite simply the best blowjob you can possibly imagine. I'm talking the Aston Martin of blowjobs. The Stanley Cup of blowjobs. If blowjobs had a World Series, this girl was Ty Cobb, Roger Hornsby, and Joe Jackson COMBINED.

I'll call her Cinnamon Buns. Because she looks as delicious and smells and tastes like the best one you've ever eaten.

. . .

This blowjob from Cinnamon Buns was clearly a gift from the heavens, and I feel strongly that the gods bestowed it upon me because they knew I would act benevolently. Thus, I share with you my experience not to inspire envy or resentment, but in the hopes that you can find a way to get your girlfriend's eyes on this article and inspire her to blowjob brilliance as well.

In return, gentlemen, you will please follow this link to an article called 10 Ways to Get Her Off Tonight (You're Doing It Wrong, Asshole).

OK. Let's begin. You with me, ladies?

First, I want to commend you for reading. You're clearly smart, sexy, and fun, which makes you the hottest woman he has ever known even before you put that gorgeous mouth on his unworthy dick. You are a goddess. (See what I'm doing here, guys?)

Now, I'm just going to come right out and say it: I've had a lot of blowjobs.

But this one.

This one.

As I watched Cinnamon Buns get to her knees on the floor in front of me, my dick sprang up like one of those inflatable Bozo the clown bop bags I had as a kid. I'd push it down and it would pop right back up again, ready to go.

Not that there is anything funny about my dick, of course. It is very serious. Let me rephrase.

. . .

My dick stood tall like a proud soldier ready for duty, weapons locked and loaded.

Much better.

I had a feeling before she even got started that this was going to be a blowjob of epic intensity, and I was right. Now, partly it was because of our great chemistry, and partly it was because she's just magic, but here are five things I can't stop thinking about today, things that you can do tonight to create a little magic of your own for your guy—just make sure he deserves it.

1. Take Control…Then Give it Up. Cinnamon Buns pushed me into the bedroom, shoved me down on the bed, and bossed me into a blowjob like it was for *her*, not me. She came at me like it was her birthday and all she wanted was a great big piece of birthday cock, and I was gonna give it to her or else. But she knows I like submissiveness too, and when I took charge, she let me.
2. Look Up. One of the reasons guys love blowjobs is it's fun to watch. We are visual creatures, and your mouth on his dick is the best movie he's ever seen. It's his favorite, in fact, and he can't watch it enough times. And when you, the beautiful star, look up and make eye contact with him, he feels like a million fucking dollars. Sometimes Cinnamon Buns looked up at me with this innocence in her eyes, as though she couldn't believe how big I was, how hard I was, how deep I was. Other times, the look in her eye was pure salacious delight, and she'd moan or laugh or sigh, like the pleasure was all hers.

3. Use Your Hands on Him. Yes, it's mostly about his dick, and no man will complain if that's all you want to focus on. But while you are merrily sucking him into oblivion, don't be shy about touching him other places. Balls. Nipples. Ass. (Cinnamon Buns was not shy.) If he doesn't like it, he'll let you know, but I'm gonna venture a guess he does.
4. Use Your Hands On Yourself Too. At one point, Cinnamon Buns got so turned on by what she was doing, that she touched her body the way I would have if I hadn't been so paralyzed with joy by the sight of her doing it. In fact, I nearly fired the canon before I could properly warn her, which a gentleman should never do. (Are you listening, gentlemen?)
5. Swallow. You don't have to pretend it's the nectar of the gods, but it sure makes us feel good when you do. I don't actually recall the expression on Cinnamon Buns's face when she swallowed because I was too blinded by rapture, but when I recovered the use of my eyes, she looked delighted. Sated. Pleased with herself and with me.

I was pleased as well.

And I showed her by returning the favor before she even caught her breath.

Sound good?
    You know what to do.

. . .

(Guys? That goes for you too.)

Oh my God.

I finished the article and read it again three more times. My mind whirled, my heart beat crazily, and I couldn't keep the smile off my face. Not only because the me he'd described was so hot and alluring or because he was so cute and funny or because his words brought back the memory of last night in breath-stealing detail, but because of three little words he'd said about me...

She's just magic.

I wasn't magic, but *we* were.

I felt it too.

CHAPTER 15
Miles

WHY WAS SHE SO QUIET? Did she hate it? As she read, I kept trying to get a glimpse of her expression, read her body language, but she was sort of turned toward the window. She gasped once or twice and brought one hand slowly to her mouth, but I couldn't tell if it was because she was shocked, embarrassed, or touched. Fuck, maybe I shouldn't have written about her. Natalie wasn't show-offish like other women, who sometimes begged me to write about them. A lot of them even asked me to use their real names too, which I never did. Not only for their protection, but also because real names suggested a level of intimacy I wasn't comfortable with.

"Hey," I said, tapping her head. "What's going on up there? Do you hate it?"

"No, I love it!" she said, turning toward me with bright eyes. "Are you kidding? Thank you for saying all those things. Really, it was the best blow job you've ever had? The Stanley Cup of blowjobs?"

"Definitely." I nodded, relieved she wasn't angry. "You're the top. And I've had a lot of blowjobs, I mean seriously a lot, and by some really hot women. I remember this one girl who—"

"OK, OK. Enough." She held up her hand. "I get it. Thank you. I'm flattered, and you should stop talking now."

I grinned at her. God, I was even starting to adore the frowny face. "Sorry. Anyway, she was nothing compared to you. That was my point."

"So you really meant all those things you said?" She sounded surprised.

"Like I told you, I always mean what I say, Nat. Especially where you're concerned." I wondered which things in particular had her curious, but didn't ask. "Now my problem is that you've ruined blowjobs for me forever because nothing will ever compare."

"Oh, right." She shook her head and sighed. "Something tells me you'll be just fine, Miles Haas. And considering you just explained exactly what you like in a blowjob to any woman who reads your stuff, I'm sure you'll have plenty of qualified applicants to replace me."

"Doesn't matter. You'll always be my favorite." I tugged a few strands of her hair, happy at the sweetly surprised expression on her face.

For about five seconds.

Because I realized it was true—no matter what happened, no matter how many hot girls lined up to blow me, I'd forever compare them unfavorably to her. And what about sex? Had she ruined that for me too?

Quickly I tried to think of another girl I'd rather go to bed with than Natalie, another pussy I'd rather taste, another body I'd rather be inside. And I couldn't.

A sweat broke out on the back of my neck.

Because I realized I'd *never* been able to think of another girl I'd choose over Natalie. Ever.

And now that it had happened, I never would.

What the fuck was I going to do about that?

For one crazy moment, I wished we weren't so good together. I wished the sex was average, the chemistry lackluster, the feeling I got when I came inside her something less than fucking transcendent.

For an even crazier moment, I thought about promising her everything and all of me if only she'd say she wanted it.

Then I shook it off.

That was fucked up.

We stopped once for lunch and once for more coffee and gas, and arrived in Detroit around four o'clock that afternoon. Natalie wanted to see my apartment before we did anything, so I parked in the garage adjacent to the building and took her up to the twenty-third floor. I unlocked the door and let her in first.

"Wow," she breathed, setting her bags down. "This is beautiful."

"Thanks." I set my keys on a small table against the wall and kicked the door shut. "The guy who rents it to me said it was built in the twenties but abandoned for years before they renovated."

"That's amazing." She walked over to the huge floor-to-ceiling windows and looked out. "I love the view."

"Cool, isn't it? The guy asked me if I wanted shades on those windows and I said no way."

She turned around and took in the furniture, wood floors, and two-story ceiling before wandering over to the kitchen. "Holy shit," she said, running her hand over the shiny granite counter. "This is gorgeous."

"Yeah, he's a chef, so this kitchen is totally decked out." I went to the huge stainless fridge and took out two beers, taking the caps off before handing one to Natalie. "Actually he owns a restaurant called The Burger Bar in Corktown that I love. Maybe I'll take you there for dinner."

"Why'd he move out?" she asked, her wide eyes taking in the dark wood cabinets and stone tile floor.

"He got married and bought a house in Indian Village."

"Oh." She took a sip of her beer and meandered into the pantry. "What the hell, Miles? You have, like, nothing in here."

"I've got the basics." I leaned back against the counter and tipped up the bottle.

"What basics? Cap'n Crunch, Doritos, and Twinkies? Oh wait, I do see a bag of flour in here."

"Yeah, I think he left that."

"Oh my God." She came out, shaking her head. "Let's go to the grocery store while I'm here. I'll help you fill up your pantry and show you some easy things to make." She put her hand on the fridge handle and looked at me. "Do I even want to open this? Is six months' worth of moldy takeout food going to attack me?"

"It might."

She opened it up and sighed. "No mold. But what do you live on? Beer and cereal?"

I shrugged. "I could probably live on that."

She shut the fridge and stuck a hand on her hip, looking adorably concerned for me. I let myself fantasize for a moment that she lived here too, that we shared things like beer and Twinkies, that she'd cook for me and I'd...well, I'd think of something to do for her. There must be something I had to offer.

Your dick! That's what you have to offer, asshole. So stop with the stupid silly shit and go have sex.

"That diet cannot be healthy." She threw a hand up in exasperation. "How are you in such good shape? It's so annoying!"

Smiling, I set my beer down and tugged her toward me by the hem of her shirt, setting her hips against mine. "How about cinnamon buns? Are those healthy?"

"No."

I buried my face in her neck, kissing her hungrily, licking her throat. "But they taste so good."

She giggled. "I suppose they're all right for a treat. Every once in a while."

"How about now?" My hand slid up her stomach, palming her breast as I kissed my way to her mouth. My dick came alive, pushing against the crotch of my jeans. "Can I have some now?"

She set her beer on the counter and took my face in her hands, sliding her tongue along my lips. "Yeah. Want to show me your bedroom?"

Without another word, I took her hand and led her up the stairs to the loft bedroom, which was above the kitchen.

"Aha. You have a shade on this window, at least." Natalie went over and pulled it down, and the room into shadow.

"Only because I like to sleep in, and that window gets morning sun." I wrapped my arms around her waist and pulled her away backward. "Come here, you. It's been hours since I've seen you naked. That's not right." Lifting her shirt at the bottom, I pulled it over her head, then undid her shorts and yanked them down.

She turned to face me, sliding her shoes off her feet before taking off my shirt. For a moment, she stood silently, looking at my bare upper body. Then she put her hands on me, running them up my arms and down my chest. "I used to look at you," she said, her fingertips brushing my nipples, which made my cock surge with lust. "That last summer before you left, I used to look at you and wonder what it was like to touch you this way." She unbuttoned my jeans and slid a hand inside them. "And I felt so guilty," she whispered, bringing her lips to my chest, her fingertips playing with the tip of my cock. "I knew it was wrong, but sometimes I saw you looking at me, and I wondered what you were thinking."

"Uh, safe to say I was thinking about fucking you." I reached between her legs and stroked her softly through her panties. "I used to imagine your body naked under mine, your back arched, your legs spread." I slid my hand inside her underwear, teased her open. "I'd think about touching you this way, making you wet."

Her breaths coming faster, she wrapped her fingers around my dick and worked them slowly up and down. "And then what?"

"Then I'd have to go take a shower so I could jerk off."

She looked up at me. "Show me. I want to watch."

Oh, fuck. Was she serious? "You do?"

"Yes. Let's take a shower together." A devilish little glint flashed in her eyes. "And I'll let you watch me too."

I stared at her in disbelief. "You are *such* a bad girl right now."

"I know." Rising up on tiptoe, she whispered in my ear. "You can punish me later." Then she took her hand off me and sauntered through my closet into the adjacent bathroom, stopping to look over her shoulder in the doorway. "Well, come on, cowboy. You brought me all the way here. Don't you want to play with me?"

I stared at her in complete fucking disbelief. What the hell was this? She was out-Miles-ing me! She was so hot and had me so off-kilter, I didn't even know what to do with myself!

Get it together, Haas. Natalie Nixon is standing in your bathroom doorway in a little white lace bra and panties, and she's asking you to play. This is what you do—you play. You don't have Emotions, you don't have girlfriends, and you don't have time to stand here wondering if the life that's being upended here is yours. Now get the fuck in there and do your thing.

But even as I grinned and ditched the rest of my clothes while she watched, biting that juicy bottom lip of hers, the floor seemed to tremble beneath my feet.

CHAPTER 16
Natalie

I HAD no idea what possessed me to ask Miles if I could watch him jerk off in the shower, but now that I was here with a front row seat, I thanked my lucky stars I had. Hot water streamed down his body while steam billowed up around it. It was a feast for the eyes, and I could hardly get my fill. Where to begin? From bottom to top, he was simply delicious. I sat on the tiled bench and he stood in front of me, feet planted wide. His legs were so muscular—I'd forgotten how taut and toned they were from years of soccer and running. His cock was hard and thick, slipping through his fist in long, slow pulls, making my clit pulse with desire. Water dripped from flexing muscles in his forearm, shoulders, abs. It ran down his chest over the points of his hip bones and down his thighs, tempting me to drop to my knees at his feet and lick it up. The ink on his body was wet and shiny, and his chest rose and fell with heavy breaths. He used his right hand on himself; the other was fisted at his side. Sometimes he looked down at what he was doing, but mostly his eyes were on me.

"Is this what you wanted?" His voice was low and even.

"Yes." I moved to the edge of the bench, closer to him.

He stepped back. "Uh uh. No touching."

"But—"

"You wanted to watch; you're going to watch."

I stared at his cock, solid and slick, darker than the skin on his stomach, and lined with thick veins. Licking my lips, I looked up at him. "Please?"

"No. You want your hands on something? Touch yourself. Show me like I'm showing you."

If I wasn't so turned on, I'd have been more self-conscious. As it was, I opened my knees for him and arched my back, sliding one palm up my inner thigh.

"Fuck, yes." His eyes followed my fingers as they moved toward my pussy. He stroked himself harder. "God, that's so fucking hot. Do it."

The kick I got from seeing how much he enjoyed what he was doing while watching me was like fire in my veins. I smiled wickedly and dropped my chin, looking up at him through lowered lids, while my fingers circled my clit. Seeing as I had no toys, and sex with Dan had become a rarity the last year, I was an expert at getting myself off with my hand and rather enjoyed it. Granted, I'd never had an audience before, but I was delighted to find it aroused me even further, knowing that Miles was jerking off to the sight of me when he'd only had the *thought* of me before.

"Tell me." He struggled to speak. "What you're thinking about."

"Your cock," I said, breathless and panting. "Your cock inside me. So deep it hurts. Hitting me in that spot. Rubbing me just the right way."

"Yes. Fuck. Yes." Words hissed from his mouth through gritted teeth. "My cock in that tight, wet pussy." His eyes were glued to my hand, and my legs tingled with pleasure.

"Oh, God. Miles." I watched his hand work hard and fast, his thick solid flesh slipping through his fist, the muscles in his abs flexing. "I'm close. Do it with me."

"Christ," he rasped, leaning forward and bracing his left hand on the wall behind me. "I can't stop. Fuck…"

"Here." I flattened my palm on my chest, slid it over my breasts. "Put it here."

Thick white spurts shot from his cock onto my chest, and I rubbed it all over my breasts while he watched, wide-eyed and open-mouthed. The sight of him losing control pushed me over the edge, and my cries echoed off the tiles as my orgasm rocketed through me, my entire body clenching up before easing itself with rhythmic spasms beneath my fingers.

It took us a minute to calm down.

"Jesus." Miles breathed hard, still braced on the wall. "Who the hell are you?"

I smiled slyly and brought my knees together, hands clasped on top. "The girl next door."

"You think you know someone." He shook his head, water dripping off his dark locks.

"You know what?" I stood up, rinsed off, and we wrapped our arms around each other's waists. "You do know me, Miles. I think you knew me better than I knew myself. I don't exactly know how, since we haven't even seen each other much at all in the last few years, but you did. You do."

"I don't exactly know how, either. Just seems like it's always been that way with us." He rested his forehead against mine. "We've always had a connection."

A shiver moved through me. "Yes."

He pulled me closer, tucking my head beneath his chin, and turning me so the shower hit us both on the side. "Cold?"

"Just for a second there. I'm fine." But I hadn't been cold at all. I'd been moved by his words.

And a little bit frightened.

Because he was right—we did have a connection and we always had. What was left unsaid was that *we always would*. I felt it. But what would that mean when our three days were up and I went back to my real life? Yes, I was enjoying my newfound sexual freedom, but eventually I wanted something more lasting, didn't I?

Breaking up with Dan had been the right decision—I had no doubt about that. But I hadn't changed that much... Once my taste of freedom was complete, I saw myself wanting to be part of a couple again. Wanting to belong to someone. Wanting to fall in love. Those things made me happy.

But Miles didn't want those things, and it would be wrong of me to try to change him. He loved me in his own way, and I loved him, but he loved his freedom more. I didn't want him to resent me for asking him to be something he's not.

I sighed. No, this was it. And there was no sense in getting all freaked out and scared about it. If and when I met someone I could truly fall in love with, I had to believe that would overpower my chemistry with Miles.

But it would have to be one hell of a love.

We cleaned up, got dressed, and headed to Corktown for drinks and dinner, Miles giving me a little tour of the historic neighborhood first. I had my camera with me and took lots of pictures in the beautiful fading light—century-old row houses, colorful Victorians, the hulking, ghostly abandoned train station.

"Hey, you check that place out for your ghost sex article? Definitely looks haunted."

Miles shook his head, his eyes going wide. "There might be some souls lurking about in there, but none of them are souls I'd like to fuck."

"There's a soul you don't want to fuck?" I teased, putting my camera in my purse.

He grabbed me from behind, pinning my arms to my side.

"Yes, smartass. There are plenty. In fact, I only want one soul these days, and that's yours. So behave."

I giggled. "I'll try. You don't make it easy, though."

The Burger Bar was nice and cool inside, and pretty crowded, but we found two seats together at the bar. We ordered beers and burgers, and when I praised the menu, with its locally-sourced ingredients, Miles asked me if I thought I'd stick with the coffee shop or wanted to try something else one day.

"Oh, I think I'd like to try something else someday. Coffee Darling is a great little place, but I wouldn't mind something bigger at some point. Maybe a restaurant at one of the local wineries or farms. I think that would be fun."

"But definitely up there, huh?"

I sipped my beer, thinking about it. "Yeah," I answered finally. "I do like traveling, but that part of Michigan just feels like home to me. I love the seasons up there, I love being close to my family. Both my sisters are up there, and now with Skylar getting married, I wouldn't be surprised if she and Sebastian have kids soon."

"When's the wedding again?" Miles took a long drink from his glass.

"Three months. End of September." I was telling him more about their plans when a dark-haired guy approached us from behind the bar. He was so handsome, I forgot what I was saying and left off in the middle of a sentence. He had tattoos too, down both arms, and the short sleeves of his fitted black Burger Bar t-shirt hugged the muscular curves of his arms. Immediately I thought of Jillian, since he looked like her type—dark hair, dark eyes—and he was a little older, maybe in his mid-thirties, but then I noticed he wore a wedding band.

Rats. Was she right? Were all the good ones taken? Maybe she and I were both destined to be single forever. We'd live in my house where we'd get old and crabby together, no one to bitch at but each other and maybe a few sad cats. God, that was depressing.

The guy grinned at us and held his hand out to Miles. "Sorry, didn't mean to interrupt. Just wanted to say hi and see if you needed anything."

Miles shook his hand. "Nat, this is Nick Lupo, the owner of this place and my apartment. Nick, this is my friend Natalie from up North."

"The swimmer with the coffee shop?" Nick held his hand out to me. "I've heard a lot about you."

Warmth rushed my face as I put my hand in his. "Wow. I'm flattered." I glanced at Miles, who looked pleased with himself. "You have a great apartment and a great restaurant. I love the menu."

Nick filled up our glasses and stayed a few minutes to chat about some local farms he worked with and the farm-to-table concept he embraced—good quality ingredients, organic whenever possible, from responsible farmers he knew personally that were worth the higher price he paid for them.

"Natalie was saying earlier how she'd like to run a restaurant someday," Miles said.

Nick looked at me. "Oh yeah? I've been thinking about opening something up in that area."

"You should definitely partner up." Miles picked up his beer. "Natalie is wickedly talented and totally dedicated to what she does. Although I do think she works too hard."

I slapped his leg. "Stop it. I'm here, aren't I?"

"Honestly, I'd love to talk about working together on something in that area," Nick said, bracing his hands on the bar. "My wife's best friend and her husband have a winery up there, so we've visited a lot."

"Which winery?" I asked.

"Abelard Vineyards," he said.

I slapped a hand on my chest. "My sister works there! Is your wife's friend Mia Fournier?"

He nodded and smiled. "Yeah. Small world."

"It's a fantastic spot. So beautiful—in fact, my sister is getting married there this fall."

"I'll have to check it out," Miles said. "In fact, I told Skylar yesterday I'd come to her wedding." Then he shuddered. "Although those things give me hives."

Nick rolled his eyes and looked at me. "Good luck with him, Natalie." He pulled a card from his back pocket and slid it across the bar from me. "When you're ready, give me a call and we can talk. That way I can tell my wife I'm actually doing something about it. She'll be delighted with me."

"Maybe she'll even do something nice for you," Miles said. "You should have her read my blog post today. It's about blowjobs."

"Miles!" I hit him on the shoulder, mortified he'd said that out loud.

Nick laughed. "She doesn't need any help there. Besides, what I want takes the real deal."

Miles's jaw dropped. "You want another kid? Don't you have, like, two of those things already?"

"Three." Nick's dark eyes lit up, which I thought was really sweet, especially compared to the way Miles reacted to the subject of kids. "All boys. I want to try for a girl, but Coco gives me the evil eye every time I mention it."

"That's because children interfere with all the best things in life—sex, sleep, and drinking."

His words stung, which was so dumb. It's not like I hadn't known his views on marriage and family before. I'd just teased him about it last week!

But you didn't have these feelings for him last week.

I forced the realization from my head. It wouldn't do me any good to dwell on my growing feelings for him. They couldn't go anywhere.

Nick shrugged. "Can't argue there. But they're worth it." Our food arrived, and he stepped back to give the server room to set down the plates. "Enjoy, you guys. Nice meeting you, Natalie. Looking forward to hearing from you. See you, Miles."

"Nice meeting you too." I smiled at him and dropped my eyes to my plate.

"Think you'll call him?" Miles asked, dumping a pool of ketchup onto his plate.

"Maybe."

"What's wrong?"

"Nothing. Why?"

"Because I know you, Nixon. What is it?"

I glanced at him, and he was so cute, and so concerned, and we were such old friends that I almost figured, *fuck it—I'll tell him the truth.*

Almost.

I faked a smile. "Nothing, really. I'm just thinking about my shop. Thinking about what I'd do with it if I decided to do something different."

That seemed to satisfy Miles, and we spent the rest of dinner chatting about the possibilities. When we were done, Miles wanted to take me to a place called The Sugar House for drinks, which was just across the street and down a few blocks. We said goodbye to Nick and left the restaurant, and Miles grabbed my hand as we hurried across busy Michigan Avenue. He didn't let go when we got to the other side, my heart beat quicker as we strolled hand in hand in the dark. *God, I wish things were different. This feels so good with him, so easy.*

Inside the bar, a narrow old storefront with high ceilings, brick walls, and, oddly enough, big game heads mounted opposite the long wooden bar. Huge, ornate, floor-to-ceiling drapes on the window and a chandelier in a cozy front alcove gave the place a little Victorian hipster vibe, as did the three tattooed bartenders, who wore ties and vests, their shirtsleeves rolled up and held with garters. They all had thick facial hair, one wore a top hat, and they took their cocktail-making very, very seriously.

Miles and I sat at the bar and ordered drinks, and mine was so delicious I ordered another one right away. Maybe it wasn't wise to consume so much so quickly, especially since I'd already had two beers at dinner, but the more I drank, the hotter I was for Miles, and that was a much safer feeling than brooding about what could never be. I finished the second drink even faster than the first, and Miles asked if I wanted another.

"Oh, God. I really shouldn't." I giggled. "I'm already goofy. I'll get drunk."

"Good! You should get drunk. You should get drunk and let me do ridiculous things to your body."

I leaned toward him, put my hands on top of his thighs. "I don't need to be drunk for that, silly. You can do anything you like to my body."

"Uh, in that case. Let me get the check and get you home." He leaned in too, and spoke low in my ear. "Did you wear that short little skirt just to torture me?"

"Uh huh."

"You wicked little slut," he whispered, making all my nerve endings tingle. "I'm going to make you pay for that."

While I used the bathroom, Miles paid the bill, and by the time I came out, he was waiting for me at the door. Grabbing me by the hand, he ran through the bar, out the door, and down the street toward the parking lot so fast I could hardly keep up.

When we reached the Jeep, he backed me up against the passenger door and kissed me hard, one hand fisted in the back of my hair, his erection pressing against my abdomen.

"Feel that? I've been hard for you all night, ever since I saw your legs in that skirt." He tightened his hand in my hair, and I gasped at the needles of pain prickling across my scalp. "I want to do such bad things to you. Such bad things."

My heart threatened to pound right out of my chest as he crushed his mouth to mine once more.

"Get in." He unlocked the door and practically threw me into the passenger seat before storming around to the driver's side.

On the ride home, I unzipped his jeans and took his cock in my hand, and he slid his hand up my thigh and inside my panties.

"Already wet for me. I like that." His fingers easily slid inside me, and I grabbed his wrist with my free hand, holding him against me as I swiveled my hips.

"I want you so badly," I whispered. "I've never wanted anyone the way I want you."

"Trust me. I know the feeling." He pulled his fingers from me and touched them to his tongue. "Fuck. Your taste. I can't get enough."

He drove home so fast I was amazed he didn't get a ticket, and we ran so hard through the parking garage to the elevators I was gasping for air by the time the doors opened. As soon as they closed and we were alone, Miles and I went at each other, lips sealed, hands groping, feet stumbling. At the twenty-third floor, we didn't even stop kissing when the doors opened, and barely made it into the hallway before they closed.

We moved awkwardly down the hall with our tongues and legs tangled, hands sneaking beneath clothing, until he picked me up and I wrapped my legs around him. I have no idea how he knew where his apartment door was, but somehow he unlocked it and got us in without ever taking his mouth off mine.

Inside, he kicked the door shut and went right for the stairs without even turning on the lights. I thought he'd go right for the bed and throw me down, so I was surprised when he went into his closet.

"What's this?" I laughed against his lips. "Wardrobe change?"

"Wardrobe removal." He set me down and whipped my shirt off, breaking the kiss only to allow it to go over my head. His shirt was next, then I kicked off my flats as he removed my bra and shoes and skirt and panties. But when I reached for his zipper, he stopped me. "Wait."

It was dark in the closet but I heard hangers being shoved aside on a bar and then a drawer open and close.

Next thing I knew, he had something over my eyes and he was tying it at the back of my head. A scarf? A tie? "What is this?"

"Shhh. This is your punishment for teasing me tonight with that little skirt." Once the blindfold was secure, he took both my wrists, brought them over my head and wound something around them. "You're not allowed to use your hands."

I gasped. "I can't see you *or* touch you?"

"Not if you want to come tonight."

"Oh, God." My heart pounded as he moved me beneath the bar where he'd cleared space, and secured my wrists to it.

"Perfect." Miles pulled a final knot tight. "I'll be right back."

"What? You're leaving me like this?"

He laughed and kissed the top of each breast. "Yes. You stay here and think about what you did." A final pinch on the ass and he walked out, leaving me tied up, blindfolded, turned on, and alone. *In his closet.*

Now what?

CHAPTER 17
Miles

HOLY FUCK.

Holy. Fuck.

Natalie Nixon, good girl next door, was naked, blindfolded, and tied up in my closet.

Just seeing her standing there, arms over her head, back arched, her fair skin radiant in the dark, that head full of tousled blonde hair that always looked like she'd just been fucked...I nearly shot my load right then. But I didn't want to rush—I wanted to tease her, savor her, linger over every inch of her perfect body. What if I never had this opportunity again?

I walked out of the closet and through my room in case she could hear my steps, but then I fucking bolted down to the kitchen, where I pulled a bottle of my favorite Kentucky bourbon and a glass from the cabinet. If I'd had whipped cream or chocolate syrup or anything else to eat off her body, I'd have brought that too, but I was me, so I had nothing but Cap'N Crunch and Doritos, which I didn't think would be too sexy. But the bourbon would be delicious licked off Natalie's vanilla skin...fucking hell, I was so excited my legs were shaking as I ran back to the stairs and darted up three at a time. I slowed down when I got near the closet—just to torture her a little.

"You're back," she said.

"Yes." I moved past her into the bathroom and turned on the light, so I could see her a little. Her rosy pink nipples were puckered, and her chest rose and fell with labored breaths. *Oh, fuck, I want her.*

"Well, now that you have me like this, what are you going to do?" A hint of nerves edged beneath her tone, and it made me fucking crazy. My cock was like steel in my pants.

"I'm going to have a drink." I pulled the cork from the bottle of bourbon, and she turned her head in the direction of the pop. I poured a couple fingers and set the bottle down.

"A drink?"

"Yeah. Want a sip?"

She smiled hesitantly. "Sure."

I lifted the glass to her lips, then kissed her, stroking her lips and tongue with mine, tasting the honey-sweet bourbon on them. Then I poured a little just beneath her collarbone and watched it run down her breast. Her mouth fell open and she gasped while I licked the rivulet just as it reached her nipple, swirling my tongue around the stiffened peak, washing it in bourbon. I did the same on the other breast, and she moaned lightly when I sucked her nipple into my mouth, rubbing the hard tip with my tongue.

Next, I poured some down the center of her chest, watching it flow between her breasts and down her belly. I dropped to one knee and flattened my tongue just above her clit, and licked all the way up her body long and slow, up the underside of each breast, up her throat, tracing the shell of her ear. Her entire body shivered. "Oh my God, I want you," she whispered. "You've got me desperate for you."

I was desperate for her too, but I wasn't finished yet.

"Turn around," I told her.

She turned, presenting me with the most beautiful series

of curves any man has ever seen. From the rounded lines of her arms and shoulders to the arc of her back to the flare of her hips, she was perfection. I poured the rest of the bourbon at the base of her neck and watched it cascade down her back and disappear in the crack of her ass. Getting to my knees, I set the glass aside. "Now spread your legs like a good little slut."

She did as I requested, arching her back, and I licked and sucked the bourbon from her pussy to her ass, making her quiver and moan. I fucked her with my tongue, reaching around to rub her clit with one hand while the other held her trembling legs apart. "God, you taste so fucking good. I could do this all night."

"I love it," she breathed. "I love your mouth on me." She rocked her hips against my hands and tongue, her sighs coming closer and closer together, her voice rising, until finally she cried out in rapture, her body going slack.

"Miles," she said weakly. "I might pull this bar right out of the wall. I can't stand up."

I dragged my tongue up her ass as I stood. "Need something to sit on?" I asked, unzipping my jeans and shoving them down. My cock burst out of my pants like a jack-in-the box.

"Yes. Please," she panted. "Do it."

She was soaking wet from my mouth as well as her own desire, so my cock slid easily inside her. Both of us groaned as I grabbed her hips and buried myself deep. Oh, fuck, that body. The muscles in her back. *That ass.* I wanted it for breakfast, lunch and dinner every day of my life. Digging my fingers into her flesh, I watched myself move in and out of her, slowly but forcefully. Each thrust was punctuated by a gasp from her as I tested the limits of how far I could go.

I'd planned on teasing her a little more, playing a game, making her wait. But with my cock so hard and her pussy so wet and her ass so pretty, I lost all control. My body moved purely on instinct. "Christ," I snarled, fucking her hard and deep, so hard she rose up on her toes with every thrust. "I want to come on your ass." I wanted to come inside her too, but *that ass*. And she was so vulnerable and helpless, bound and blindfolded like she was—even if she said no, I could still do it. She couldn't stop me. Was I a total fucking asshole because that turned me on?

I needn't have worried.

"Yes!" she begged. "Do it."

"Fuck!" My balls tightened up and I waited until the last possible second before I pulled out and took my cock in my fist, working my hand up and down as I came all over her.

I swear I lost vision.

I might have lost my hearing too.

When I could see again, I flattened a palm on her upper back and blinked in amazed, grateful disbelief at the sight of what I'd just done to her. Truthfully, I'd done dirtier things to other girls, but it hadn't felt nearly so illicit. Doing this stuff with Natalie was like stealing a priceless work of art and getting away with it.

If only I could keep it.

But I couldn't. I had to give her back the day after tomorrow, which meant that I had only one more day and night to spend with her.

Unless…

No. Don't start making any promises you can't keep. This sweet, beautiful girl you adore just let you tie her up in your closet, lick bourbon off her body, and come all over her ass. She's your friend. Enough.

Gently I slipped her wrists from the tie I'd used to bind them and pulled the blindfold off as well. Taking her hand, I led her into the bathroom where I ran the shower, slipped in beside her, and washed her off from head to toe.

Clean and damp, we slid between the sheets of my bed and snuggled up together, her head on my chest, her leg over my waist. I put an arm around her shoulders and a hand on her thigh, pressing my lips to her head as we drifted off to sleep.

It felt so good. What the fuck was the matter with me that I didn't want this forever?

The next morning, I woke up to the sound of rain against the window. Immediately I felt around for Natalie, but she wasn't there. I reached for my glasses, and once they were on I saw her standing at the window peeking out the side of the shade, stark naked.

I was speechless. She looked so beautiful in the soft gray light filtering through the shade. My plan had been to let her sleep in and go get us some breakfast, but I'd woken up semi-hard and now the sight of her had me at full mast.

She looked over her shoulder and smiled at me. "Morning."

"Morning." My voice cracked, but something inside me was cracking too.

"It's raining."

"I hear it. What time is it?"

"A little after nine. I thought I'd sleep more, but I'm so used to getting up early, I can't help it. Hope I didn't wake you."

"You didn't. Come here." My entire body was aching for her. This was so uncool.

But I had to have her near me.

With the smile still on her face, she came back to bed, sidling up next to me. "So what do you do with your rainy days?"

I took off my glasses and set them aside. "Usually, I write.

Go to the gym. Hang out. I was thinking of going to get us some breakfast just now. I don't have much food here."

"I know," she said, giggling as she threw that arm and leg over me again. "But I don't think you should go out like this." She rubbed her inner thigh over my dick, making me groan. "And we can't let it go to waste."

Climbing on top of me, she straddled my hips and looked me right in the eye as she licked her fingers and touched herself.

"Jesus, Natalie. Do you want me to shoot my load in my own eye?"

She laughed, getting up higher on her knees and taking my cock in her hand. "No. Although it might be funny to watch."

"It would be pathetic and juvenile, trust me. Oh, God." I had to close my eyes as she placed the tip of my cock between her legs and slid down one inch at a time until I was entirely sheathed. It was too much. I twitched inside her.

"Look at me."

"I can't."

"Look at me, Miles."

I opened one eye, and she dropped her chin and smiled devilishly, one blue eye peeking out from behind her hair. "No. You're too fucking hot. I'll come too fast this early in the morning."

"No, you won't."

"Trust me. I will embarrass myself."

"I know you. You always make sure the girl comes first. Isn't that your rule?" She put her hands on my chest and began to circle her hips, sighing with pleasure.

"I try," I said weakly, unable to resist putting my hands on her tits. She closed her eyes as I teased her nipples into stiff little peaks. "But you're messing with my rules right now. And I have no control over this situation."

She leaned forward, grabbing the headboard and putting her breasts in front of my face. "That's because I have it."

As she rocked her hips over me, moving at just the angle and rhythm she wanted, I buried my face in her tits and tried to pace myself. But my usual tricks weren't working. I couldn't concentrate on anything that wasn't sexy—for fuck's sake, who could? And then she started talking. *Talking!*

"God, Miles, fucking you is like nothing I have ever felt."

"Yeah?" Giving up on holding back, I grabbed her hips and watched her. Her skin was flushed and warm, her breathing fast, and I prayed she was as close to orgasm as I was. "Tell me."

"I can't stop thinking about it. All day yesterday I felt like a fiend because I just couldn't wait to get you inside me. I couldn't wait for you to make me come again."

My cock pulsed with need. "Oh, Jesus." Reaching between us, I rubbed my thumb over her clit in tight little circles. "I love making you come. I love watching it. I love feeling it happen."

"Yes!" she cried, her eyes closing, her body thrashing above mine. "It's so good—I can't—I can't—"

I could tell she was right there, and I was about to explode, so I lifted my hips, pushing even deeper inside her and she screamed so loud, I thought the walls shook, or maybe it was the climax that thundered through my body at that moment, paralyzing me as I came inside her in powerful, surging throbs.

When the tremors subsided, she pitched forward and collapsed on my chest, her skin warm and soft.

I ran my hands up and down her back. "I like when you take control."

She laughed softly. "Me too."

Our breathing synced, and I was lulled by the feeling of our lungs and chests moving in tandem. Again, I closed my eyes and wished that things were different. That I trusted myself not to be an asshole to her. That I was the kind of guy who'd pick a place and settle down, like she had. Be a husband. Be a father. Be a grown up.

How the fuck did you even go about it?

And did she even want that from me?

I had no idea, and I was too scared to ask.

What if the answer was no?

CHAPTER 18
Natalie

AFTER WE GOT DRESSED, Miles drove to the grocery store and I filled the cart with healthy staples for his pantry and refrigerator, some chicken breasts and ground beef he could store in the freezer, some deli items, a loaf of bread, and plenty of fruits and vegetables. "I'll leave you some easy recipes, OK? That way you're not eating junk all the time."

"Cinnamon buns. Cinnamon buns. Cinnamon buns," he panted as he pushed the cart.

"Oh, for heaven's sake. OK, I'll grab the ingredients for buns. Want some bacon and eggs with them?"

He nodded happily. "Yes please."

We went back to his apartment and put everything away, then I started breakfast for us while Miles made coffee.

"I'm glad to see you have a coffee pot. And one decent pan." I shook my head. "Tell me I'm imagining things and that's not all plastic in your silverware drawers."

Miles winced. "Ummmm…"

"Jesus, Miles!" I opened and shut several cupboards and drawers. "Not even a spatula?"

He looked offended. "I have a spatula." He opened the dishwasher and pulled out a wooden spoon. "Here."

"Oh my God. Forget it. At least you have measuring cups."

"Yeah, I think my mom gave me those. I've never actually used them."

I managed with one pan, a wooden spoon, and some plasticware, and we stuffed our faces with scrambled eggs and thick-cut bacon and strawberries dusted with powdered sugar and cinnamon buns dripping with glaze.

"Told you it would taste just as good with plastic forks," Miles said with his mouth full. "And think how fast the cleanup will be without real plates."

I rolled my eyes. "Now I know what to get you for Christmas."

When we were done, we lay on the couch, rubbing our full bellies and swearing we'd go for a walk as soon as the rain let up.

"This rain is killing all my plans for today," Miles complained. "I wanted to take you to a game at Comerica Park, but it looks like a rain delay. Do you want to go to the art museum or something?"

"You know what? I'm fine just hanging out here if you want. I'm so busy on the days I work, I don't really need to do anything but be lazy today."

"That is perfect, because it just so happens that I am awesome at lazy. I fucking *own* lazy." He rolled to his side and put his arms around me. "Let's do this all day. But take breaks for sex."

I laughed. "Don't you want to write?"

"If I feel like it, I will. Right now I'm happy."

"Me too." I couldn't remember the last time I'd taken a nap so early in the day, after I'd done nothing but eat breakfast, but I was so relaxed and comfortable, I shut my eyes and let it happen.

We fell asleep to the sound of the rain, and when I woke up, his arms were still wrapped around me. It surprised me about him—that he liked to cuddle this way. I'd have thought he was one of those guys who likes the sex but not the closeness, but it seemed as if he liked both. I did too.

For a moment, I let myself wonder what life might have been like if we'd kissed on the Almost Night. Would we have fallen in love? Stayed together? Miles wouldn't have been able to get the reputation he had, so what would he be writing about instead of sex? Would we live together? Would this be my apartment too? I swallowed hard. Would we be married by now?

Or maybe it would have gone the other way. Maybe we would have broken up while he was at college because he couldn't keep it in his pants. Maybe we'd have fought and I'd have gotten back together with Dan. Maybe we wouldn't even be friends now.

My throat squeezed. I didn't want to think about that. I liked the other scenario better—the one where we fell head over heels and made it work somehow, even though we were so different. Too bad our timing had never been right. We might have been good together.

We would have been good together.

I sighed, and Miles shifted behind me. "You awake?"

"Yeah." My voice was weak.

"Everything OK?"

"I guess so."

"What is it?" He pulled my shoulder back so he could see my face.

"I don't know. Maybe the whole breakup thing is hitting me now." It was a lie, and I felt guilty about it since he was always swearing he told me the truth, but how could I admit that I was sad about us? That we'd never been given a chance? He'd tell me I was nuts, wouldn't he?

"Hm. Well, we can't have that." He tapped a finger on his chin. "What should we do? Want to watch cartoons? Or porn?

The internet has such a good selection of both, sometimes I have a hard time deciding between them."

I laughed. "You don't say."

He looked out the windows. "Or, you know what? I think the rain let up a little. Want to go out for a walk? Grab a drink?"

"Actually, that sounds nice."

"That means we have to get off the couch though. And this is really fucking comfortable." He squeezed me tight, laying his head on my shoulder. "Never leave me."

Stop it, Miles. I'm confused enough.

"OK. Now let me up."

He sighed dramatically, but he released me from his grip and I forced myself to get off the couch.

Upstairs, I went into the bathroom and took a few deep breaths, reminding myself to keep this time with him in perspective. No good would come of falling for a playboy like Miles Haas, especially so soon after breaking up with Dan. That had disaster written all over it. Yes, I'd promised to let myself make some mistakes in the future, but that could not be one of them. I plastered a smile on my face as I went down the stairs. "Ready."

We walked down Woodward through a light drizzle and ended up at the Grand Trunk Pub, where I got tipsy on mojitos and tried not to think about going home tomorrow.

"So what will we do for my last night here?" I asked.

"I'm going to take you out."

"Out where?"

"To one of my favorite places in the city. It's old school Detroit, a classic."

I clapped my hands. "The dress-up date?"

He nodded and took out his phone. "I should probably make a reservation, although on a Tuesday night, it won't be that crowded."

"Go ahead," I told him. "I'm going to use the bathroom

before we leave. And let me buy the drinks this time. You've been treating me long enough."

"I enjoy it."

"My turn," I said firmly, pulling a twenty from my wallet. "Tell her to use this please." I walked away before he could argue.

In the bathroom, I fussed with my hair in the mirror and wondered what I should do with it tonight. The dress I'd packed was strapless, and sometimes I wore my hair up when my shoulders were bare. *Maybe I'll ask Miles what he prefers.* I got a little flutter in my belly thinking about getting ready for a night out with him—almost like we were back in school and he'd asked me to the Prom or something. Or like we were a married couple going on a date night.

Stop it. The more you fantasize about this stuff, the more disappointed you're going to be when the magic wears off and you're just friends again.

But the flutter stuck with me as I walked back through the bar, and intensified when I saw him stand up and wait for me. I couldn't keep the smile off my face.

Then he handed me my twenty. "Here. Save your money. You need it for your loans."

"Miles!" I slapped his arm. "You were supposed to use it for the drinks."

"Well, I didn't." He tucked it into the back pocket of my jean shorts, taking the opportunity to feel my butt.

I giggled, pushing his hand away. "You're terrible. There are people in here who don't want to see you grabbing my ass."

"Only because they are jealous." He took my hand as we walked to the door. "Oh fuck, look at that rain."

While we'd been inside, it had started pouring again. I looked up the street. "How far are we?"

He shrugged. "About a ten minute walk. And you've got your camera. Want me to call a car?"

"Nah. It's in the case, and I like rain. Let's just run."

Suddenly his face lit up. "Remember the time we camped out in the orchard with your sisters and it started to rain?"

"Yes, and they were such babies about it and went inside and we stayed out there until my mom realized it was thundering and made us come in too?"

He nodded. "You were furious that your mom made me stay on the couch because you wanted me to sleep in your room."

I laughed. "Yes! I totally remember that. We were what, like ten and eleven at the time? I didn't understand why she wouldn't let you."

He leaned close. "But you know now."

"Yes." My cheeks warmed as I thought about our last few nights together, and a little rush of desire swooshed inside me.

"Then let's do it. Because now I'm thinking about being in bed with you and your mom can't tell us what to do anymore. Want to go get naked?"

I didn't even hesitate. "Yeah. I do."

Without another word, he grabbed my hand and we ran out into the summer rain, Miles groaning and me squealing as it drenched us in under a minute. We moved quickly, skirting Campus Martius and racing up Woodward hand in hand. When we got to his building, our shoes squeaked across the floor as we hurried for the elevator, both of us anxious to get up to his apartment.

Out of breath and soaking wet, we stood at the back as a few more people got on, and Miles brought our hands in front of his dick, pressing them not so subtly against his bulging erection. I gasped. To torture him—and myself—a little, I braved rubbing the back of my hand up and down on it, keeping my eyes straight ahead. Next to me, I heard Miles stifle a moan by clearing his throat, and I hid a smile.

When the doors opened on the twenty-third floor, he yanked me through the crowd and pulled me roughly down the hall. We barely made it inside before we went at each other, our mouths crushed together and tongues lashing inside, our hands tearing wet clothes off and flinging them any which way. Unable to wait, we dropped to the wood floor right there in front of the door.

He was inside me in less than thirty seconds, his cock driving hard and deep, his eyes dark and wild with lust. My head knocked against the door and I flattened my palms against it, pulling my knees up alongside his ribs and wrapping my legs around his back.

"This feeling," Miles panted. "Right here. Being inside you after all this time, your legs around my body, your skin against mine, your pussy around my cock. Seeing you look at me that way. It's all I want."

"Me too." I fought for control of my breath, of my voice, of my heart. It was pounding inside my chest, clamoring like a caged animal trying to escape—but I couldn't let it. I couldn't let it.

"What are you doing to me?" he rasped. "Why can't I get enough of you? What is this?"

"I don't know." I bit my lip to keep from saying more. *But I feel the same, and I'm confused and scared and it's crazy and impossible and I'm out of control.*

He brought his mouth to mine and I greedily sucked his tongue into my mouth. Faster and faster he drove into me, his cock grinding against my clit, until the world turned silver and started to hum.

No longer caring about my head banging the door, I grabbed his ass and pulled him into me, rocking my hips beneath him. He buried his head in my neck as he came, his body going still as his cock pulsed inside me, and my body answered in kind, contracting around him over and over again in blissful harmony.

When his body had gone still, I held him close to me, stroking his back, his hair, his neck.

"God, I'm going to miss you when you're gone." Still breathing hard, he picked his head up and looked down at me quizzically. "What the fuck is that about?"

I smiled, but a pang of longing shot through me. *I'll miss you too.* "No, you won't. You'll have some other girl on your couch as soon as you're back."

He tipped his head to one side, like he was thinking about it. "Probably. But I'll still miss you."

I rolled my eyes to cover up how hurt I was before squirming out from beneath him. "I better go shower. We'll be late for dinner."

He let me go.

CHAPTER 19
Milees

FUCK, *I shouldn't have said that to her.*

After Natalie went upstairs to get in the shower, I pulled on my jeans and sat on the couch with my head in my hands, trying to regain my sense of balance, figure out which way was up. I knew I'd hurt her feelings just now, I'd seen it in her eyes, but fuck! She had me all out of whack. The entire day had been perfect, from the wake-up sex to the breakfast to the nap to the walk in the rain to the floor sex. Too perfect. So perfect I was off my game. She was making me FEEL things, and I was not OK with that.

For example, I felt like I didn't care if I never had another girl on my couch if only I could have her forever.

WHAT THE ACTUAL FUCK.

And I felt like I'd never get enough of her body, her face, her brain, her voice, her laugh, her cinnamon buns.

HER FUCKING CINNAMON BUNS.

I felt like I was ready to give up anything I had to in order to have a chance with her—and it wouldn't even be a sacrifice.

I felt like I wanted her. Like I needed her.

Like I loved her.

I WAS MESSED THE FUCK UP!

As if I'd been caught doing something wrong, I jumped to my feet and paced in front of the couch. Now what was I supposed to do? I had no experience with Feelings. What if she didn't feel the same way? And why should she? My timing sucked fucking hairy balls—she was just getting out of a relationship. And I'd told her she was too serious all the time and needed to just relax and have some fun. I fisted my hands in my hair. Why the fuck had I done that?

Because you were right. She does need time off from a relationship. She does need to have fun. What she doesn't need is another guy telling her he loves her right away, putting pressure on her. Especially a guy like you who doesn't want any of the same things she does in life. So slow the fuck down.

It was true. As much as I cared for Natalie, I wasn't ready to promise that I'd be up for the role of homeowner, husband, and father. And she wanted that. She deserved that.

I'd only disappoint her.

I heard the water go off upstairs, and I knew I had to go get ready for dinner or we'd be late. I scooped up the rest of my clothes and headed upstairs, reaching my room just as she opened the bathroom door.

Something gripped me hard at the sight of her standing there in a towel, hair dripping, face flushed, skin damp. My stomach knotted, my throat went dry, my hands flexed.

Oh, Jesus.

I couldn't speak. I felt sort of sick to my stomach, too. And my chest—what the hell was going on in there? Was it love or cardiac arrest? Fucking hell, did people actually like this feeling? It was horrible!

I was going to die.

CHAPTER 20
Natalie

THE LOOK on his face was one I'd never seen before, somewhere between shocked and nauseated.

"You OK?" I asked, holding the towel tightly around me as I walked toward him. I'd spent the last ten minutes feeling kind of aggravated with him, but he really did look bad.

"Uh. No. Yes." He swallowed hard. "Maybe."

"We don't have to go out if you don't want to."

"I'm fine." Now he just looked frightened. "I want to go out."

"OK." He didn't look fine at all. Had I done something wrong?

He went into the bathroom without another word, shutting the door behind him.

What the hell? I threw my hands up. *I get that you don't do relationships, but could you please do civilized, if not friendly?*

Men.

Seriously, why did women even bother?

Grumpy, I towel-dried my hair and pulled on my panties and dress, zipping it up as far as I could. I took my blow dryer and makeup bag to the downstairs bathroom, and while I blew out my hair, I let my resentment stew and gave myself a good ten minutes of envious grumbling that Skylar had managed to find someone like Sebastian—gorgeous, sweet, smart, kind, and totally devoted to making her happy. I knew it hadn't been easy for them, but they sure made it look that way now.

When my hair was dry, I pinned it up in a twist, brushed my teeth, and put on my makeup. Upstairs, the door to the bathroom was open, and my breath caught when I saw Miles standing at the mirror in a blue suit, fussing with his hair. I'd never seen him in a suit before. He looked so…mature. Classy. Stylish.

Like a real gentleman.

He caught my eye in the mirror. "You look beautiful."

"Thanks," I said, feeling the heat in my cheeks. And my panties. "You look very handsome. I love the suit."

"Thanks."

"Can you zip me up all the way?" For some strange reason, I felt shy as I walked into the bathroom and turned around. For heaven's sake, we'd been naked and sweaty less than an hour ago.

"I think I can manage that. Although usually I'm *un*zipping dresses."

"Ha, ha." I didn't exactly like the reminder of how many dresses he'd unzipped, but I was glad he'd made a joke. He seemed so on edge. And was it my imagination, or did he touch me as little as possible while zipping the dress? *Now you're just making shit up. Relax.*

"Ready to go?" he asked.

"Yes."

He didn't take my hand as we walked down the hall, he didn't stand too close to me in the elevator, and he barely spoke to me on the ride to the restaurant. Something was definitely off with him. "Are you OK?" I asked as we pulled up at valet parking.

"I already answered that question. Yes." He didn't even look at me.

A doorman ushered us down the stairs into a dark, cozy underground space. Intimate booths lined the walls, black linens topped the tables, and candles gave the room a soft warm glow. We were seated at a table at the edge of the dance floor, and I hoped maybe Miles would ask me to dance at some point in the evening, just for fun, but he never did. In fact, the night was just one disappointment after another where he was concerned. The setting was romantic and elegant, the food and wine delicious, the jazz standards played by a trio next to the small dance floor enchanting—it should have been the perfect date, and it would have been, except that Miles was kind of an asshole all night.

Never mind the limited conversation and eye contact. Once he got a drink in him, he made several comments about our waitress's awesome rack, he took two phone calls from his editor, he texted at the table, and he flirted openly with the female bartender when we moved to the bar after our meal. He even gave her his number! Right in front of me! By the time we paid the bar tab, I was fuming. I'd known he was a flirt and player, but he'd never been so disrespectful to me. It wasn't like him at all.

Clearly the magic was gone.

My throat constricted, and I swallowed hard. *Is this it, then? This is how he pulls away?*

It pissed me off, actually. I got that I wasn't his girlfriend, but I wasn't just another one of his blog bunnies or whatever. Or wait...was I? After all, there was a post about me now. Good old Cinnamon Buns. I chewed my bottom lip.

Still, he shouldn't treat me this way. And if he thought I was going to jump into bed with him when we got back to his apartment, he had another thing coming.

The ride home was uncomfortably silent, as was the elevator ride up to his floor. I could have laughed aloud thinking about how different our earlier return to his apartment had been—we couldn't keep our hands off each other. What the hell had happened since? I racked my brain trying to come up with what I must have said or done to scare him off, but I couldn't think of anything.

It's nothing. This is the way he is. He's the kind of guy who just wants sex and once he gets it, he's done. Even with you. Why are you surprised about this? You've known this about him for years!

You never should have slept with him.

Angry at myself and him, I stomped down the hallway and waited stiffly for him to unlock the door. When he opened it, I stormed through the apartment and went right upstairs to pack my stuff. I wanted to be ready to go first thing in the morning. Biting back sobs, I folded up clothes, wound the cord around my hair dryer, and tossed everything in haphazardly. Once everything was packed, I took off my heels and dress, but realized I hadn't brought anything to sleep in.

Of course, Miles chose that moment to come upstairs, and he found me standing there over my suitcase in my underwear, arms folded across my chest. "Hey," he said grimly.

"Do you have a shirt I could sleep in, please?" I asked, careful to keep my tone and expression impassive.

"Sure." Moving slowly, he went into his closet and came out with a folded gray t-shirt.

"Thanks." I grabbed it from him, turned away, and threw it on.

He sank down onto the bed and sighed. "Natalie, I'm so sorry."

"For what?" Avoiding his eyes, I pulled the pins out of my hair and dropped them into my makeup bag.

"For being an asshole tonight. I've been downstairs hating myself ever since we got back."

"Whatever. No big deal." I breezed by him and went into the bathroom, where I pulled a clean washcloth from a bathroom drawer, wet it with warm water, and started scrubbing off my makeup. I had no intention of letting him see how much he'd hurt me.

He came and stood in the bathroom doorway. "It is a big deal. You're angry."

"I was, earlier. But now I realize that was stupid. You were just being you. You don't owe me anything."

He flinched. "Yes, I do. An explanation, at least."

I shrugged and rinsed out the cloth, hanging it on a towel bar.

"Hey. Look at me." He took me by the shoulders and forced me to face him. "I need to tell you something."

"OK." I hoped my expression read Cool and Detached, but my stomach was churning.

"I've been a dick all night, and I can't keep it up." He cocked his head. "But that will be the *only* time I ever say something like that. I can *always* keep it up."

I remained stone-faced.

"Wow. You're really mad. OK." He cleared his throat. "Here's the thing. I'm…"

His eyes searched mine, for what I don't know. It almost seemed like he was going to make a big announcement, but couldn't find the words.

"You're what, Miles?"

"I'm moving to San Francisco," he blurted.

"Huh?"

He dropped his hands from my shoulders. "Yeah. I'm moving to San Francisco. I've always wanted to check out that area, and I'm kinda done with Detroit, so I figure now's the time."

I crossed my arms over my chest. "Good for you. I hope you're happy there. That still doesn't explain your behavior tonight."

"Oh, right. That. Um…I was concerned."

I raised my eyebrows. "About?"

"About your feelings. These last few days have been…" He rubbed the back of his neck. "Intense."

"And?" I wondered if he was going where I thought he was going with this, and if so, I might be up for kicking him in the nuts. *He better not blame me for that intensity. It was his idea to bring me here.*

"And you're in a really weak and vulnerable state right now, having just broken up with Dan, and things with us just sort of got serious quickly."

"Serious?" I rolled my eyes. "We fucked in your closet last night, Miles. That isn't serious." I knew that wasn't what he meant, but I couldn't let him see he'd been right to worry about my growing feelings for him.

His face went a little red. "OK, maybe that part wasn't serious, but it seemed like…feelings got serious. And I think we should just take a moment to remember that we're friends, that in the end, we don't want the same things. I don't want the whole marriage and house and kids kind of life, and you do. So we just have to make sure things stay friendly."

I screwed up my face. "So that's what you were doing tonight? Being an asshole so I didn't get *feelings* for you and you wouldn't leave me heartbroken when you go to San Francisco?"

He looked a little relieved that I'd explained it better than he had. "Yeah. That's it. Exactly."

"Oh my God." I shook my head. "Well, you can relax, Miles. Despite the nice time we've had, your little display of assholery tonight was quite sufficient to remind me that we are not compatible for the long haul. And yes, I did just break up with Dan, but I have to say, I'm not feeling all that weak and vulnerable right now. In fact, I feel stronger than I have in a long time."

"Good. I'm really glad to hear that." He gave me a hopeful smile. "Does that mean we can still have sex tonight?"

"No. We will not be having any more sex. Not because

your dick is some kind of mystical love wand that will put me under your spell, but because you're right—we are friends and need to remember that. This last week has been totally insane, but it's time to go back to reality." I put a hand on my chest. "I'm going back up North, where I own a home and a business and have roots and family. Those are the things that are important to me." I poked his chest. "You can go flying off to anywhere you please and fuck all the girls you like, watch cartoons and porn, eat cereal, drink beer, and never have to worry about me again."

His face fell, and I swear to God his eyes teared up. "I'll always worry about you, Natalie. I just...can't be what you want."

"Stop it, Miles. Just stop it." I was doing my best to control my emotions, but he wasn't making it easy. "I've never asked you to be anything other than what you are. Do I think we could have been good together once upon a time? Yes, I'll admit it. Do I think it would work now? No. Because you were right—we don't want the same kind of life. You're not capable of it, and you've shown me that repeatedly." I put my hands on his chest and pushed him backward. "Now get out. I need to pee and then we are going to sleep. I'd like to leave early tomorrow."

I shoved him out, shut the door, and locked it. Then I stared at myself in the mirror, hands gripping the edge of the sink, legs trembling.

Don't cry. He will hear you.

And you have nothing to cry about.

I got on the toilet, like peeing might distract me from crying, but instead I found myself peeing and crying, which, if you've never done it, is probably the most pathetic you will ever feel as a human being. You realize you have no control whatsoever and everything is horrible and you might as well just give up.

Angry with myself, I balled up some toilet paper and

wiped my nose. I wasn't even sure why I was crying. Was I sad about the argument? Was I sad about Miles moving to San Francisco? Was I just scared of being alone? I thought about it for a moment, and decided it wasn't that. I could've handled being alone after the breakup with Dan. What I couldn't handle was this crush on Miles that couldn't go anywhere. But it was my own fault—I'd let myself think I could turn off the emotional switch and just fuck around, but that wasn't me. And now I was left with these powerful unrequited feelings for him, feelings that he'd never return. I dissolved into tears one more time, and gave myself permission to mourn something that could never be.

After a few minutes, I pulled myself together, cleaned up and opened the door, switching off the bathroom light. The bedroom was completely dark, which I was glad about because I didn't want him to see my puffy, tearstained face. I felt my way along the foot of the bed to the side I'd slept on last night, crawled in and pulled the covers up to my shoulders, totally focused on not touching him.

Except that once I was there, I missed him. I wanted to touch him. But I couldn't let him know I missed him. The touch had to be accidental.

I let one foot stray toward him. It strayed, and it strayed, and it strayed…nothing.

I bolted upright. Felt around.

He wasn't there.

What an asshole!

Really? He wouldn't even *sleep* next to me if there was no promise of sex?

Fuming, I threw myself back onto the pillow and punched it a few times. *Good! I'm glad you're not here, asshole! I didn't want your stupid amazing body next to me anyway! I'd have probably ended up banging you in spite of myself!*

Wide awake, I shoved my face into the pillow. It smelled like him. I missed him. I wanted him. Even though I knew exactly what he was and that sex would probably only make me feel worse afterward…I still wanted him. What the hell was the matter with me?

After lying there sleeplessly for at least a half hour, battling with my urge, I got out of bed and tiptoed down the stairs. The TV was on with no sound and Miles was asleep on his back on the couch. He'd taken his jacket and shoes off, and his white dress shirt was unbuttoned and untucked. I bit my lip, wishing more than anything it was my place to take his hand and guide him up the stairs. Peel the rest of his clothes off him. Pull the sheets up to his chest and tuck my body in next to his.

But it wasn't. He didn't want that.

He'd made that clear tonight.

So I went back up to his bed and curled up alone, telling myself this was how it had to be.

CHAPTER 21
Miles

I AM *the biggest asshole on the planet. I know this.*

I knew it while I was acting like a dick at the restaurant. I knew it on the unbearably silent ride home. I knew it while I sat berating myself on the couch as she packed her bags upstairs. I knew it as I lied to her about San Francisco—where the fuck had I come up with that, anyway? I had totally been about to tell her I loved her, and panicked—and I knew it when I heard her feet on the stairs a moment ago.

Now she was standing there at the foot of the couch, looking at me. Wondering. Possibly wanting me.

Silently, I begged my dick not to give me away, because if she saw it move, if she touched me, I was gone. I wasn't a good liar. It took everything out of me. Keeping up the facade at the restaurant and then making up that bullshit story upstairs had totally drained me. And it killed me to think I'd hurt her feelings.

If she put a hand on me, if she kissed me, if she whispered to me right now…that was it. I'd give in. I'd tell her the truth. *We could still be good together. Somehow.*

But she didn't.

She left me alone, tiptoeing back up the stairs as quietly as she'd come down.

It was just as well.

Christ. Love sucks.

The next day was rough. I think she spoke a total of five sentences to me on the ride home, and they were all something like this.

"I need coffee."

"I have to go to the bathroom."

"Do you want to stop for lunch?"

"I'll have the chicken sandwich."

"Thanks for the ride."

In her driveway, she pulled her keys from her purse and opened the door.

"Natalie, wait." I put my hand on her leg. "Shut the door, please."

Reluctantly, she closed the car door and sat looking straight ahead.

I love you. "You're still mad."

"I'm not. Really."

I love you. "Tell me I didn't ruin our friendship."

She sighed, turning to look at me. "You didn't ruin our friendship."

"Good." *Because I love you.* "Because I'd never forgive myself."

She lifted her shoulders. "Nothing to forgive. You are who you are, Miles."

Ouch. "That doesn't sound like a good thing."

She pressed her lips together. "Sorry. I'm in a weird place

right now. Just trying to reconcile everything that's happened in the last week with who I am. Who I want to be. The truth is, I do think I started to get a little confused about us. Like you said, we've always had a connection, and then the sex was so good—"

"*So* good." I put my hand on her arm. "*So* good."

She smiled, her cheeks blooming with pink. "Yes. Well, it all started to feel a little too good. Probably a good thing you're heading out west. I need some time to myself, so I think stepping back at this point is a good thing. But don't be a stranger, OK?"

Something weird and horrible squeezed my throat, like it was trying to choke me. "I won't."

She leaned over and gave me a hug, and I nearly lost it. Clutching her to me, one hand on the back of her head, one arm wrapped around her back, I took a deep breath and held her scent inside my lungs, wishing I could bottle it somehow. Take it with me. Curl up with it at night when I missed her, which would be all the fucking time now. But that would be no good because if I could smell her, I'd want her body next to me. And if I had her body next to me, I'd want to touch it. Claim it. Devour it. Bury myself in it.

Oh great, now I was hard. Just great.

She released me and sat back. "Now make a dirty joke or say something about your dick so I know we're really OK."

"Um. That hug got me hard."

She laughed. "Good. Hate to think I lost my effect on you just because you had my buns for five days straight."

Her buns. Oh, God. "Not at all. You'll always do something to me. That's just the way we are." I took her hand and kissed her fingers.

She nodded slowly, her eyes shiny, and gently pulled her hand from mine. "I better go in. Safe travels, OK?"

"OK. Want some help with your bag?"

"No, thanks. It's small, I've got it." She reached into the

back for her little suitcase and shut the door, giving me a little wave before heading toward the house.

I watched her let herself in and close the door behind her, then thumped the steering wheel twice. "Fuck!" Fisting my hands in my hair, I reconsidered my decision to let her go. It wasn't too late—I could knock on the door, tell her the truth. Tell her I loved her, but I didn't know how to be the man she deserved. Tell her I wanted to be the stranger who upended her life, *and* the one who helped her put it back together. Tell her I'd do anything to have the chance to make her happy.

Are you fucking crazy? No! You can't do that. She just told you she wanted time to herself. She wants to step back. Don't go running in there and make a fool of yourself. The truth is, you're not good enough for her. You're not what she wants. You can't have her.

You never could.

CHAPTER 22
Natalie

I SHUT THE DOOR—*THE* door—behind me and leaned back against it, waiting to hear his Jeep pull away.

Go, Miles.

He didn't.

What the hell are you doing?

I went into the bathroom and peeked out the window. His Jeep was still there in the driveway, and he had his head in his hands.

My heart ached for a second before I thought, *He can't handle emotions. No surprise there.*

But what was he feeling? Regret? Sadness? Indecision? Maybe he was just waiting for his hard-on to go away. I bit my lip, wondering what would happen next. I wasn't even sure what I wanted to happen... If he got out of the car and knocked on the door, would I let him in? And for what? More sex? What the hell else did he have to offer?

And the more sex we had, the more attached I got.

No. I couldn't do it.

Go, Miles. Before I fall in love with you.

The next second he was peeling out of the driveway and taking off down the street.

Backing away from the window, I grabbed my suitcase from the front hall and avoided looking at the door. I trudged upstairs and unpacked, telling myself that this was for the best—a clean break while we were still on good terms. I needed time to heal, and he needed to time to grow up.

Something told me I'd get there first.

I didn't hear from Miles for three weeks, nor did I reach out to him. I thought about it a million times, but each time I picked up the phone, something told me not to do it. He'd probably just think I was trying to rope him into a relationship, pressure him to be someone he's not. And since he wasn't texting me, I figured he didn't miss me like I missed him.

And I missed him *so much*. It shocked me how much—after all, I was used to short, intense bursts of his company and then nothing for long periods of time. But this time when we said goodbye, he took a piece of me with him, and I felt the loss like a sickness. I missed his eyes, his laugh, his voice, his terrible dirty jokes, and his obscene mouth. I missed the way he smelled, the way he breathed, the way he looked at me. I missed sexy things like the roll of his hips, the stroke of his tongue, the depth of his body inside mine. I missed silly things like the way he reached for his glasses when he woke up, the way he defended his plastic forks, the way he panted for cinnamon buns. Didn't he miss them? Maybe he was really just a *love the one you're with* kind of guy, and he was on to the next breakfast pastry.

Then he called me.

It was a Saturday night in mid-July, and Skylar and Jillian were over helping me paint the kitchen a soft gray color that reminded me of the t-shirt Miles had given me to sleep in. I'd left that t-shirt on his bed after giving it a little spritz of my perfume, just to torture him. *Wonder if he washed it yet.*

"Nat, your phone's ringing." Skylar glanced at me over her shoulder. She was standing on a ladder near the sink, and my phone was on the counter. "It's Miles."

"It is?" My heart immediately started beating faster, but I took a deep breath and kept concentrating on my brush strokes where I was cutting in around the base molding.

"Yes. Don't you want to answer it?"

"Not really. I'll call him later." Not only did I not want to talk to him in front of my sisters, but I didn't want to seem too available. Better to let him think I was busy on a Saturday night.

Jillian, who was taping off the wall behind the kitchen table, poked her head up. "So what happened with you guys, anyway? I've been so busy, I haven't had a chance to ask you about the trip to Detroit."

I shrugged and tried to play it cool. "It was fun."

"How fun?" she wanted to know.

"Very fun," Skylar put in. "She told me she was sore for days afterward."

Jillian gasped. "Is that true? You slept with Miles?"

"Oh, they did more than sleep." Skylar set her roller in the pan and came down the ladder. "Anyone want some wine? It's about that time."

"Me," Jillian and I said together.

Skylar pulled a bottle of white out of my fridge and unscrewed the cap. "Tell Jilly about the closet."

My face went hot as my phone pinged with a voicemail. What had he said?

"Closet?" Jillian went to the cupboard and pulled three wine glasses down. "What happened in the closet?"

"He tied her up!" Skylar squealed before I could even get a word out.

"Eeeeeep! Is that true?"

"True," I admitted, painting over the same spot for the tenth time. The memory of being tied up and blindfolded in the closet rendered me breathless for a moment. Miles's tongue running up my body, his hard cock lifting me up from behind, the way he'd come all over my ass...*oh, God.* I'd probably never experience anything that hot ever again. "And blindfolded me and talked dirty and did amazing things with his tongue."

"Wow." Jillian's voice was wistful. "I'm impressed. And jealous."

"Nat was due some hot sex." Skylar handed me a glass where I was sitting on the floor, but I got up and joined them at the table. "It had been months or something since she'd been with Dan."

Jillian blinked at me in surprise. "Seriously?"

"Yeah." I took a sip of wine, but it tasted off to me. "Skylar, was this already open or something in my fridge? It doesn't taste right to me."

"Really?" She drank from her glass and then from mine. "Tastes fine to me."

Jillian sipped hers. "It's fine. Now let's get back to the sex thing. Why hadn't you been sleeping with Dan for that long?"

Frowning, I set my glass down. "Because things weren't good with us, and they hadn't been for a while. I was just too stubborn to admit it." I told Jillian what I'd told Skylar about the breakup, what I'd learned about his cheating, how he'd apologized but I'd decided breaking it off was the right thing.

"Have you guys talked?" she asked.

"Yeah. It was hard," I admitted. "We met for coffee last week and talked some things out. He was up for trying to make it work, but I think that's more laziness than anything else. He's not crazy in love with me, and I'm not with him. He went about it the wrong way, but he was right in seeing that we weren't happy."

"And Miles?" she pressed. "What about him?"

I shrugged, but my stomach clenched. "Miles just came around at the right time. He was there when I needed a friend, someone to talk to, someone to tell me I was doing the right thing—"

"Someone to fuck you in the closet," Skylar finished, smiling from behind her wine.

"Exactly." I toyed with the stem of my glass. "But really, it was too soon for me to start up with anyone."

"Why? Are you in some kind of Victorian mourning period?" Jillian asked.

"No." Thinking about Miles had me warm all over. God, I missed him. "But Miles isn't into me that way, anyhow."

"What?" Jillian rolled her eyes. "Yes, he is. He's just too stupid to know it."

"Or he's too scared to admit it." Skylar shrugged. "But I agree with Jilly. I think he's way into you and always has been, and I think he was the handsome stranger Madam Psuka was talking about."

"Please. Not that again." I tried another sip of wine, but it still didn't taste right to me. "It's not Miles. Besides, he's moving to San Francisco anyway." Ending any chance for us before it even began. Why did he have to be such an ass when he was so hot and sweet and funny too? It was so unfair, the feelings I had for him, the chemistry we had. It would never amount to anything more than one hot weekend when we could have been *so much more*.

"He is?" Skylar looked surprised. "When? He told me he wanted to come to my wedding. He can't move to California."

"The world doesn't revolve around your wedding, Skylar," I snapped harshly.

She looked annoyed. "I never said it did, Judy Moody. Sheesh. What's with you lately?"

"I'm going through shit, OK?" I stood up and carried my glass to the sink, tossing the wine down the drain. "And you're constantly talking about the wedding and honeymoon and gifts and seating arrangements and flowers and I'm just tired of it!" I stared into the sink, ashamed of myself.

"What the hell, Natalie?" I heard the plunk of a glass being set on the table.

"OK hold on." Jillian came over and put a hand on my back. "You're definitely going through shit, Nat, and it sucks, but don't be an asshole to Skylar. She hasn't been that bad about the wedding."

I closed my eyes. "I'm sorry, Sky."

"It's OK," she said quietly. "I should be more sensitive to the breakup."

"No, really. I'm fine about the breakup. I'm just…" Tears welled, and a few spilled over before I even knew what was happening. "I'm just emotional lately. And tired." So, so tired. Every morning this week it felt like my alarm went off earlier and earlier, and even naps didn't take the edge off my fatigue. "You know what, you guys? Let's be done with this for tonight. I'll clean up and you guys can go do something fun with your Saturday night."

"Are you sure you're OK?" Jillian rubbed her hand along my spine.

"Yes." I wiped my nose with the back of my hand. "I'm fine. And I kind of just want to be alone."

They helped me clean up, hugged me tight, and left.

The minute I shut the door, I grabbed my phone and ran up to my room, where I curled up in bed and listened to Miles's voicemail.

At the sound of his voice, my entire body shivered.

"Hey you. Haven't talked to you in a while. It rained here today and it reminded me of you. Then I had to jerk off in the shower because I couldn't stop thinking about that morning."

I smiled as my belly fluttered. Some things would never change.

"I thought of you in the shower too, in case you were

wondering. And on the couch, and in the kitchen, and in my bed…"

The smile faded as I thought about his bed and wondered if he'd had anyone in it since I left. The thought made me sick to my stomach.

"Anyway, I miss you and want to hear your voice. Give me a call if you want."

I played the message again and again and again, missing him more each time, that ache in my chest growing stronger. *That's why you can't call him back*, I told myself. *You'll only want him more.*

Setting the phone aside, I switched off my lamp and rolled on to my belly. But my breasts were sore because I was about to get my period, so I flipped over onto my back. *That must be why I've been so moody this week. I didn't even think about that. Maybe that's why I've been tired too, although I've never had PMS this bad before. I bet it's the new pill.* I'd switched brands last month because I'd had too much spotting, but was this one going to make me feel awful every month? I couldn't win. Maybe I'd go off it altogether. Not like I had a lot of sex on the horizon anyway.

Cranky at the thought, and suddenly hot under the covers, I kicked them off and lay like a starfish, making a mental note to call the doctor next week after my period was over.

Except that it never arrived.

CHAPTER 23
Natalie

TEN DAYS after Miles's voicemail, I sat on the edge of the tub and stared at the plus signs. There were four of them because I hadn't believed the first test could be right, nor the second or third. But the fourth…the fourth was the kicker.

I was pregnant.

By Miles Haas.

A huge wave of dizziness and nausea rushed through me, and I quickly knelt in front of the toilet until it passed. Then I sat on the cold white tiles with my hands cradling my stomach, sweaty, hot, and shaking.

OK, think. Just think. One step at a time.

First, I needed to make a doctor's appointment and get a blood test to make sure I really was knocked up. Maybe the tests were defective.

Four tests? And what about the fact that you're a week late? You've never been a week late, not ever.

I looked down at my belly in disbelief. Was it possible that Miles had gotten me pregnant?

Of course it's possible! You had sex without a condom, didn't you?

But…but I was on the pill! It always worked for me and

Dan! For eight years! Had I fucked up the cycle when I'd switched brands? I knew I'd missed a pill the night I slept at Miles's house, but I'd taken the missed one right away the next morning. And I'd taken another one that night. I'd done that before and it had been fine!

Moaning, I got off the floor and stood in front of the full length mirror on the back of the bathroom door. Flattened my hands over my belly. It didn't feel any rounder than usual, but then again, even if I *was* pregnant, I wouldn't show for a while yet.

If I kept it.

Don't think about that yet. You don't even know for sure.

But I felt like I did.

Trembling, I went down to the kitchen and dug my phone from my purse to call the doctor.

The next day, I left my OB's office and drove straight to Skylar and Sebastian's cabin. Beside me on the seat was a stack of pamphlets about prenatal vitamins, breastfeeding, and my "options."

My stomach churned as I thought them over.

I could terminate the pregnancy.

I could proceed with the pregnancy and give the baby up for adoption.

I could have the baby and…have a baby.

I'd already cried buckets in the exam room, but the tears flowed again as I drove up the highway, and I reached into my purse for the wad of tissues I'd stuck there. After blowing my nose, I called Jillian.

As expected, I got her voicemail. "Hey, Jill. It's Natalie. I'm on my way to Skylar's for dinner and I know you're working, but if there's any way you can head out there when you're off, I'd love it. I need you guys. The blood test was positive." My voice was shaky and the entire message was punctuated by sobs, but I got it out.

Last night, I'd called my sisters and told them about the home test results. They both agreed I shouldn't panic until I saw my doctor, although I could tell by what Jillian said, she thought those home tests were accurate. Skylar had gone dead silent, and I imagined she was picturing me fat as a rhinoceros coming up the aisle in my lavender bridesmaid dress. But maybe that was unfair. Right away, she'd offered to take this afternoon off and go with me to the doctor's, but I said it was OK, I could handle going alone. I'd probably have to go to a lot of things alone in the near future. The thought brought on a fresh round of tears, and I blubbered into my sopping tissues.

Ten minutes later, I parked in front of the cabin and got out. Skylar ran out onto the porch before I even shut the car door.

"Well?"

I was crying too hard to speak.

"Oh, honey." Skylar opened her arms and I ran into them, feeling every bit the baby sister I was.

I sobbed on her shoulder, keening so loud Sebastian came out to see what he could do.

I took one look at his big, broad chest and threw myself at him, needing to feel a pair of strong, masculine arms around me, even if they were my future brother-in-law's.

He was a good sport about it and held me loosely in his arms while I slobbered all over his shirt, patting my back while Skylar stroked my hair. I was glad they didn't say anything like *It's OK* or *Don't worry* or *Everything will be fine*. I needed to wallow in my stupidity and misery for a moment before I faced the facts and made a plan, and they understood.

But after a couple minutes, Skylar tugged on my arm. "Come on inside."

We went into the living room, and Skylar dropped down next to me on the couch. "So now what?"

"Now I have to decide what to do," I said, my breath coming in gasps.

"You should tell Miles right away." Sebastian spoke quietly from where he stood near the door, hands in his pockets. "He needs to know."

"I know," I said, reaching for the box of tissues on the end table. "God, I'm dreading that."

"I don't blame you." Skylar continued to stroke my hair. "You think he'll freak out?"

"Uh, yes. *Duh.* He's like a big kid himself. You should have seen his refrigerator. His cupboards. He didn't even have a spatula!" I wailed.

"What does a spatula have to do with a baby?" Sebastian sounded confused.

I threw a hand in the air. "It's another sign that he doesn't have his shit together."

"Well, maybe he could get it together by the time the baby is born," Skylar said hopefully. "I mean, if you end up having it. When's it due?"

Oh, God. A due date. This was so real.

It's real. Get used to saying it. "March."

"March what?" Sebastian asked.

"Seventeenth."

He winced. "Ooh. That's a bad number."

"Sebastian!" Skylar glared at him. "This isn't the time."

"Sorry." He held up his hands. "Sorry, Natalie."

"It's OK." I sniffed. "Everything about this is bad, so it doesn't matter."

"Maybe it won't be that bad." Sebastian perched on the edge of the couch and touched my shoulder. "Sometimes guys are ready for these big things in life and they don't even realize it."

"Maybe, but Miles Haas isn't one of those guys. He flat out told me he never wanted a family. That kids wreck everything fun in life. That he'd never be able to love someone completely and forever." Miserable, I dropped my face into my hands.

"But he doesn't know you're pregnant with his child," Sebastian said. "That makes a big difference. And I saw the way he looked at you that day at your parents' house. I think he might surprise you."

I shook my head. "I doubt it. But I have to tell him, anyway. And then he'll tell me I ruined his life, and I'll feel horrible."

"He would never say that to you," Skylar said firmly. "Never."

"How *do* you feel, Natalie?" Sebastian asked quietly. "You're talking a lot about his feelings, but what are yours?"

"I don't know how I feel. It's just such a shock." I put my hand over my belly and tried to explain all the tears. "I'm sad, mostly. I'm sad because I've always wanted kids but this isn't how it was supposed to happen. By accident, with someone who won't want it. And it's going to hurt when he says that to me."

"Because you want to keep it?" Skylar asked.

Because I love him. "I don't know yet."

"Hey." Jillian knocked on the screen door and then opened it. "I heard your message. You OK?"

One look at my oldest sister and I burst into fresh tears, getting up from the couch to weep into a third pair of arms for the day, a fourth if you count the poor nurse at my OB's office.

But I couldn't help it. Everything about this situation was miserable. If I ended the pregnancy, I'd feel terrible and possibly regret it every day for the rest of my life. That kind of decision was irreversible and terrifying. If I continued the pregnancy and gave it up for adoption, I'd be judged by everyone in town as I waddled around, pregnant and single, Dan would despise me, and I'd always wonder if I'd made the right decision. If I kept the baby, my life as I knew it was over. I'd be a single mother, and that child would be my days and nights for the next eighteen years—probably more. Would I be able to support us? Would I ever meet someone willing to marry me and complete a family? What kind of role, if any, would Miles want in the child's life? What kind of father was he capable of being?

Maybe they can watch cartoons together. Ride bikes. Build sand castles. Because that's about all Miles Haas is qualified to do as a parent beyond donate the sperm.

It was an angry thought, but it made me sad too—the image of Miles playing with our child. Because he'd probably never do it. Even if I had the baby, I didn't see him moving up here to take an active role in a baby's life. More likely he'd fly in from San Francisco or New York or Amsterdam or wherever he was living and awkwardly pet the baby once or twice a year, and then he'd fly out again, and go back to his free, fun, sexy life.

And it would hurt. God, it would hurt.

CHAPTER 24
Miles

I ONCE FELL OFF A ROOF, losing my footing on some slippery shingles and bouncing off a prickly shrub before hitting the ground hard. I broke my arm, cracked a few ribs, and had scratches from that fucking bush all over my body. It was growing needles, I swear to God. I was drunk at the time, of course, and didn't feel too much when I landed, but the next day—the next month—I was in a lot of fucking pain.

That was nothing compared to what I felt after leaving Natalie. Nothing.

I would jump off a thousand roofs, bounce naked off a thousand prickly bushes, break every bone in my body willingly, if I thought it would ease the pain of pushing her away.

I couldn't write. I didn't feel like eating. I had trouble sleeping.

Sleeping! How can you fuck that up?

But every time I got in bed or lay on the couch, I thought of her. Didn't matter if my eyes were open or closed—I saw her in front of me. Didn't matter if I was alone or in a crowd—I could smell her. Didn't matter what I ate or drank—nothing came close to the sweet taste of her, and nothing could erase it from my memory.

I spent long hours holed up in my apartment, watching cartoons or porn, not wearing pants, eating cereal with a plastic spoon and drinking beer, trying to convince myself that this was the good life. I jerked off to her constantly, but since I'd had the real thing, even that wasn't as satisfying as it used to be. It made me even madder at myself that I'd fucked things up, although I still did it—the self-service equivalent of an angry hand job.

I called my friends to go out, but the ones with girlfriends seemed content to spend their nights in, and the ones without just wanted to troll for an easy fuck.

I was over it. I only wanted Natalie.

Finally, I broke down and called her. Got her voicemail. I tried to be casual and make jokes, but maybe I came off as pathetic or desperate, because she didn't call me back right away. Ten days went by. The ten slowest, saddest, most agonizing days of my life.

I had to face it—she didn't want me.

And why should she? Nothing had changed in her eyes. *I* hadn't changed, although I wanted to. I just didn't know where to start.

Should I show up on her doorstep? Admit I'd lied about California? Tell her I was in love with her and wanted to try one of those relationship things? I had no fucking clue. But every day without her was more miserable than the last, with no end in sight.

And then she called.

At the sight of her name on my screen, my body reacted like I'd just sniffed two lines of cocaine. I came alive instantly, my heart beating hard and fast. For a second, I debated making her leave a message and calling her back later, but then I thought, fuck it, I'm through playing games. I was unhappy, and she could make it better.

"Hello?"

"Hi, Miles. It's me."

"Hey, you." I smiled and leaned back on the couch. "Took you long enough to call me back."

"Sorry. I've been busy."

"Yeah? I've missed you. What have you been doing?"

"Um, working. Painting the house. Helping Skylar with some wedding stuff."

"Cool. When's the wedding again?"

"September twenty-fourth."

"That's right. I'm supposed to go to it, I think."

"That's OK, you don't have to. I know those things give you hives."

Had I said that? I couldn't remember. Sounded like me, though. "I might brave one, if you want me there," I said, feeling like the biggest person ever.

Silence.

What the hell? Was she still upset with me? "Natalie? Do you want me to come to the wedding?"

"Um, before we talk about that, there's something I have to tell you."

Oh fuck. She got back together with the Douchebag.

I braced myself. "You're back with Dan, huh?"

"No." She paused and took a shaky breath. "I'm pregnant, Miles."

I had to have heard that wrong.

"I'm sorry. What did you say?"

"I'm pregnant."

"Like, with a baby?"

"Yes. Like with a baby. Your baby."

I held the phone away from me and stared at it in shock. I had a baby? What the hell was this?

"Miles?"

Slowly, I put the phone to my ear again. I'd never had an out-of-body experience before, but this is what I imagined it would be like, where everything around me, even the air I breathed, felt foreign and wrong. Was this real?

"Miles? Did you hear me?"

I cleared my throat. "Yeah…but I don't understand."

"Not much confusion about it. We had sex. I got pregnant."

Silence.

I had no fucking clue what to say. This had never happened to me before. What did she want to hear? Sorry? Congratulations? There were any number of possibilities but none of them seemed right.

I finally found my voice, and of course I said the wrong thing. "Are you sure?"

"Yes, I'm sure," she snapped. "I wouldn't have called you otherwise."

I closed my eyes. A sweat broke out on the back of my neck. "Natalie, don't be mad. I'm just…I need a minute to take this in."

Actually I needed more than a minute. I needed the world to stop turning right now. I needed a pause button—no, I needed a stop, rewind, and do-over button. Why the fuck had we had unprotected sex? I never had unprotected sex!

"Didn't we… I mean, aren't you on the pill?"

"*Yes*, I'm on the pill. What do you think, I *lied* to you about that? I don't know what happened, OK? I thought I followed the directions just like always, but it didn't work. Your super sperm broke through the barrier."

Absurdly, I felt proud of my super sperm for exactly two seconds before reality sank in again. And fuck, I kept saying the wrong things. "Sorry…I'm just…" I sat forward and tipped my head into one hand. "I don't know what to say, Nat. What are you going to do?" God, now I'd just made it sound like it was her problem. I didn't mean that, I just—fuck, this was hard! I needed a script!

"I don't know." Her tone was cold.

"What do you want me to do? Tell me and I'll do it."

Silence.

"Nothing, Miles. I don't want you to do anything. The whole thing was a mistake. *We* were a mistake."

"But—"

"Look, neither of us planned this, Miles. This is the worst possible timing for a pregnancy and the worst possible combination of factors. We're young. We're not married—we're not even a *couple*—you don't want kids, you're moving across the country, I own a business, and I will have to answer everyone's questions for the next nine months if I go through with this pregnancy, not to mention the next eighteen years."

Oh my God. Nine months. Eighteen years.

The world was spinning too fast. Days and nights were flying by. I closed my eyes and tried to breathe. "Jesus. I can't handle this."

"You think I don't know that?"

"What's that mean?"

"It means, I know exactly how you're feeling right now. You're hoping I'll just get rid of it so it won't be your problem and you can go on with your life."

I jumped off the couch, enraged. "Natalie, I never said that!"

"You didn't have to!" she yelled. "I know how you feel about kids, Miles. They get in the way of everything. They're expensive and they disrupt your sleep and your drinking habits and your sex life!"

Fuck, I had said that, hadn't I? *Fuck!* "Well, how was I supposed to know this would happen?"

"You weren't. Forget it, it doesn't matter anyway."

Oh God, now she hated me. "Natalie, wait. I'm sorry—"

"I'm sorry too, Miles. I'll let you know what I decide, but don't worry. I won't ask you for anything. You can go ahead and move to California."

"Don't say that. Please." *I love you. I'm just terrified right now. Give me time to think.*

"Goodbye." She ended the call and I stood there, frozen,

the phone still at my ear. I was sweating buckets, but started to shiver.

"Fuck!" I threw my phone on the couch and fisted my hands in my hair.

Natalie was pregnant. Pregnant! With a baby! An actual baby!

I fell back onto the couch and lay there with my hands over my face.

"Fuuuuuuuuck," I groaned. This was so far beyond my adult zone I couldn't even form a sentence. A relationship was one thing, but a child… I was the least qualified person I knew to be a dad. My own hadn't been around that much. I had no uncles I was close to. The truth was Mr. Nixon was probably the best example of a good father I'd seen in my life. And he'd always been so nice to me—what would he say when he learned I'd gotten his daughter pregnant?

Oh God, I was such an asshole.

And she knew it. She'd thrown all my stupid remarks about being a husband and father right back in my face. But a guy could change his mind, couldn't he? If he met someone who made him feel something he'd never felt before, if he learned something about himself—like that he was capable of falling in love—he should be allowed to take back what he said. Suddenly I was angry. She wasn't even giving me a chance to do the right thing. She was just assuming I was the same old Miles I'd always been.

Because she doesn't know you love her. You never told her.

Chills swept over my entire body, and I felt as if everything I'd ever wanted was right in front of me, and I had to grab it now or risk losing it forever. Was I scared? Fuck, yes. But what if this was my chance? If I blew this, Natalie would never forgive me, and some other guy would come along and fall in love with her and do things right. She'd always be the one that got away. But what if this baby happened for a reason? What if this was the universe banging me over the head with the best thing that had ever happened to me?

This wasn't a mistake.

I grabbed the phone off the couch and called her back, but she didn't answer. Her voicemail picked up as I was running up the stairs to pack a bag. "Hey," I said. "I need to see you. I'm driving up."

A bit short and not exactly heartwarming, but fuck it, I was flustered.

Five minutes later, I raced back down the stairs and grabbed my phone charger, computer bag, and the keys to the house up there. Frantically, I looked around, feeling like I needed more things, a better plan, a fucking clue what I was doing. But I couldn't think of anything.

I locked my apartment and flew down the hall, tapped my foot impatiently in the elevator, and ran like mad through the parking garage. Thankful I had a full tank of gas, I was on the road within minutes, and figured if I didn't hit terrible traffic, I could be there by nine o'clock tonight.

That gave me just over four hours to figure out what the hell I was going to say to her to convince her to let me in. To let me love her. To let me be a father to my child.

My throat closed up, and my vision went a little blurry.

I had no idea how to be a father, but I would sure as hell try.

CHAPTER 25
Natalie

I LET his call go to voicemail, mostly because I was crying too hard to answer, but also because I didn't really want to hear him talk anymore. Maybe that wasn't fair, since it was his baby too, but his reaction had been exactly what I thought it would be, and even though it wasn't a surprise, it still hurt.

Ten minutes later, I listened to it, but it didn't make me feel any better. Why was he coming here? What did he need to do, crush me in person? Would he try to sweet talk me into getting rid of it? Offer to write me a check so I'd just go away? My stomach churned just thinking about it.

I called Skylar.

"Hello?"

"It's me. I told Miles."

She gasped. "What did he say?"

"Not much. He was in shock."

"Of course. So were you. So was I."

"Right."

"And wait 'til you tell mom and dad."

I frowned. "You're not helping, Sky."

"Sorry. So what happened with Miles?"

"He basically said he couldn't handle this and didn't know what to do, and we hung up."

"Ugh. Not helpful or supportive."

"Nope, no surprise there. But then five minutes later, he called back."

"And?"

"And said he needs to see me, and he's driving up."

Another gasp. "Really?"

I grimaced. "Really."

"What do you think he'll say?"

"I think he's either going to be all sweet and persuasive and try to convince me to get rid of it because life is all about fun and games and we're too young to be saddled with this, or he'll offer me money."

"Money for what?"

"I don't know. To leave him alone so he can skip out to California unencumbered?"

"I think you're selling him short, Nat. I'm on your side no matter what, but I do think you could maybe cut the guy some slack. You just told him you were pregnant. You've had days to think about this—he's had minutes."

"Yeah," I said grudgingly. "Maybe."

"What do you want him to say?"

I sighed. "I don't know. This is such a fucking mess."

"Just hear him out. He deserves that, at least."

"Why?" I snapped. "Because his dick has good aim?"

"No, crabbypants. Because you've been friends forfuckingever, and you care about each other, and no matter which way you look at it, this is his baby, too."

Baby. I sighed. Every time someone referred to it as a baby, I melted. There was no way I could end this pregnancy—deep down, I knew that. I believe in a woman's right to choose, but politics aside, this was something Miles and I had done willingly. We'd taken the risk because we trusted each other. We cared for each other and always had.

"Fine. I'll listen."

"Fair enough. You need anything? I'm just getting to the grocery store. I could bring you some dinner."

"No, that's all right."

"OK. Call me tomorrow."

"I will. Night."

We hung up, and I puttered around the house for a while, aimlessly wandering from room to room, picking things up and putting them down, idly wondering where I'd put things like a crib, a high chair, a rocker. Pretty soon, I felt too restless to be contained by the walls, and I grabbed a swimsuit and went to the gym. A swim always cleared my head, and it had never felt more muddled than it did right now.

But what was I going to do about my heart?

CHAPTER 26
Miles

I CALLED her when I was five minutes from her house.

"Hello?"

"It's me. I'm just getting here. Can I come over?"

She sighed. "I guess so."

"Are you feeling OK?" Fear gutted me, and I realized I'd better get used to that feeling. I'd be worried about her all the time now.

"I'm fine. Just tired."

"Can I bring you anything? Are you hungry? Thirsty?"

"No, thank you."

"OK, I'll be there in five."

We hung up, and I pressed my lips together, going over in my mind what I wanted to say. You'd think as a writer I'd have a good enough command of my vocabulary to string something solid and convincing together, but every time I thought about Natalie being pregnant with my baby, my brain went to mush. What did she want to hear? Would she believe me if I told her I loved her? Would she take me seriously when I told her I wanted her to have this child? That I'd do anything to help her? That I'd never let her be alone?

When I pulled up in her driveway, I still had no clear strategy.

My heart thumped hard as I knocked on her door. Fuck, I'd showered today, right? But had I put real pants on? Was my shirt clean? I looked down at myself. OK, the jeans were fine, and the light blue t-shirt appeared to be in decent shape, although I wished I'd have put a nicer one on.

She opened the door, and I couldn't breathe. That feeling struck me again—that surge of longing to do everything at once. Hold her, kiss her, touch her, tell her everything, wrap her up in my arms and keep her there until she believed how much I loved her, how much I needed her, how hard I'd work to deserve her.

"Hi," she said, her expression neutral. "Come on in."

I followed her through the kitchen to her family room, noting not only the nice furniture but the books on the coffee table, the pictures on the walls, the healthy-looking plants in the corner. Damn, a white couch. Grownups had things like white couches and managed not to ruin them, didn't they? I'd have already spilled salsa, dripped pizza sauce, and dumped beer on it. I sat down on it cautiously.

Natalie stared at me like I was nuts. "It's a couch. It's not going to bite you."

"I know. It's just so nice."

She flopped down on the other end, not touching me, her legs tucked beneath her. "Thanks."

"How are you feeling?" I sat forward and focused intently on her, eager to show her I could be less selfish than I'd been in the past.

"Fine, thanks."

I stared at her, unnerved by her cool demeanor but also by her beauty. She wore no makeup and her hair drifted around her face in its usual unfussy waves, but her skin was smooth and radiant, her blue eyes wide and clear, her mouth full and soft. She was so alluring, I had to move closer and put a hand on her knee. I felt my dick jump in my pants and begged it not to bother me right now.

"Natalie, I'm sorry about earlier. I should have reacted better."

"It's OK." She shrugged. "I know you were stunned. I certainly was."

"Have you told your parents yet?"

She shook her head. "Just my sisters. I'll tell them soon. After I decide what to do. But Miles…" She hesitated, playing with the hem of her loose black top. "I'm going to have the baby. I don't know if I'll give it up for adoption yet or not, but I've decided against the other alternative."

I nodded, totally relieved. "I fully support you. And I'll go with you when you tell your parents. You are not alone, Natalie. I'm going to do the right thing."

Silence. "The right thing?"

I knew right away it wasn't what she'd wanted to hear. But why not? Didn't that prove I was a good guy? Someone worthy of her and the baby? I tried again. "Yes. I want to be here for you."

She shook her head. "You can't, Miles. You're moving, remember?"

"Um. About that." I rubbed a hand over my jaw. Crap, I should have shaved too. This was all so rushed! "I made that up, Natalie. I'm not really moving to San Francisco."

"What? Why would you make that up?" Her eyes clouded with confusion.

"Because I was scared. I realized I had feelings for you that I'd never had for anyone before, and I panicked. I couldn't tell you because you'd just broken up with Dan, and I knew you were just hanging out with me for fun."

"Because that's all you do," she snapped. "You've told me repeatedly. Your life is about fun, not feelings."

I held up my hands. "Fair enough. I know I have said that in the past. But Natalie. Things are different now." I could feel the sweat under my clothes, and my pulse was racing. "I love you."

Her eyes went wide. "What?"

"I love you." Goosebumps were breaking out all over my body.

"No, you don't. You love yourself. You love cartoons and porn. You love your life. You love women."

"I love *you*, Natalie. I've always loved you. Deep down, you know that." This was not the way I imagined things went when a guy told a girl he loved her for the first time. Wasn't she supposed to be happy about this? Wasn't there kissing involved?

But Natalie was shaking her head. "That night at the restaurant. You were such a jerk to me. And later you told me it was because you were scared that *I* had feelings for *you*. And you wanted to protect me."

The back of my neck got even hotter. "I know. That was bullshit. I was only protecting myself."

Her lips made a straight line. "And the next day. When you drove me home and we said goodbye. That was another chance to tell me the truth. But you didn't—you stuck with the lie."

"It was a mistake!" I put both hands on her knees. "I was scared, OK?"

Her eyes teared up. "Too many games, Miles. And what were you afraid of? Did you think I didn't feel the same?"

"I *knew* you didn't. You told me you wanted space. Time to yourself. Time to process the end of your relationship. For all I knew, you were still in love with Dan."

"I hadn't been in love with Dan for a long time. I wouldn't have slept with you if I had been."

"It wasn't only that. I was also scared I wouldn't be able to make you happy even if you did feel the same way."

"Because you don't want a monogamous relationship. You don't ever want to get married or have a family."

"But that was before I knew you were pregnant. Now I want to do the right thing. I want you. I want the baby. We could get married."

She shook her head, her eyes tearing up. "You're a good guy, Miles, and I appreciate that you came all the way up here tonight, but I don't think you know what you're saying, and I don't want you to make promises you can't keep."

"Natalie." I got to my knees in front of her. "Maybe I'm saying this all wrong. I'm not good at this stuff. But please give me a chance."

"A chance at what? Being a family? How? You making a living writing about sex and the single guy. How does a family figure into that?"

"I don't know," I admitted.

"And you hate being tied to one spot."

"But I'd try it for you. For the baby."

"You'd try it. Oh, God." She put her face in her hands, and when she picked up her head, tears were dripping from her eyes. "Look, Miles. A family is not something you can sample and send back like a bottle of wine. It's a permanent commitment. You don't do those."

"I haven't in the past," I admitted. "But I want to start. I can change, Natalie."

She hesitated. "I want to believe you. I want to think that we could be happy together."

My chest felt strapped tight. "But you don't love me?"

She took my face in her hands. "Of course I love you. You know I do."

Relief coursed through me, but it was tempered with fear too. She was still holding back—or else she didn't feel what I felt, which was even worse. "But you're not *in* love with me. Not the way I am with you."

"I'm scared to love you like that, Miles. I'm scared because you've always been there, always been this amazing *what if* in the back of my mind, ever since that night we almost kissed.

But you told me yourself you weren't capable of loving someone completely and forever. You weren't capable of the sacrifices it would entail. And I want that."

"You deserve it." I kissed the palm of her hand. "Tell me what to do to prove to you I can be the man you want."

She pulled her hand away and wiped her eyes. "I can't tell you that. I don't know. I just know that it's not enough to hear you say you want to do the right thing. I'm sorry."

She let me hug her goodbye, and I held her for a long time. I'd stopped talking, because clearly I wasn't saying the right things. And why would I? I'd never talked this way to anyone in my entire life. I didn't pay attention to those scenes in movies, I didn't read those kinds of books, and people in porn and cartoons don't really talk about the future. I'd thought saying I wanted to do the right thing would indicate to her that I was ready to grow up and be the kind of person she wanted, but I'd been wrong.

But I wouldn't give up. As I embraced her by the front door, I vowed to try harder. I thought about the little life we'd created, a life that she was protecting inside her body, and I wrapped my arms around them both.

Suddenly my chest hollowed out like it was cleaving in half. It was similar to the feeling I had when I realized I was in love with Natalie, and yet different. Just as compelling, just as shocking, just as relentless, but more ferocious, more possessive, more instinctive. It came from a place inside me that hadn't existed until this very moment, an empty space that was rapidly filling with the most powerful emotion I'd ever experienced.

Somehow I knew it was the beginnings of the fierce, protective love of a father for his child.

I don't know how I knew, but I did.

I held her closer.

Mine. This was mine, and I wouldn't let it go.

Somehow I'd find a way to prove it to her.

CHAPTER 27
Miles

ON MY WAY to the house, I called Nick Lupo.

"Hey, Miles. What's up?" The clatter and conversation in the background told me he was at work.

"Hey. You know that winery you were talking to Natalie about? The one where her sister works?"

"Abelard Vineyards?"

I thumped the steering wheel. "That's it. Thanks. I just needed the name."

"Are you up there?"

"Yeah, and I need to get ahold of Natalie's sister Skylar but I can't ask her for the number."

"Uh oh. Why not?"

"It's a long story, but I fucked things up somehow and now I have to get her back."

"Sounds serious. Is this really Miles Haas I'm talking to?"

"Ha. Yes. Hey, what did you say to get Coco to marry you?"

Nick made a choking sound. "You want to *marry* her? Are you drunk?"

I smiled. "Nope. Totally sober."

"Jesus. Well, Coco wanted nothing to do with me when I originally asked her. I had to do it bigger. Better."

"What did you do?"

"I got on the airport loudspeaker."

I frowned. "Hm."

"But you can do anything—it just has to be meaningful to her. And women always like a grand gesture."

"A grand gesture?"

"Yeah, something kind of public. You know, to show her that you're not afraid to let the world know how you feel."

I thought for a moment. "She's pregnant."

"Oh, fuck."

"Yeah."

"You OK with that?"

I smiled. "You know what? I fucking am. I really fucking am."

"Good." He paused. "This might sound crazy, Miles, but I kinda feel like this is exactly what you need. That girl is way too good for you, but you might be able to have her forever if you do this right. Go get her."

"Thanks. I will."

I barely slept that night. The next day, I went over to Abelard Vineyards around eleven. It was Sunday, but it was summer, so I figured they'd have so much weekend tourist business, they'd be open, and I was right.

In the tasting room, I found Skylar pouring wine behind a long wooden bar. She looked surprised to see me.

"Hi. What are you doing here?"

"I came to talk to you. When are you off work?"

She scrutinized my face. "You look awful. Did you sleep last night?"

"No. I can't sleep. And I can't eat, and I don't even feel like drinking, which is a serious sign that something is wrong with me. I need your help."

Her eyes went wide. "Damn. Why don't you come over tonight? We can talk." She gave me directions to the house she shared with Sebastian, and I told her I'd be there at six.

I spent the rest of the day moping, fretting, and trying to come up with ideas to get Natalie to see me in a new light, but mostly I just walked around in dazed circles, opening the fridge when I meant to open the pantry, going into the library and then forgetting why I was in there, losing entire chunks of time staring aimlessly into space.

For fuck's sake, someone please tell me love gets easier.

At five o'clock I took a shower and got dressed, then hit the wine store on the way to Skylar's so I wasn't empty-handed.

Sebastian let me into their house, which turned out to be a sort of pimped out one-room cabin with a loft, set in some secluded woods on the water. He gave me a tour while Skylar was changing out of her work clothes.

"This is amazing," I said, standing on the stone patio and taking it all in. "So quiet and private." In the past, that wouldn't have appealed to me so much, but now that I was looking ahead, I could see how living in a place like this with Natalie would be heaven.

"Thanks. Can I get you a beer? Or a glass of wine?"

"I'll take a beer, thanks."

Sebastian went in the house and came out a minute later with two beers, Skylar at his heels with a glass of wine in her hands.

"Let's sit," she said, dropping down in a patio chair and tucking her legs underneath her, just like Natalie had sat last night. "Tell me how it went. I haven't talked to Nat yet."

I sat opposite her and Sebastian chose a seat to her left. They listened intently while I told them what I'd said.

"You said you wanted to do the right thing?" Skylar's lower lip twitched. "Hmm."

"What's wrong with that?" I asked. "Wouldn't a nice guy do the right thing?"

"She doesn't want a nice guy. She wants you." Skylar frowned. "OK, that came out wrong. But you know what I mean. She doesn't want to feel like she's forcing you into being someone you're not. She doesn't want to be your obligation. She wants the real you to want her."

"I do," I said helplessly, squeezing the beer bottle tightly in one hand. This was so fucking *frustrating*. "I swear to God. And I know I've said all kinds of things in the past about how I don't want a wife and kids, but now when I think about it with her, it's different."

"Did you actually propose?" Sebastian asked.

I cocked my head. "I don't think so."

Skylar's eyebrows went up. "You don't know?"

"Well, I didn't exactly ask her to marry me, if that's what you mean."

"That's what a proposal is." Skylar threw a look at Sebastian. "Not that you asked either."

I glanced at him, too. "You didn't propose?"

He looked a little sheepish. "Ah, no. I think I just said, 'Marry me.' It was a bit spontaneous. I hadn't really planned on doing it right then."

"But it was perfect." Skylar reached over and patted his leg. "And heartfelt. And I knew that he meant it."

A look passed between them that made me so envious I wanted to throw my beer bottle against the stones beneath us just to hear it shatter. "I guess I just sort of implied it."

"Not good enough." Skylar shook her head. "Natalie might be strong-willed and independent, but I guarantee she still wants that question."

"Do you love her?" Sebastian asked quietly.

"Yes," I said without hesitation. In my mind, I saw her smile change from a playful little girl's to a gorgeous grown woman's. God, when had I not loved her? "I'm crazy about her. I'm just an idiot about it."

"Does she love you?" he asked.

"She said she did last night." I exhaled, thinking about how sweet those words had sounded on her lips. I wanted to hear them again, wanted to feel her whisper them in my ear as I slid inside her, wanted to hear it over and over again.

"She does," Skylar said confidently. "I believe that. When she came home from Detroit, she was so weird. Just mooning around all over the place, like she was sad about something, but it definitely wasn't the breakup."

I frowned, slumping in my chair. "So now what? She doesn't believe anything I tell her. And I know that's my fault, because I once told her I was too selfish to love anyone forever."

"Man." Sebastian tipped up his beer and shook his head. "You are definitely your own worst enemy."

"I know. Help," I begged, sitting up straight again. "You guys are good at love. I am horrible. I'm only good at sex."

"We've heard." Skylar wiggled her eyebrows.

"I didn't mean like that—I meant that when people write in and ask me about sex, I'm good with the answers. But the emotional stuff is killing me." I ran a hand over my hair. "Not even joking, sometimes I think about her, and I can't even breathe. It's like I'm suffocating."

"Yeah, that's the feeling all right." Sebastian nodded. "What do you say when people ask about sex?"

"Slow down. Pay attention. Give a fuck."

He shrugged. "OK. Go with that. Go home and think, really think, about what would be meaningful to Natalie. About what she wants to hear and how she wants to hear it."

"OK. Yeah, maybe rushing right over to her house without a plan was a mistake."

Skylar tapped her chin. "But you have to do something big."

I sat up straight. "That's what my friend Nick said. A grand gesture." I looked at Sebastian. He seemed to have all this figured out. "What did you do?"

"He got on a plane," answered Skylar. "Which I knew he did not want to do."

"More airplanes," I grumbled. "Should I book a flight somewhere?"

"Not necessarily." Sebastian leaned forward on his knees. "That was my issue, because I'm anxious about flying. I'm anxious about a lot of things, and to show her that I was willing to try to be better for her, I had to get on that plane."

Skylar patted his leg again. "I had to drag you on that plane, honey. But you let me." She turned to me. "You have to think of something that's unique to you—something that would show her you mean what you say. Something that would show her you're still the Miles she loves, but you're also the one who loves her back enough to change."

It hit me. "I could write about her."

"Write about her?"

"Yes. I could use her real name," I said, warming to the idea even more. "That's something I've never done before."

"There you go." Skylar nodded.

"But I'm not going to propose online. I need something better."

"Think about it. Think about her and what's important to her. It'll come to you." She clapped her hands together. "And then I'll plan your wedding!"

"Oh, Jesus." Sebastian put up a hand. "Let's get through ours first please."

She nudged him with one bare foot. "Party pooper."

They invited me to stay for pizza, but I said no, thanks, I

had some work to do. My brain was whirling with possible things to write about, and I wanted to get the ideas down on paper before I forgot them. I also had to think of a way to propose to her that wasn't forced or clichéd or impersonal.

Propose. Marriage.

Me.

I grinned as I started the Jeep.

That was fucked up. But I loved it.

Later that night I called Skylar, who had given me her cell phone number and told me to reach out if I needed help.

"Hey, it's Miles. I have an idea."

She squealed. "What can I do?"

"Do you have a decent camera?"

"Yes."

"Great. Are you working tomorrow?"

"Nope. I'm off Mondays."

"Can you come to my house in the morning?"

"Yes, but I'm dying. What are we going to do?"

I smiled. "I'll tell you tomorrow. Bring the camera, please. Hey, do you by any chance have another day off this week?"

"No. But I could take one."

"What about going in late? Could you go in a little later on Tuesday morning?"

"Sure. My God, Miles. You're *killing* me. *What* are you planning?"

"To upend her life," I said. "In the best possible way."

CHAPTER 28
Natalie

ALL DAY SUNDAY I expected him to get in touch, but he didn't. I worked that morning, and every time the door opened, I thought it might be him, but it never was. We stayed so busy, I was able to get through the day without breaking down, but the moment I got home, I ran up to my room and crashed onto my bed, sobs wrenching from my throat.

Had I been wrong last night to turn him away? Was I just being stubborn? Refusing to give him a chance to prove he could change because I was scared of being hurt? Had I made him feel like he'd never be enough? Maybe it was my fault and this would be just another almost, another missed opportunity to be happy. Maybe I was too stuck on what I *thought* my life would look like. But how could I know for sure?

Needing to clear my head, I went to the gym.

I felt a little better after my swim, but my stomach was growling. I thought maybe I'd pick up some takeout from O'Malley's, so I parked and walked down the block, the summer breeze ruffling my damp hair. I passed the bar where just over a month ago, my sisters and I had gotten drunk on vodka martinis and gotten the reading from Madam Psuka.

Instinctively, I looked up at her window and saw the same sign.

I stopped in my tracks.

Had she been right after all?

Let's see.

Life upended? Check.

Handsome man? Check.

Stranger? Maybe…

Granted, I hadn't known his real first name was Edward, but maybe more significant was that he was trying to change, to be a different kind of man. Was he capable of it? Maybe I didn't know him as well as I thought.

On impulse, I pushed open the door to Madam Psuka's building and walked up the stairs. "Ew," I said, holding my nose. It had smelled bad the first time, but now that I was pregnant, bad smells were even more offensive. And I was only like five weeks along! What the hell would happen at ten weeks or twenty or thirty?

Oh, God. Pregnancy was so long.

Heaving a sigh, I reached the top of the steps and knocked. The door opened a moment later, and the acrid, herbal smell wafted out. It was pungent, but better than the cat pee scent in the hall. Madam Psuka appeared, looking much the same as she had last month, only wearing soft, flowing black pants and a loose-fitting top slipping off one shoulder.

"You are back." She nodded, her eyes narrowing. "I knew you would be."

I fought the urge to roll my eyes. "May I come in?"

"Yes. Please." She stepped back, and I entered the colorful room, which was, again, lit only by candles. "Sit down."

I lowered myself onto the rug, and she sat opposite me, legs criss crossed, feet bare. "So," I began.

"You are vith child."

I blinked at her, then touched my stomach. "Is it that obvious?"

She shrugged and gave me a smug little smile. "Maybe only to me."

"Wow."

"The handsome stranger?"

I swallowed hard. "Yeah."

"Interesting. You vant reading?"

"Uh, yes. I'll pay you this time. How much?"

"For you, twenty dollar."

"OK. Should I pay you now?"

She flipped her wrist. "You can pay after. Give me your hands."

I held them both out, and she took them in hers, closing her eyes. Again I felt the hum of energy between us, as unbelievable as it sounds. My hands and forearms grew warm with it.

"Things are uncertain," she said.

"Yes, that's why I'm here," I said, a bit peevishly. "I need to know what to do."

She opened her eyes. "I cannot tell you what to do. I can only tell what I see."

"OK, fine. What do you see?"

"You have important decision to make."

I clenched my teeth. Twenty dollars for this? "And?"

"And the stranger is involved."

"But...he's not really a stranger. I know him. I've always known him."

She cracked one eye open. "You don't know everything."

I huffed out a breath. "OK, fine, I don't know everything, but I know enough. He's totally immature. He's never even had a girlfriend. He doesn't understand commitment."

She shrugged. "Maybe. Is possible."

Frustrated, I shook my hands. "What else is there?"

"Love."

"What love?"

"Love between you and the stranger. Love between you and the baby. Love between the baby and the stranger."

"That's crazy," I said, but my heart was beating hard.

"Tell me. Have you had any odd dreams lately?"

"Have I? No, not really." Then I remembered something. "But Miles…the stranger, the baby's father…Miles did, a while back."

"Tell me."

I thought hard about the details. "Um, he was in my coffee shop eating a bagel."

She nodded. "The bagel was something missing from his life. Key element. He vas not complete and whole. Also…" She opened one eye again and gave me a sly look. "It can mean sexual urges."

My face burned. "Uh."

She closed her eyes again. "Go on."

"OK, um…he was eating a bagel and I was taking his picture. No! I was looking for my camera, and I couldn't find it."

She nodded. "He wanted you to focus on him, see a big picture. Possibly a memory."

"And then I turned into a bear."

She opened her eyes. "A bear?"

"Yes. What does that mean?"

"A bear is a symbol in the cycle of life. Perhaps it was his cosmic energy recognizing he would create new life with you." She glanced down at my stomach. "Or perhaps he just vanted to see you *bare*. There is that."

I grimaced. "There was that."

One eyebrow peaked. "Obviously."

"Look, I need to know what to do. Is there some sort of sign there? Something to indicate what direction to take? This is serious!"

"As I say, I cannot tell you what to do. I can only intuit.

But." She closed her eyes and concentrated hard, breathing deeply. "You must be willing to bend. You must be willing to change."

"But it's not me that has to change!"

"Yes. You must be willing to see things not as they have been or as they are, but as they could be." She leveled me with her gaze. "All that is real is not visible. And all that is visible is not real."

I sighed. I was getting nowhere, and frustration was making me sweat. Taking my hands from hers, I pulled a twenty from my purse and gave it to her.

She walked me to the door, and I thanked her for her time. As I was leaving, she put a hand on my shoulder. "You have come a long vay since last you were here. I sense it. I see it."

I nodded as tears filled my eyes. "I just don't know where to go next."

She tilted her head. "You will figure it out. Be strong, be brave, be open to all possibilities. Everything you vant is there for you to find."

Everything I vant.
Right.

On my way home, I picked up the phone and called Jillian. Skylar was too happy in love to appreciate my misery. I needed someone who would abet it. Someone who would agree with me that love was hopeless and no one knew what they were doing. Someone to tell me men were clueless apes who didn't understand anything. Someone who would commiserate with me on my desolate future and let me wallow.

"Natalie?"

"Hi."

"Everything OK?"

"No. Everything is terrible."

"Are you home? I'm coming over."

"I'll meet you there in fifteen."

Half an hour later, she walked in and found me curled up on the couch. "Hey. How are you feeling?"

"Shitty." I sat up and put both hands on my stomach. "But I decided to have the baby."

"You did?" She sat down and threw her arms around me. "That's so exciting! To keep?"

"I don't know." I sighed. "Probably. Once I start a project, I don't like to give up on it."

She laughed ruefully. "True."

"I just went and had a psychic reading from Madam Psuka."

"Shut up. Did you really? Why?"

I threw my hands up. "Because I'm confused! My life is a wreck! It's turning out to be nothing like what I thought it would be, and I'm totally lost. I was hoping she'd tell me what I'm supposed to do!"

"And did she?"

"No," I said angrily. "She just gave me a bunch of nonsense about being more flexible and brave and seeing things that aren't there."

Jillian sighed. "Sorry, kiddo. I wish I could help. Hey, are you hungry?"

"I was before. But then I wasn't."

She stood up. "You need nourishment. Let me get you something to eat."

"I just said I wasn't hungry."

"Doesn't matter. Your body needs sustenance." She gave me the look. "Now come in the kitchen and talk to me."

I followed her into the kitchen, and while she rummaged in the fridge and fiddled with the microwave I sat at the table and ranted about men and apes and cluelessness and misery. She let me go on for about ten minutes, nodding and clucking her tongue in sympathy.

"I hear you." She set a bowl of chicken noodle soup down in front of me, along with an orange and a glass of milk. "So I take it Miles was a jerk about the baby?"

"No, not a jerk exactly." I picked up the spoon and poked at some noodles. "Not a jerk at all, I guess."

She sat down and looked at me, perplexed. "What did he say?"

Taking a deep breath, I filled her in on what had transpired yesterday.

"Wait a minute." She sat back and held up her hands. "He drove here right away and told you that he loves you?"

"Yes, but—"

"That he wants to be with you? And raise this child?"

"Well, yeah, but—"

"That he's willing to change his life for you? Move here? Get married?"

"Not in those exact words, maybe, but yeah. I guess that's what he meant."

"And this is the guy who tied you up in his closet and talked dirty and did amazing things with his tongue?"

"Um…yes."

Jillian sat back. "So where's the ape, Nat? Where's the cluelessness? Where's the misery?"

"I don't know, OK?" I stabbed the noodle into bits. "It just wasn't right."

"Forgive me, little sister, I know you're going through some shit, but maybe you're being a little too picky here. I think Madam Psuka might have been right."

I looked up at her. "What do you mean?"

"I mean, this wasn't exactly planned. You guys haven't been together for a decade. Miles didn't have ten years to come up with the perfect proposal. So maybe it wasn't the perfect pitch, but guess what? You're pregnant. With *his* child. And you guys are going to have to sort of feel your way from here. I know that's hard for you, but life threw you a big fat curveball and you took a big hard swing."

It was big and hard all right. "Yeah. We did."

"So maybe you need to be a little flexible. Cut Miles some slack. Let your life take this new direction—it's not what you planned, but maybe it's meant to be."

I bit my lip. "You think so?"

"Yes." She reached across the table and put her hand over mine. "And you guys love each other. You've been friends for twenty years. Maybe it's not the perfect love story, but it's yours."

Tears filled my eyes. "God, Jilly. I'm so fucking tired of crying."

"It's the hormones," she said, coming around to hug me. "It will get better."

"When?" I sobbed into her stomach.

"I don't know. Eighteen years?"

I choked out a laugh. "Jesus. Eighteen years."

"You won't be alone, honey. You'll have Mom and Dad, me, Sky and Sebastian. And you'll have Miles, too, Nat. I feel it. I see it in the way he looks at you. How he's always looked at you. He loves you—you just have to let him do it his way."

I lay awake most of the night wondering if Jillian and Skylar and even Madam Psuka were right. Was everything I wanted right there in front of me and I just didn't recognize it? Was I too stuck on the idea of what I *thought* the fairy tale would look like? After twenty years of being just friends, had a few days of crazy bound Miles and me for life?

Was this our story?

How did it end?

I sort of felt like the prince had come to rescue me, and I'd turned him away from the castle. But you know what? I didn't want to be rescued by the right thing.

I wanted to be swept away.

I went to work the next morning, tired and emotional and still uncertain what would happen next.

We got busy fast, and again I looked up every time the door opened, hoping to see Miles walk in. Around ten, I was surprised to see Skylar come in, a big grin on her face.

"Hey," I said, pouring coffee for someone from behind the counter. "What are you doing here? Not working today?"

"I'm going in late. Can you take a break? I have to show you something." Her eyes twinkled, and I wondered what she was up to.

"OK. Sure, come in the back."

She came around the counter and followed me through the kitchen into my little office. "Have your phone?"

"It's right here." I reached into my purse, which was sitting on the desk. "What's going on?"

"Did you see Miles's post today?"

At the mention of his name, my heart quickened. "No. Why?"

"Look at it."

"Why?" I asked again, but I was already searching for it.

"Just look."

I searched his name with trembling fingers and fidgeted impatiently while the results loaded. Scanning the top hits, I clicked on the right one and gasped when I saw the title.

It Happened. I'm in Love.

I know what you're thinking.

It's impossible. The only thing that guy loves more than his dick is...well, nothing.

And a couple months ago, you'd have been right.

But there's this girl, see? Remember Cinnamon Buns? It's her.

Her name is Natalie. I don't remember not knowing her. We've been friends forever. But I've always wanted to be more.

I'm glad I had to wait, though. I needed to wait.

I don't think I would have appreciated her enough five years ago, or one year ago, or even six months ago.

But now...

Now I can't breathe when I see her.
    Now I can't sleep without her next to me.
    Now I can't be happy without her in my life.
    Now I can't believe I ever thought she wasn't the one.

. . .

I once told her I wasn't capable of loving someone completely and forever, but I was wrong.

I was so wrong.

Now I want to spend the rest of my life proving it to her.

I just hope she'll let me.

CHAPTER 29
Natalie

MY PHONE WAS SHAKING in my hand. "Oh my God." I looked at Skylar. "Oh my *God*. He published this?"

She nodded.

"Hey, Natalie?" Hailey called from the kitchen. "Can you come out here? I need you."

"Oh, shit." I put a hand to my cheek. "Is my face flushed?"

"Yes." She giggled and fanned it. "But you better get out there."

I moved past her and went through the kitchen into the shop, my pulse skittering out of control.

Then I gasped. The entire place was silent, all eyes on me. On the wall opposite the counter, where the pictures of Skylar usually hung, were four huge new photos.

Of Miles.

He wore the same jeans and t-shirt in each one, as if they'd all been taken the same day, and in every photo he held up a different hand-painted sign.

I moved closer, my hands covering my mouth, as I read each sign.

The one on the left said WILL.

The next said YOU.

The third said MARRY.

The last one ME?

Heart pounding, I looked around the room. Was he here somewhere?

"Pssst." Seated at a table near the door, a little old lady pointed outside. "I think that's what you want."

I turned, and sure enough, out on the sidewalk and framed in the window, was Miles. Down on one knee. Holding a ring box.

"Oh my God." On wobbly legs, I walked to the door and pushed it open. "What are you doing?"

He smiled and took my hand. "Isn't it obvious? I'm upending your life."

I laughed as a few tears splashed down my cheeks.

"Did Skylar show you the post?"

I nodded, swallowing hard. "Did you mean it? What you said?"

"Of course I did. I love you, Natalie. Let me show you how much."

"But—"

"Just listen. I know I'm not what you planned on," he said, his expression turning serious. "And believe me, I never thought I'd be down here on one knee, begging to love someone forever. But *this is not a mistake.*" He squeezed my hand, his eyes filling. "I feel it in my bones, Natalie. You've always been in my heart. You've always been the one I couldn't forget. And all last night I kept thinking that this—you and me and this baby—it wasn't an accident. It was exactly what was supposed to happen all along."

"Miles," I said, a sob breaking lose.

"You told me you were lost that first night we spent together," he went on, rising to his feet. "And do you remember what I said?"

I nodded. "You said, 'You're not lost. You're right here with me.'"

He opened the box, spoke low and soft. "You always have been. Stay with me?"

The sunlight winked off the big round diamond at the center of the ring's setting, and I gasped.

"Is that a yes?"

I burst out laughing. "Yes!" Holding out my hand, I watched through tears as he slid the beautiful ring on my finger. It was a little big.

He looked at me sheepishly. "Sorry. I guessed at the size. It almost fits."

I smiled. "Almost."

He kissed me deeply, stealing my breath, our arms twining around each other. From inside the coffee shop and on the street, cheers and applause erupted. Miles lifted me right off my feet and swung me around, and I squealed in dizzy delight.

"This is crazy," I said in his ear. "Are we really engaged?"

He set me down. "Well, I'm not too familiar with the concept, but I believe when you give a girl a ring and ask the question 'Will you marry me?' and then she says 'Yes,' that means you're engaged."

I lay my head on his shoulder. "I can't believe it."

"Told you your buns were worth matrimony."

I picked up my head. "This was all a ploy for my buns, wasn't it?"

"It was, and you said yes, so now I get to glaze those buns as much as I like. And also butter your muffin and polish your fine china."

Skylar opened the door poked her head out. "We're dying in here! You guys coming in or what?"

I turned to her, arms flailing. "Sorry! Yes, we're coming."

"Hard and often," murmured Miles from behind me as he steered me through the door.

Giggling, I looked at him over my shoulder. "Promise me you'll always make dirty jokes in my ear."

He spanked me lightly. "With pleasure. Easiest promise I've ever made."

The entire day, I floated around on a cloud, happier than I'd ever been, giddy every time I looked down at my hand. The feeling actually reminded me of being a kid and seeing a car in the Haas's driveway for the first time each June. I'd know that my summer fun was about to start, and I'd go running across the orchard to play. We weren't playing anymore, and we had a lot of important decisions to make, but for once it didn't drive me nuts not knowing exactly what the next step was. Or the next ten steps. I had Miles. He had me.

That's all I needed to know.

I knocked on the door, and when he pulled it open, I prayed those butterflies at seeing his face would never go away. "Honey, I'm home."

He grinned. "Took you long enough."

Before I could say another word, he pulled me inside, shut the door, and pushed me back against it, crushing his mouth to mine. Dropping my bag at my feet, I threw my arms around his neck and held him tight, reveling in the feel of our bodies pressed together, our hearts beating closely, our uncertainty gone.

"God, Natalie," he murmured, taking my face in his hands. "I missed you so much. I missed you every fucking minute we were apart, and I hated myself for it."

"It wasn't all your fault." I kissed his chin and his cheek and his lips. "Just mostly."

"Hey." He caught my bottom lip between his teeth, biting down gently. "Be careful, little girl. Just because I asked you to marry me doesn't mean you're off the naughty list."

"What's this? An overly amorous husband already?"

"Yeah. What's your advice book say to do about that?"

I smiled. "Run." Ducking beneath his arm, I took off running through the living room, squealing as I raced through the dining room and kitchen, Miles hot on my heels. Breathless with laughter, I looped back through the front hall and bolted up the stairs. Miles took them at least two at a time, grabbing me just as we reached the top.

"That's it, little girl. You're in trouble with me." He threw me over his shoulder and I pounded my fists against his butt.

"Let me go!" I howled, kicking my legs.

"Never." He went into his room and tossed me onto the bed, set his glasses on the table, then crawled on top of me, kissing my chest and throat and lips. "Do you hear me? I will never let you go."

I dug my heels into his ass, pinning his erection between my legs. Desire swept through me. "But will you let me come?"

He gave me a wicked smile. "First and often."

"Oh God, Miles," I murmured as he kissed his way down my body. "I missed you. I missed this. I missed everything."

"Then let me take care of you." Getting to his knees at my side, he pulled off my shorts and panties, and pushed up my shirt. "Poor baby," he said, low and sweet, moving aside the white lace cups of my bra to expose my breasts. He kissed each hard, tingling nipple as his hand moved up the inside of one leg, hitching up my knee. "All this time and no attention. Let me make you feel good."

I arched my back and closed my eyes, bringing one arm over my head. His fingers trailed up my inner thigh, making my core muscles clench. "Did you wait for me to make you come? Or were you a bad girl? Did you do it yourself?"

"I waited for you." I reached down with my other hand and rubbed his cock through his jeans. "And I wanted you so badly."

He teased me open and rubbed my clit with one fingertip, making my whole body twitch. "Does that feel better?"

"Yes," I panted as all the angst and tension and misery I'd felt over the last few weeks centered beneath his nimble fingers. "*Yes*."

Dipping one fingertip inside me, he spread my wetness over my clit in tight little circles that made my stomach quiver with desire. His other hand whispered across my chest, barely brushing my nipples, trailing between my breasts. I kept my palm over the bulge in his jeans, torn between begging him to fuck me right now and letting him get me off with his hand. He was just so fucking good at this! The thought that I got him to myself for the rest of my life was nearly enough to push me right over the edge.

My breaths came faster and louder, turning to moans and sighs as he took one nipple between his fingers and gave it a series of little pinches before holding it firmly. "Yes," he whispered as I began to writhe under his hands. "That's it. Let me watch you lose control." He switched to the other nipple and increased the pace and pressure of his fingers on my clit, and my entire body seized up.

"Oh God—yes…" I dropped my head to the side, my hips moving involuntarily, my cries loud and unabashed.

"Fuck yes. Come for me," he growled, and his voice sent me soaring over the peak, exploding beneath his fingertips in hot, frantic pulses.

Within seconds after the climax the pressure was too much, and I grabbed his wrist, curling onto one side. "Miles." I couldn't catch my breath. I could barely open my eyes.

"You. Are so. Fucking. Beautiful." Eyes on me, he tore off his clothes while I watched, my insatiable body shivering with want. When he was naked, he stood next to the bed, grabbed my legs and turned my body ninety degrees. Hooking his hands behind my knees, he hitched them up alongside his hips, my heels resting on the edge of the bed.

"I want you inside me," I panted. "Now."

"Shhhhh." He lowered his mouth to my mine, and I grabbed his head, holding him to me. Our tongues tangled and tasted and teased. Slowly he kissed his way down my chest to my stomach then my thighs, kissing one and then the other. "I'm making my way inside you, believe me." He brought his mouth between my legs, teasing me with warm breath and soft lips brushing gently back and forth. I moaned as he stroked up through my pussy with a firm, flat tongue that felt like velvet against my skin, once, twice, three times. Finally he lingered at the top, kissing and sucking gently on my clit, his hands pressing my thighs open.

"Oh, God," I murmured, grabbing handfuls of my hair. "That feels so good, soft like that. I love it."

"I like hearing what you want," he said, his breath on my wet pussy making my toes curl. "I want to give it to you."

"Just like that," I said as he swirled his tongue over the sensitive little bud. It tingled and throbbed, bringing me closer to another orgasm. "Yes, yes, yes. Now more. Harder."

He did exactly as I directed, and within seconds I came again, my hands yanking my hair, his name falling from my lips.

"Please." My voice was weak as he straightened up, kissing a path up the inside of one leg and setting my heel on his shoulder. "I want everything. Give me everything."

"Always," he said, his eyes dark with desire as he pushed inside me. "Everything I have, everything I am." He brought the other leg up and kissed my calf and ankle and instep before putting it on his shoulder. I touched my knees together as he gripped my hips. Holding me still, he thrust in and out with steady, rhythmic strokes. "I love watching my cock slide inside you, nice and slow. I love how wet and warm and tight you feel. I love that I can make you come with my fingers and my tongue first, then fuck you so hard you'll come again." Each time, he pushed a little harder, reached a little deeper, until finally he buried himself completely and leaned into me, bracing his hands on the bed and crushing the tops of my legs to my breasts.

At that point, something about the angle and depth made my insides start to contract and I lost the ability to string words into a coherent thought. My entire being was reduced to just my physical self, every nerve ending on fire, every muscle tense, every inch of my skin humming. Breathless and near delirious with want, I waited, suspended on the moregasm plateau, in that sublime marriage of ecstasy and frustration, desperate for that moment of release. Our eyes met.

"Oh, fuck," he breathed, rocking his hips a little faster. "It's been too long, and you feel so good, and you're so fucking beautiful. I can't stop."

"No! Don't stop!" I cried, feeling myself begin to tip. "I want you to do it. I want to feel you throb inside me. It makes me come so hard."

My words sent him over, and he cursed and growled and gasped as he lost himself to me, my insides gripping his driving cock like my body couldn't get enough. When he'd regained control, he slipped my legs off his shoulders and slid an arm under my back, moving me further onto the bed so he could lie next to me. Tears dripped from my eyes as we clung to each other, arms and legs tangled, my head buried in the crook of his neck.

"God, I love you," Miles said, kissing my head. "I fucking love you so much. Now I get it."

"Get what?" I pressed my lips to his collarbone, breathed in his scent.

"Being in love. Why people like it. When I first realized I was in love with you, I felt sick. I thought I was having a heart attack. It was terrible."

I had to laugh as I wiped away the tears. "And now that you know I love you back?"

"It's the best high I've ever felt, the most intense. Now I

get why people want to live together and take care of each other and get married and have kids. It's this feeling."

Shocked, I propped my head in my hand and looked at him. "You even get having kids?"

"Yes." He looked as amazed as I felt. "I look at you, and I love you so much I want to *do* something about it, but nothing is big enough, nothing is good enough, nothing is extreme enough."

I smiled wryly. "Having a baby *is* pretty extreme."

"Yes. It is." His hand moved between us, and he brushed the back of his fingers against my stomach, making me shiver. "And I know we didn't plan on it. But I want this, Natalie. I didn't even know how much until right now. I *want* to have this baby with you. I want us to have something with each other that we don't have with anyone else. I want us to be a family. In fact, if you weren't pregnant right now, I'd keep you right here in this room and fuck you until you were. That's how bad I want this baby."

I burst out laughing and rolled onto my back. "You're insane. This whole thing is insane. Are we really doing this?"

"We are." He moved down and kissed my stomach. "Hi in there. I hope I didn't wake you up with all that pounding."

I played with his hair. "He'll get used to it."

He looked up at me and blinked. "You think it's a boy?"

"No idea, babe. Sorry."

"Don't be sorry." He laid his cheek on my belly. "I'll be happy either way, boy or girl. Hey, I think I feel it moving."

I laughed. "You don't. Not yet. A few more months on that."

He grinned, his eyes wide like he couldn't believe it. "This is so fucking amazing, Natalie."

"You're going to be a great dad, Miles." And he was, I could feel it. That playful, wide-eyed side of him that found so much joy in the world, found something to be happy about every day, found pleasure in little things like cinnamon buns and big things like love and family—that's what would make him a good father. My throat got tight as I realized how lucky I was.

"Thanks." Kissing my stomach once more, he sat up and reached for his glasses. "So should we go tell *your* dad that I knocked you up?"

"Um, no. We will not be saying it like that."

"Why not? I'm planning to make an honest woman out of you."

I picked up a pillow and clubbed him with it.

"Hey." He took the pillow from me. "At least now I can admit it was me who threw that baseball and cracked your mom's kitchen window that time. That will no longer be the worst thing I've ever done in their eyes."

I sat up. "You know, you don't have to come with me if it's too awkward. I can tell them myself."

He jumped off the bed and started pulling on his pants. "No. You're not doing this alone. And I know you don't want to hear me say this is the right thing to do, but fuck you, it is, and I'm going."

Smiling, I watched him pull his shirt over his head. "OK, OK. You can come. We'll do it together."

Twenty minutes later, we walked across the lawn toward my parents' house hand in hand. My stomach was a little jumpy, but all in all I wasn't as nervous as I thought I'd be. My parents would be surprised, but they loved Miles, and I knew they'd be happy for us and thrilled to have their first grandchild on the way.

"Hey." I squeezed his hand. "You know what I just realized? I gave you a first!"

"You sure did. Many of them. And you know what I just realized?" He tugged me in front of him, wrapped his arms around me from behind, and whispered in my ear. "You'll give me all my lasts too."

Epilogue

NATALIE

At the sound of Mia's voice, we turned to see her standing in the doorway, a smile on her face. Jillian and I were upstairs at the winery in what Mia called The Bride's Room, which had a couple sofas and chairs, several full-length mirrors, and plenty of natural light streaming through the windows.

"OK." Skylar took a deep breath and looked in the mirror one last time. "This is it. Am I good?"

"You're absolutely stunning." My voice hitched as I said it, and for the millionth time, I wondered when this pregnancy would stop making me so emotional. I cried at everything these days! Although seeing our middle sister in her wedding gown and veil, holding her bouquet, in the moments before she married the love of her life, even had Jillian near tears.

"You are," she echoed, sniffing. "No one will be able to take their eyes off you."

"The only eyes I care about are Sebastian's." Skylar's smile was bright and her eyes clear as she picked up the bottom of her frothy white dress with one hand. "And I can't wait to see them, so let's do this thing."

Sebastian's two young nieces were serving as flower girls, and they were already giggling at the top of the steps, waiting to be told they could go down. When Mia gave them the nod, they took off, bounding down the stairs in a fit of excited laughter. "Here, let me take your flowers so you can hold your dress up as we go down," she said to Skylar.

Skylar handed them over and used both hands to ensure she didn't step on the bottom layers of tulle. She'd chosen a strapless tiered lace dress with a mermaid shape that showed off her hourglass figure, and wore her hair in a loosely braided mass of curls pinned to one side. Her veil floated behind her, and Jillian handed me her flowers so she could pick up the lace-edged tulle and make sure it didn't catch on anything.

I was last coming down the stairs, carefully keeping my eyes on my feet. The last few weeks, I'd been a little dizzy, but other than that and the out-of-control emotions, pregnancy was treating me pretty well. I was about fourteen weeks along now and just barely starting to pop. My dress, also floor-length tiered lace in a dusty lavender, had a wide eggplant-colored sash that probably emphasized the fact that I no longer had a waist, but at least I could breathe in it. It looked much better on Jillian, whose slender frame was perfect for its slightly vintage look.

As we neared the bottom of the steps, I saw our father waiting and heard music from the string quartet playing outside. My heart beat quicker.

"Hey, Dad." Skylar held up a hand and he high-fived her. "Ready to do this?"

"I sure am." He smiled at Jillian and me, offering me a hand as I neared the bottom step. "You feeling OK?"

"Yes. Promise."

As I'd expected, my parents had been shocked but not

unhappy about my pregnancy and engagement, and once they'd had a few days to let it sink in and see Miles and me together, they'd both taken me aside and said how happy they were for me. Although we were living in my house for now, they were hoping we'd move into the Haas vacation home so they could see the baby whenever they wanted. Neither of them seemed bothered by the fact that we weren't planning to be married before the baby was born, and my mother was already talking about a shower. Miles and I often remarked how lucky I was to have the parents I did. His parents seemed happy for us, if a bit unsettled by the news that Miles was getting married and making them into grandparents, but they still hadn't come to visit.

"This way, please." Mia led us over to some large glass doors leading to the terrace and we peeked out over the flower girls' heads. Rows of chairs had been set up and an aisle created on the stone patio, with everyone facing away from the building. The terrace was strewn with soft pink rose petals, and strands of lights were strung above it, looping from the building to the surrounding trees.

"OK," Mia said smoothly, handing Skylar her bouquet. "They've seated all the parents and grandparents. Skylar and the girls will stay here with me. Natalie and Jillian, you go out, and when you see Sebastian and his brothers line up at the front, you walk slowly toward them and take your places opposite. Got it?"

We nodded, grateful for her cool head and professional experience. The three of us would have been a mess back here alone. For a moment, I wondered about my own wedding—would it go something like this? Miles and I still hadn't decided what we wanted, but we knew we'd wait until after the baby was born, so we had time to think.

I turned to Skylar and took her hand for a second. I wanted to say something, tell her how beautiful she was, how happy I was for her, how much I loved her, but my stupid throat closed up again and tears welled. She understood, and it made her smile. "I know," she said, squeezing my hand. "I love you too."

Jillian fared better. "You're breathtaking, Skylar. We're so happy for you, and we love Sebastian like a brother. You're perfect for each other." Pressing her cheek to Skylar's, she smiled. "OK, Nixon sisters. Let's do it."

I followed her out into the warm September afternoon, managing to hold my tears at bay. Standing at the back, we watched as the three Pryce brothers came from around the building and walked together to the front of the terrace, where the officiant waited. Jillian reached behind her back, and I grabbed her hand when we saw how sweetly nervous Sebastian looked. He was clean shaven, hair neat, and his tall, muscular frame filled out his black suit like nobody's business. He had a face that rivaled Skylar's in its classic beauty, and for a moment I imagined the gorgeous children they'd have.

Once the men were in place, Jillian took a breath and started up the aisle, heads turning to watch her. When she was nearly to the front, I started out, my legs a little shaky, my fingers gripping my hydrangea bouquet tightly. Halfway up the aisle I saw Miles, and surprisingly enough, his handsome smile and adoring expression didn't make me tear up. Victory! Maybe I could get through the ceremony without weeping!

As I passed him, he mouthed the word *beautiful* at me, and my stomach fluttered. I passed my mother, seated at the front, and she smiled before bringing a clump of tissues to her nose. Glancing at Sebastian, I flashed him a big grin and he gave me a small one back. I took my place next to Jillian, and we held hands as we watched the flower girls come up the aisle, all ribbons and giggles and gap-toothed smiles.

Finally, the music changed and our dad and Skylar appeared at the base of the aisle. The guests rose, and a collective gasp sounded as everyone took in how beautiful the bride was. They started up the aisle, and I had to laugh to myself because it looked like Skylar was moving even faster than our Dad, like she was so eager to get married, she was hurrying him. Jillian squeezed my hand as he kissed her cheek, and we both sighed at the way Sebastian looked at Skylar as he took her hand, as if she might not be real.

The ceremony began, and as I listened, I looked out at the love of my life, at my family, at this perfect, sunlit day that felt like such a gift. Putting a hand over my stomach, I caught Miles's eye and smiled at the pure joy in my heart. It was almost too good to be true.

Almost.

The End

Next up in the Happy Crazy Love series, SOME SORT OF LOVE! Don't miss this second chance romance, in which oldest sister Jillian Nixon falls for Levi Brooks, the hot bearded single dad she had a college fling with and never forgot…get your copy here and read on for a sneak peek at the opening chapters!

Bonus Epilogue

MILES

"You ready, babe?" I snuck up behind Natalie, who was frowning at her reflection in the full-length mirror on the back of the bedroom door, and kissed her shoulder. "We should probably go. Dinner's at seven."

"I guess so."

I wrapped my arms around her waist—or at least where her waist used to be—and placed my palms flat on her hard, round belly. "How's he treating you?"

"He's being difficult today." She sighed, settling against me as if exhaustion was melting her bones. "He can't get comfortable, and neither can I."

I kissed her shoulder again, then the side of her neck. "Well, you look perfect." I breathed in the scent of her skin, which always smelled delicious.

"I don't look perfect. I look like a hippopotamus." She caught my eye in the mirror and gave me an angry glare. "And don't try to argue with me."

"OK fine. You look like a hippopotamus." I sniffed her neck again. "But you smell divine, so I'm going to go out with you tonight."

"Very funny." She closed her eyes and inhaled sharply just as I felt her stomach stretch and roll beneath my hands. "Jesus. Can you please tell your son to stop the assault on my bladder, or whatever organ it is that he's abusing? I can't take it."

Even though I loved feeling the little life we created moving inside her, I knew how difficult the last few weeks of pregnancy had been for Nat. Time after time I told her how much I wished there was something I could do to relieve her from the burden, and I meant it, but secretly I was like fucking hell, I'm glad men don't have babies. That shit looks hard! But I couldn't have been happier that Natalie was having mine. Just two weeks to go, and then I could pitch in and share the load.

I took her by the shoulders and gently turned her toward me before leaning over to address our belligerent baby. "Listen, Gotham. You need to stop all this hibernation crap and just get out here already. You're driving your momma here crazy, and I'm getting really fucking impatient to see you."

"His name is *not* Gotham." Natalie put her hands on her belly as if she could cover his ears. "And don't say fuck," she whispered. "He hears you."

I straightened up and took her face in my hands. "Of course he does. He probably even knows what it means. He's brilliant."

"Oh?"

"Can't miss." I dropped a kiss on her cute round mouth. "You're the smartest person I know. And my sperm was genius enough to scale the walls and penetrate all your defenses—so genius that your body was like, 'Oh yeah, this is the one. Fucking astrophysicist here. Brain surgeon. Virtuoso. This is clearly sperm prodigy.'"

She cocked her head. "Sperm prodigy?"

"Definitely." I kissed her lips again before dropping to my knees, lifting up the flowing hem of her maternity dress, and pressing my mouth to her belly. "Are you listening, wunderkind? You found your way in, now complete the maze and get out. The fit might be a bit tighter through the hedges, but I think you can do it."

"Oh, God." She laughed and pushed her dress back down, but a moment later, she gripped her lower back, and the giggle turned into a groan. "Don't make me laugh. It hurts."

"It does?" I hopped to my feet and studied her, trying to assess how serious this was. Natalie wasn't one to complain about anything, or get dramatic. "Maybe we should call the doctor. Or stay home tonight."

"No, no. We have to go. It's Jillian's engagement party; I don't want to miss it. And even if we stayed home, I'd still be uncomfortable."

"Are you sure? I can go get you a pint of Ben and Jerry's Cake My Day and give you a foot massage while we watch Netflix. Or a butt massage. Those are nice too."

She smiled, but I saw pain flicker across her face, and she had to take a deep breath before she spoke again.

"No, let's get going. I need the distraction. Will you grab my purse? It's on the bed."

I grabbed it, but I saw the way she walked toward the door, using the edge of the dresser for support, slowly shifting her weight from one leg to the other and wincing with effort. Something buzzed up my spine—a warning. She looked gorgeous, but something wasn't right with her tonight. "Hey, we're calling the doctor in the car, OK? Just to make sure."

She nodded, exhaling slowly. "OK."

\#

On the twenty minute ride to the restaurant, Natalie spoke with the doctor, who didn't think her symptoms sounded like anything more than end-of-pregnancy discomfort, but said we could head over to the ER if she wanted to be seen tonight. Natalie hated that idea, of course. "I want to go to the party," she said when she hung up, her eyes filling with tears, as they did so often lately.

"Then we'll go to the party," I said, taking her hand and kissing the backs of her fingers. "And if you start to feel worse, tell me."

"I will. I'm sure this is nothing. Dr. Baldwin said she often gets these calls from first-timers thinking they're in labor when it's really just the buildup," she said sheepishly.

I gave her hand a squeeze. "Exactly. Everything is going to be fine."

"It is. And don't tell anyone I'm not feeling well, OK?" Her voice got stronger. "I don't want my family to worry, and I don't want anything to take away from Jillian and Levi."

Our baby, of course, didn't give a shit about taking away from Jillian and Levi, and decided to arrive early.

Natalie had been shifting uneasily in her chair all evening before finally leaning over during the meal and saying, "Uh, I think this baby is coming tonight."

For a second, I totally panicked. I mean, I completely freaked out internally.

No! No! I'm not ready! I can't be a dad! I'm not qualified! I'm a child myself! I've never even had a dog! I'll probably forget to feed the baby! Or drop it! Or damage his frail little psyche with my foul mouth! Oh my God, whose idea was this? Why did I ever think I could be a father? I have to get out of it! I'm a menace to society! I can't be trusted! What is wrong with the universe that someone like me is entrusted with ensuring the health, safety, and happiness of a helpless human being? Where's the exit row? Can my seat cushion be used as a flotation device? I need the oxygen mask!

"Miles. I'm scared." Natalie put a hand on my arm, and as soon as I looked into her eyes, my anxiety was replaced with the fierce need to protect her, make her feel safe, keep her calm. Maybe I wasn't qualified, or even deserving, but I was this woman's husband and this kid's dad, and I loved them more than I'd ever be able to express. They were everything to me.

"Don't be scared, honey." I patted her arm and spoke quietly. "I'll totally take you to the hospital as soon as I finish eating. The chicken piccata is amazing."

"Miles!" she hissed. But a smile ghosted her lips, and I was grateful I knew how to make her laugh. If the baby really was coming, this could be a long night.

"OK, OK, fine. Let's get up and go right in the middle of dinner." I helped her to her feet and said to the other guests at our table, "Gotta run. Nat's decided now would be the perfect time to go into labor. Some people are such attention hogs."

"Oh my God." Natalie shook her head and leaned on the back of her chair. "I'm going to kill you."

She probably said that at least ten more times throughout the night, but by eight the next morning, when we finally welcomed our son into the world, both of us were crying happy tears. I couldn't even speak. I'd been scared for nearly nine months about actually watching the birth, wondering if I could handle it, but when the time came, I couldn't look away for a moment. It struck me how incredibly lucky I was in so many ways—to have Natalie for a wife, to be a part of this huge, loving family as we started our own, to become a father at a time when dads are not only allowed in the delivery room but encouraged to take part. It was scary as hell, but I'd stayed strong for her, keeping my fears and emotions in check, making her laugh when I could, staying quiet when she rested, telling her constantly how much I loved her—but at that moment when I heard our son cry out for the first time and then they placed him in my arms, the lump that had been building in my throat dissolved, and I let the tears fall without shame.

A little later, when we were finally alone in the room, I sat at her side while she held him, overcome with love and gratitude, and found myself choked up again.

"Jesus, you're worse than I am," Natalie teased when I had to get up and get a tissue.

"I'm a modern man, Natalie," I said, blowing my nose. "We are not afraid to let our feelings show, because we know that our manhood is not threatened by showing emotion. In fact, we recognize that it only makes us sexier. Look at you, you're panting for me right now, I can tell. You're so hot for me."

She rolled her eyes. "You just stay over there. I'll let you know when you're welcome to penetrate my defenses again. It'll be about six weeks. In the meantime, you're on diaper duty. Go practice."

"Purgatory," I moaned dramatically. But I went to her and reached for the baby, who was surprisingly little, all wrapped up in a blanket like an enchilada. Or was it a burrito? The nurse had given me a lesson on it once already but I'd probably need another one. Maybe another five. "He's so small," I said as I carefully walked to the changing table. "And so light."

"Well, he's only, like, an hour old."

"I know, but your stomach was so mammoth, when he came out I was like, 'That's it?'" I joked as I gently laid the baby on the table.

"I just added another week to your purgatory."

"I take it back. No wonder you were so huge. This baby's an elephant."

She laughed. "That's not taking it back."

I glanced over at her. "You know I think you're perfect. I always have."

A smile lit up her face. She looked more beautiful than I'd ever seen her, even with no makeup and sleep-deprivation-induced dark circles under her eyes. "You're gonna be a great dad," she said.

I looked down at the baby, who had Natalie's big blue eyes and little round mouth, and my dark hair. A perfect combination of the two of us. How fucking crazy was that?

Love rushed me, filling me up. "I'm gonna try."

Also by Melanie Harlow

The Frenched Series

Frenched

Yanked

Forked

Floored

The Happy Crazy Love Series

Some Sort of Happy

Some Sort of Crazy

Some Sort of Love

The After We Fall Series

Man Candy

After We Fall

If You Were Mine

From This Moment

The One and Only Series

Only You

Only Him

Only Love

The Cloverleigh Farms Series

Irresistible

Undeniable

Insatiable

Unbreakable

Unforgettable

The Bellamy Creek Series
Drive Me Wild
Make Me Yours
Call Me Crazy
Tie Me Down

Cloverleigh Farms Next Generation Series
Ignite
Taste
Tease
Tempt

Co-Written Books
Hold You Close (Co-written with Corinne Michaels)
Imperfect Match (Co-written with Corinne Michaels)
Strong Enough (M/M romance co-written with David Romanov)

The Speak Easy Duet

The Tango Lesson (A Standalone Novella)

Want a reading order? Click here!

Don't miss a thing!

For exclusive behind the scenes information, sales and freebies, cover reveals, recommendations, and sneak peeks to what's coming, subscribe to my mailing list using the QR code below!

About the Author

Melanie Harlow likes her heels high, her martini dry, and her history with the naughty bits left in. She writes sweet and sexy contemporary romance from her home outside of Detroit, where she lives with her husband and two daughters. When she's not writing, she's probably got a cocktail in hand. And sometimes when she is.

Find more at www.melanieharlow.com.

Printed in Great Britain
by Amazon